# FIRES
# OF
# ALEXANDRIA

## BOOK ONE
## OF THE
## ALEXANDRIAN SAGA

THOMAS K. CARPENTER

# Fires of Alexandria
## by Thomas K. Carpenter
### v5

Published by Black Moon Books

Cover design by Rachel J. Carpenter

Cover Images by
© Bonsa | Dreamstime.com
© Irochka | Dreamstime.com
© Zoom-zoom | Dreamstime.com

Discover other titles by this author on:
www.thomaskcarpenter.com

ISBN-13: 978-1463653705
ISBN-10: 1463653700

Also by Thomas K. Carpenter

## THE DIGITAL SEA TRILOGY
The Digital Sea
The Godhead Machine
Neochrome Aurora

## GAMERS TRILOGY
GAMERS
FRAGS
CODERS

## ALEXANDRIAN SAGA
Fires of Alexandria
Heirs of Alexandria
Legacy of Alexandria
Warmachines of Alexandria
Empire of Alexandria
Voyage of Alexandria
Goddess of Alexandria

## HERON OF ALEXANDRIA SHORTS
The Price of Numbers
The Weight of Gold
The Blood of the Gods
The Virtues of Madness
The Curse of the Gorgon

## MIRROR SHARDS ANTHOLOGY
Mirror Shards: Volume One
Mirror Shards: Volume Two

*This is for Rachel.*

# FIRES OF
# ALEXANDRIA

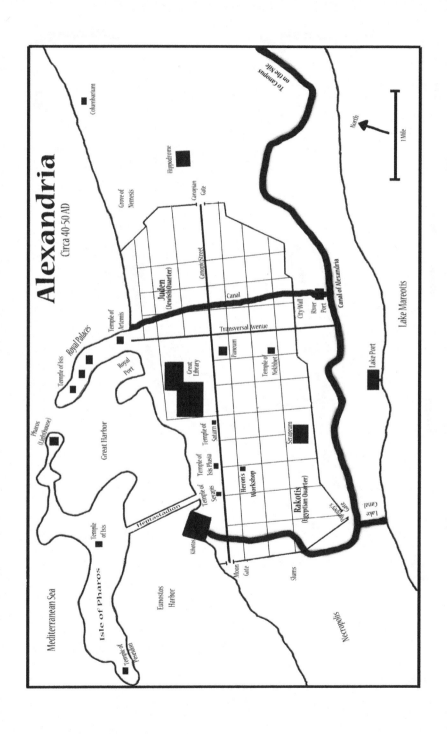

# Alexandria
## Circa 40-50 AD

Mediterranean Sea

Pharos (Lighthouse)

Isle of Pharos

Temple of Poseidon

Temple of Isis

Great Harbor

Eunostos Harbor

Heptastadion

Royal Palaces

Temple of Isis

Temple of Artemis

Royal Port

Great Library

Paneum

Temple of Nekhbet

Canal

Transversal Avenue

Grove of Nemesis

Hippodrome

Columbarium

Canopian Gate

Canopic Street

Juden (Jewish Quarter)

City Wall

River Port

Canal of Alexandria

Lake Port

Lake Mareotis

To Canopus on the Nile

North

1 Mile

Kibotos

Temple of Serapis

Temple of Isis Plusia

Temple of Saturn

Heron's Workshop

Serapeum

Rakotis (Egyptian Quarter)

Moon Gate

Slums

Lochias's Gate

Lake Canal

Necropolis

# 1

The sun blistering in the sky silenced the simmering rage that Agog had carried with him from the North. He sunk his teeth into the hunk of burnt meat he'd bought on the last street.

Spices littered his tongue, setting his nose to itch. The man who'd sold him the meat had killed the flavor with too much taste. Agog threw the half finished meal to the dirt and wiped his greasy hands on his furs. A scrawny dog snatched the meat and skittered back into the sea of legs.

Agog wound his way toward the Sun Square, admiring the orderly nature of the Alexandrian streets, criss-crossing in perpendicular lines like soldiers arrayed in battle. White-crested parapets, gilded turrets, and solitary towers stretched into the faded blue sky, filled in with colorful flags, streamers, and strange bronze cups on poles spinning madly in the upper breezes.

Beyond the edge of the city proper, the white marble Lighthouse reached high into the sky, flaunting the engineering knowledge of Alexandria. Built upon the island of Pharos, across the bay from the city walls, the Lighthouse commanded the skyline.

Agog had marveled at the light from it during his travel across the Mediterranean. Its beacon had reached across the sea, guiding their ship in, well before even the hint of land could be seen. Like the Great Library, the Lighthouse was a symbol of Alexandria's power.

He squeezed the dirt with his toes, feeling the thrum in the soil, as if a herd of beasts thundered past the city. Agog wished to yoke that energy to his needs.

The square heaved with people, amplifying the heat from the midday sun. Using his great bulk, he shouldered through, ignoring the stares and using their hesitations to make his way.

A gaggle of dark-skinned beauties wrapped in colored scarves, baskets perched on their heads, blocked his view. Agog grunted and a portly fellow in sea-blue trousers and open-shirted vest, gave him berth to pass, eyeing him suspiciously.

His nose set to itching again. The conflation of scents overwhelmed his nose. He had not the time nor the inclination to sift through their various subtle charms. Agog preferred the smell of cold wind, of charred wood in a hearth, of the sharp tint of salty air.

A slight reed of a fellow, dressed in purple silks, settled next to him. The man's perfumed aura wrinkled Agog's nose.

Agog abhorred the fellow's presence, shoulder leaning against his side, but there was little he could do in this crowd. New people streamed into the square, squeezing them like slaves in a hold.

The meat seller had told him a tale of miracles in the square at the sun's zenith. Agog had chortled and paid the man for the meat.

Still too far away from the center to witness the miracle, Agog wiped the sweat from his brow and prepared to push further in. A delicate touch under his skins alerted him to the thief.

Agog grabbed the perfumed fellow's hand, now dipped inside his skins, cozily next to his coin purse, and squeezed. The thief screamed a high willowing yelp as his bones crunched under the pressure.

The crowd, sensing trouble, gave them room, as if they were a fire too hot to stand by. Agog leaned down and put his bearded face up to the thief's, holding the broken hand in his own. The man's eyes were all white, covered in fear, spittle forming on his lips.

"Not a good idea," said Agog in fluent Greek.

Agog held up the man's offending hand and all nearby eyes followed. He snapped the man's wrist back, breaking it, while removing his coin purse in the same movement. Agog pushed the perfumed thief backwards to fall on his rear, cradling his mangled hand as he hit.

Sensing the anticipation of the crowd, he left, slipping the man's coin purse into a hidden pocket beneath his furs, next to his great belly. The purse the thief had been trying to steal was filled with worthless ceramic chips.

When Agog finally reached the spectacle in the center, he grumbled his disappointment. While the faces around his seemed in perfect adoration to the statue, he could not gather the reasons why.

Agog had seen statues before, especially ones of Roman soldiers with shield and gladius. He'd even seen bronze statues in Byzantium and Corinth before he'd taken passage. The stone statues of his lands in Old Gotar with a proper Suebian knot like his own, towered over these, but lacked the artistic detail captured in the softer metals.

Sticking out from the soldier's head, a metal pole climbed high above the square. The strange four cup spinner adorned the top, rotating in the breeze. This close to the statue, Agog could see that the pole did not move while the spinner did.

When the crowd gasped, Agog returned his focus to the statue in time to see its upper body rotate sideways and extend its shield. While many recoiled backwards at the sight of the moving statue, Agog leaned forward to study it.

The statue continued its movements, its head surveying the crowd. As the bronze soldier's lifeless eyes passed over Agog, he bared his teeth at it and instinctively reached for his weapon, which he had not carried in many months. Neither the Romans nor the Egyptians wanted to see an armed barbarian in their midst, so he went empty handed.

The statue continued its survey as if it were picking out a target in the crowd. As its focus seemed to gravitate to one area, the people stepped backwards.

In a sudden movement, the bronze soldier lifted his sword high above his head and thrust it forward as if he were leading a charge. A jet of water streaked out from the sword tip, spraying the people directly in front of the statue. A great cheer went up in the crowd and gentle laughter ensued, directed at the folks who'd been doused.

The bronze statue returned to its original position and the energy in the crowd released, as people filtered out of the square. Already, the strangling body heat lessened around him.

Agog grabbed an old man with sparse graying whiskers on his chin. His wine soaked breath was made potent up close.

"Who made the living statue?" asked Agog.

He wondered if he'd made a mistake, when the old man opened his near toothless mouth, eyes rolling wildly. Agog gave the old man a little shake, and he seemed to snap out of his stupor.

"Philo the Maker," said the old man.

"Is Philo the greatest of these miracle workers?" asked Agog.

The old man grinned. "For a beast, you do speak well."

In a different place, Agog might have strangled the old man for his provocation, but he knew the old man carried the tongue of a man in his decline, long past caring.

Agog returned his rueful smile. "In my lands, I'm king of the beasts. And as king, I treat with my enemies so that I may understand them. My thralls taught me the words in Latin and Greek, though they lay awkwardly on my tongue."

The clouds across the old man's eyes parted, leaving him nearly cognizant. He leaned back in Agog's grasp and regarded him fully, like trying to take in the size of a mountain from up close.

"Philo is the most well known of the makers. His family has burgeoning lands, filled with sweet grains, and coffers bloated enough to fund his gifts to the city," said the old man.

Agog sensed his seizing of the old man had been quite fortunate. He suspected he might have once been a philosopher, by the dirty robes, thread-bare and littered with wine stains. Maybe he had even once worked in the Great Library itself.

"And what else?" He shook the man again, lightly, to keep him in the present.

"Philo has wormed his way close to the Roman governor Flaccus so he can gain favorable contracts," said the old man.

Agog grimaced. Such close links to the Roman hierarchy would do him no good.

"Other miracle workers?" Agog asked. "Are there any that rival Philo?"

The old man cackled, shuddering like a beaten rug. "There is one. One who is probably greater and also in the same breath the worst of them."

Agog leaned close to the old man's face, ignoring the putrid stench. "Tell me." Agog smiled.

"They say that Heron of Alexandria is the greatest of these miracle workers. Conjuring miracles out of clay and stone and metal. Making the air speak and whole armies of metal soldiers march on their own," said the old man.

Agog smirked. This was the miracle worker he wanted. Not one to spit water from a sword. That would not help him win the battles he desired.

"And why is he the worst of them?" asked Agog, remembering the old man's previous words.

"He is cursed. Cursed by the gods for some crime we are not privy. Maybe he stole the knowledge for making these miracles from the gods and they cursed him with bad luck so his miracles would always fail," said the old man, grinning wildly.

"Are there no others?" Agog asked after some thought.

"None if you want the greatest of them," the old man replied.

Gazing at the feeble bronze statue, Agog weighed the two in his mind. Without a powerful army, he would not be able to claim his weregild.

Agog closed his eyes, ignoring the stifling heat and keeping his hand firmly attached to the old man. The visage of Aurinia floated into his mind: raven hair intertwined with feathers and other trinkets, wide, expansive eyes the color of deep ice, and soft delicate hands that held long memories of time under the furs.

Agog made up his mind. He pulled out the perfumed thief's coin purse and shoved it into the old man's gut, requesting directions before he released him.

The coin had been more than the old man deserved, but

he wanted to ensure he stayed immersed in buckets of wine, and forgot about the questions.

Agog the barbarian strolled down the wide avenue in bare feet, wearing matted, greasy furs. The heat coated him in a fine sheen of sweat, though he appeared not affected by it.

He took a great breath, inhaling the multitude of scents thickened in the streets, this time not overwhelmed by their strangeness. Agog cataloged them: the potent spices and the sweet breads, the odors of camels, and hearth fires, the braziers of incense burning in a city crowded with temples, the sharp, metallic tint of foundry fires reducing ore, unwashed bodies drenched in sweat, and the sea air cleansing them all when the breezes wind south.

He inhaled them in their entirety. To foil the Romans and snatch the city of Alexandria away from them, he needed to know these smells as if they were his own.

Agog grinned and tramped off in search of his miracle maker.

# 2

Heron wrapped the moist cloth around her chest, calling out to her niece Sepharia to finish the binding. She'd injured her shoulder last night during final preparations for the new miracle at the Temple of Nekhbet and couldn't reach back to fasten it.

Sepharia hustled into the dressing room wearing her glass blowing leathers over her chiton. Leather sleeves were connected across her chest in a half-tunic, strapped together with buckles. Gashes and burns littered her once white chiton, while soot smudged her pale face. Hidden amid the luscious curls on her head were make-shift glasses: two round cuts of darkened glass, held by copper bindings and connected by a leather strap.

Heron bounced a loose flaxen curl from Sepharia's head in her hand, while the girl worked on her binding.

"What I wouldn't give to have long hair again," said Heron.

She ran her free hand through her own hair, kept short in the male Roman style and dyed black.

"And I would cut mine so I could leave the workshop without being treated like an imbecile, Aunt Ada," said Sepharia.

Heron clamped her hand over Sepharia's mouth.  The cloth came unbound, releasing her smallish breasts.

"Hush, child," growled Heron.  "I've told you never to speak that name."

Sepharia's eyes glistened with tears as she tried to speak beneath the clamped hand.  Heron released her hand, threw an unwrapped chiton over her shoulder and wandered to the window that overlooked the busy street.

"—didn't think anyone was around."

Heron pushed the flowing lavender curtain aside.  Warm scents of baking bread flushed her senses, briefly overcoming even the salty air and pungent smells of hundreds of people passing beneath.  No one lurked beneath her window, nor would it have been possible that Sepharia had been heard amid the clatter.  Heron walked back, picked up the moist binding and set it in Sepharia's hands.

"While it's true only Punt is in the workshop and Plutarch and the rest are at the temple, we cannot, even for a moment let our guard down," said Heron.  "I must always be your father, my dead twin, to you.  Not Ada.  Never Ada."

Sepharia cinched the cloth, forcing Heron to suck in a breath, reminding her that the binding symbolized her life.  With the binding in place, she threw on a tunic and stepped into the special undergarments that created the appearance of male genitalia.

Throwing a satchel across her shoulder, Heron prepared to leave her living quarters by the spiral staircase.  She paused when Sepharia made a coughing noise.

A question lurked on her niece's lips. A question Heron knew, even before Sepharia spoke.

"No," Heron whispered. "You may not come."

Fierce longing welled up in Sepharia's brown eyes, reminding Heron of herself at that age. Heron opened her arms and her niece ran into them. She squeezed Sepharia tightly, inhaling the strong charcoal smell from her leathers.

Heron held her niece at arm length. "Be content. I know you're itching to make your mark on the world, but the Romans could have you killed for practicing a man's trade. No reason to flaunt yourself in public."

Sepharia sniffed and wiped her eyes. "But Cleopatra sparred with kings and studied from the philosophers and did anything she wanted."

Heron had heard this argument before. "*She* was a queen, which is a form of god. But in the end, she died as a woman, just as gods sometimes do."

"Gods can die?" The tears had dried on Sepharia's face.

"If no one worships them, they do. Which is why most of our earnings come from the temples these days." Heron sighed. "If it weren't for these unholy burdensome debts, we wouldn't have to conjure their miracles and subdue coinage from the masses."

Sepharia's eyes went wide and her mouth formed a little O. "I nearly forgot." Her niece backed away.

Heron crossed her arms. "What?"

"A man came to the front gate earlier when you were still asleep," said Sepharia with her eyes lowered.

Heron grabbed her niece's arm. "I told you not to show yourself."

"I was curious and you were exhausted from being up all night. And he was insistent, banging on the door." Sepharia pulled her arm free.

"Well, out with it."

"He said he was the customs man."

Heron put her hand to her head. "Did he say his name? No? Then what did he look like?"

Sepharia squinted. "He wore a richly decorated chiton with a crimson chlamys. He was short with a pot belly, black curly hair, and eyes so small I wasn't sure he was awake."

"Plato have pity. That was Alexander Lysimachus. You should not have shown yourself to him. He had only stopped by to taunt me with my debts, ones I am fully aware of."

Heron looked at her niece with the flaxen locks, high cheekbones, and wide expressive eyes. She knew what Lysimachus had seen. Sepharia was flowering into a beautiful woman, ready to be sold for a dowry.

"You cannot leave the house now and are strictly forbidden from answering the door again," said Heron.

Sepharia stifled a cry and ran down the spiral staircase, shaking the metal supports. Heron knew her niece would bury herself in her work, just as Heron had done when she was her niece's age.

Heron picked up an ornately clasped box the size of her fist. Two serpents coiled together forming the handle. She opened it again even though she knew it was empty, cursing it for being so. She licked her finger and ran it along the edge, hoping a few grains remained.

She decided to leave through the workshop in case Lysimachus was lurking around the front gate. Her debts were worse than she'd let on to Sepharia. Lys the Cruel, as he was commonly known in Alexandria, had come by to remind her that she was past due on her taxes. Running a workshop was an expensive business. She'd gone over the books before she collapsed on her bed the previous night. If it weren't for the debts that she'd taken on when she assumed her dead twin's name, she'd be solvent, but his business mistakes and gambling habits had buried him and threatened to do the same to her.

Her twin had a beautiful and creative mind, but no practical sense. She called him Sunny, her secret childhood twin-name since she couldn't think of him as Heron any longer. He'd called her Moony, as she was darker and infinitely more pensive.

A burst of light from the forge fire brought her back from her memories. Punt was charging the furnace with fresh charcoal and iron ore while orange-red light played across his glistening bald head and broad back. He wore a leather wrapping around his waist, darkened goggles over his eyes and nothing else. His bronze skin seemed to soak up the light that poured like honey from the combustion chamber.

The unmanned bellows fed the furnace with fresh air, heating the combustion chamber to a fierce white light from which she had to shield her eyes.

Heron smiled at the mechanism she'd built for the bellows. It captured the warm air flowing across the top of her workshop from the sea with huge spinning sails and converted the energy into a crank that pumped the bellows endlessly.

Even when the winds were dead, which weren't often, she'd made a rope and pulley system that Punt could wind up. Working a forge fire usually required assistants, but her mechanisms made it possible for Punt to work alone.

Heron pushed through the curtains that separated the foundry from the assembly warehouse. In comparison, the air felt cool against her face.

Even though most of the creations in the next room were of her design, walking through always set her heart aflame and made her feel like a child full of wonder. Only the Curiosity Rooms in the Great Library also made her feel this way.

The haphazard clutter conjured images of forgotten behemoths readying themselves for ancient battle. The shoulders and head of a bronze Horus sat precariously over a scaffolding of heavy timbers, falcon face leering across the warehouse. A nearby structure of tubes would, when filled with water and set inside the Horus statue, produce a falcon cry or mute silence - depending on the position of the rotating notched discs inside - and give the oracle-seeker his fortune.

Other constructions, in various states of assembly, littered the warehouse floor. Bronze tubes sprung from barrels like bushels of grain, polished stone blocks were strewn across tables, implements of measurement seen nowhere else in the world than in Heron's workshop, sat precariously amid other building materials.

Heron meant to make drawings of them so they wouldn't be forgotten if they were accidentally destroyed, but there was never enough time with all her projects. She'd hoped to teach Sepharia, but her niece was more inclined to delicate artistry, rather than practical mechanizing.

As she left the workshop, the layered scents of the busy streets – incense, bodily musks, and cooking fires –contrasted with her smoky workshop. A slender man with a basket balanced on his head rammed into her as she pushed into the crowd.

The streets were more crowded now than when she first came to Alexandria. Recent census had put the population near a million. Only Rome claimed more residents.

Newcomers were flooding into the city at high rate. Temporary cities were popping up outside the walls until the east and southern sections of the city could be expanded. The influx brought with it a certain air of expectation. Pushing through the crowds, Heron could feel it. Like an electricity passing through them all. It was enough to erase the morning's concerns. A good miracle would bring enough to make a sizable dent in her debts to Lys the Cruel.

Avoiding an overturned cart, Heron detoured through Fountain Square. A huge fountain commanded the center of the cross-street. Four versions of the cat goddess Bast sat at the four directions, representing her four aspects, holding: a ceremonial sistrum, an aegis, a solar disc, and empty handed. From the mouth of each statue poured glistening water. A huge windfan, suspended on a center pillar, spun lazily in the morning breeze.

A dark-skinned man in a richly colored full length robe stood near the fountain with a young boy at his side. He appeared to be from regions deeper south, past the deserts. A trader, perhaps. They were getting more of them every day.

"This is truly the City of Wonders," she heard him tell the boy. "This must be the work of their greatest miracle worker."

Heron cursed under her breath. It was hers, of sorts. Philo had bought her designs from a former disgruntled worker and had placed the fountain in the square as a *gift* to the city, along with a few other attractions. He'd been buried in work after that, taking half her customers.

The other half had left during a series of unfortunate mishaps. It seemed like someone was sabotaging her work, but each time she investigated the failure, it rang as a simple accident.

She practically had to beg the Temple of Nekhbet to let her make their miracle for them, doing it at a substantially reduced cost when compared to her rivals. Even still, the design had intrigued them and would fetch an ample profit if all went well.

It helped that the temple priests had been desperate, too. New gods, brought by the hordes of immigrants, were springing up in the city every day. Nekhbet was an ancient Egyptian goddess, sometimes presented with a vulture head, and the sister of Wadjet. But she had fallen out of favor and the other temples had better miracles as of late.

Heron reached the temple gates. A massive stone statue of Nekhbet poured water from a jug into a pool. The pool represented the waters of chaos, which the goddess had been in charge of before creation.

Below the pool, a huge brazier waited unlit. The brazier was her creation, one commonly used throughout the city. When the fire was lit, the heat forced air into a pit of water beneath the brazier. The pit would overflow into a large bucket and the weight would activate a series of pulleys, opening the door.

Heron walked up the steps past the brazier and the statue and past the big red doors that wouldn't open until later. She cut around the stone building to a hidden entrance behind a hedge.

She took a deep breath before she went in, praying that the evening's miracle didn't turn out like the last few had. If she didn't pull it off, then she might have to take Sepharia and flee the city before the debts crushed her like they did her twin.

# 3

Agog banged on the double doors. When he put his ear to the wood, he could hear the faint sounds of metal on metal. Closer, creaking metal gave away someone lurking inside.

He slammed his fist against the double door, rattling them together, and called out Heron's name. Movement from a window above him drew his gaze, but whoever was spying on him slipped away before he could get a good look.

Agog thought he'd saw a pale creature with half clothes and two dark eyes on its head. He shrugged and banged once more on the doors. He'd seen stranger things in the lands east of his. Animals that could talk and houses that walked. The former had taught him grave secrets about the world and the later had been how he'd found Aurinia.

Circling the workshop, he found gates into a courtyard. Leaping to peer over the edge, he spied building materials stacked into piles. Further in, the reddish-orange glow of foundry light poured out of the darkness.

Agog chuckled as he imagined his lieutenants watching

him hop like a mad ibex. They'd feasted him on the day of his leaving, declaring their intent to attend him on his journey, but he forbade it, under penalty of singular combat with him. None of his lieutenants had ridden with him.

Parched from a day spent sweltering in the sun, Agog left the workshop in search of covered stalls and cool drinks. He found an open-air café and carried a handful of spiced meats on a stick and an earthen mug full of beer to an empty table.

Agog questioned the freshness of his meats, but the spices and charred skin hid the rank flavor. His shoulder blades itched after a time, letting him know he was being watched. His lieutenants claimed he had eyes in the back of his head during battle, always spinning around at the last second on a charging foe.

Upon craning his neck around, he found a table of three men in togas watching him intently and whispering under their breath. The shortest, obviously a Roman by his aquiline nose, stood up and walked towards Agog's table when they made eye contact.

The man strode up and Agog supposed he was being analyzed along the way. The Roman man spoke a phrase in Burgundian, a language Agog was familiar with, but not fluently. Agog thought he might have asked him if he could sit at his table.

"Please join me," said Agog in Latin.

The man flinched, checked back with his fellows and promptly sat in the chair across from Agog. The other two were watching wide eyed as if their friend was feeding olive leaves to a bull.

"I'm Gnaeus Genucius Gurges," he said, offering his hand.

Agog captured Gnaeus' hand in his own and shook, careful not to damage it.

"Agog."

"You speak very well for one of your kind," said Gnaeus.

Agog's feet had been propped onto a chair next to his. He pulled them off, set them down and put his hands on the table around his drink.

"And what kind is that?" he asked.

"A barbarian, of course," said Gnaeus, clearly not realizing his words were insulting. "A northerner. One of the uncouth races. It's so obvious, isn't it?"

Agog grunted and took a drink from his beer.

"Go on," said Agog, switching to Gallic. "I assume you have questions for me."

The switch in languages goosed Gnaeus again, but he went on without acknowledging it otherwise.

"Well, I am the foremost scholar at the Library in barbaric studies," said Gnaeus proudly. "And I wish to ask you a few questions. In return, I would buy you a meal."

Agog looked down at the empty sticks. "I will answer your questions if you answer a few of my own."

Gnaeus nodded enthusiastically, the wealth of questions practically brimming at his lips.

"But first," Agog said. "Which library?"

The Roman scholar appeared insulted at his question.

"Why, the Great Library of Alexandria herself! Are you that unwise?" Gnaeus held his hand to his chest in mock injury.

Agog let the smile rise to his lips slowly. "Which library within the Great? The Mausoleum, Paneum, Mithereum, or the Serapeum?"

Gnaeus coughed. "The Mausoleum, of course. The oldest and most important studies are housed there, which includes my own."

Agog grunted, informing the scholar he was ready for his questions.

"Is it true that you barbarians allow your women to have a say with whom they mate?" Gnaeus asked.

The question brought memories of Aurinia leaning from her hut high above, clad in white with a flaxen cloak and a bronze girdle, taunting him with jabs about how the Suebian knot on his head had been bound too tight, making him dull. He tried to climb the poles the house had been built upon to set her right, but she knocked him loose with a long staff.

"They have a way with words," Agog replied.

Gnaeus nodded sagely. "Are you not concerned with their deceptions? They are despicable creatures."

"Despicable? No. Deceptive? Yes." Agog rubbed the parallel rope scars along his forearm. "One tricked me into killing a particularly dangerous black bear for her."

"Did you punish her for her indiscretions?" he asked.

"Yes." Agog letting a grin rise slowly to his lips. "I married her."

Gnaeus began laughing hysterically, knocking over his mug with a flailing arm. While Gnaeus wrung the beer from his toga, Agog ordered two more beers.

Gnaeus' scholarly friends departed the café, making wild glances as they passed.

"I would like to press you further on your knowledge of Northern women," he said. "But for now, I wish to know the answer to a question that has vexed me for some time."

"Ask," Agog said simply.

"You are as a barbarian familiar with the Cimbrian War?" Gnaeus asked.

Agog let his face stay neutral.

"I am familiar," he answered.

Gnaeus puffed up, as he prepared to release his hard won knowledge.

"Over a century ago, when Consul Marius defeated the

bastard King Boiorix upon the Raudine Plain, killing him and driving his troops back north, was it ever known if King Boiorix had an heir?" asked Gnaeus.

"Would it matter if he did?  A king who cannot hold his kingdom is not a king at all.  Who begat who matters not," said Agog.

"No...no..." said Gnaeus, waving his hand.  "I do not suggest that his son should have been a king, only that we are missing links in the genealogy of the northern barbaric tribes. Finding his heirs would clear up a host of other questions."

"If you know these other questions, you should not need me," said Agog.

"Well, you see," Gnaeus said.  "We lost so much in the Great Fire.  I have reconstructed what I can, but too much was lost.  I need that missing information."

"Take your complaint to Rome then, since it was Caesar that burned it down," said Agog.

Gnaeus became wide eyed, ducking his head down, listing back and forth.  The scholar became very concerned about a pair of Roman soldiers walking past the café.

"Do not say that so loudly," whispered Gnaeus.  "It is a crime to say that Caesar caused the fire.  The Romans are concerned that Alexandrians, given enough reason, could overthrow the Governor."

"If they know he burned it down, then why don't they act?" Agog asked.

"They have no proof.  The fires happened during a battle in the city.  Blame has been thrown widely," said Gnaeus.

Agog made noises of interest, the scholar's words weighing heavily on his mind.  He got up from the table to leave.

"Agog," said Gnaeus.  "Can you not answer any more of my questions?"

Agog stopped, mind whirling.  "Another time.  I will come

by the Mausoleum."

Gnaeus seemed perplexed as Agog prepared to leave. Then Agog stopped, remembering an earlier errand. "Are you familiar with the miracle worker Heron?"

The scholar nodded.

"Do you know where I can find him? No one answers at his workshop," asked Agog, clicking his tongue in thought.

"I've heard he has been seen frequently at the Temple of Nekhbet. They have been losing followers for some time now, so it would make sense," said Gnaeus.

Agog left the scholar staring into the litter of empty mugs. Gnaeus would have much to think about from their conversation and so did Agog.

The heat of the day had peaked and the streets had emptied somewhat compared to the morning. He didn't have to elbow one person on his way to the Temple of Nekhbet.

Outside, a crowd had gathered before the stone building. Water poured from a woman's statue into a pool lined with turquoise stones. A brazier set upon a bronze pillar, quite inexplicably to Agog, garnered the attention of the crowd.

Men and women in simple tunics, mostly Egyptians with their bronze skin soaking up the sun, clamored about restlessly. Though Agog had been in the south for months, his skin still paled against theirs. The assembled carried sticks and lumps of charcoal.

Agog judged the people waiting outside the temple as common folk: artisans, merchants, and the like. Those with a jingling bag of coins and ambition to spare.

A few well dressed scholars hung off to the side, debating in their obliviously arrogant manner. Agog was instantly reminded of Gnaeus. The scholar might provide some future benefit, but it would likely be trifling small and impractical.

The patrons of the temple harassed the priests in violet

robes on the stairs. He gathered from the hurled insults that the temple had been faring poorly in exciting its followers.

North or south, once a god had a building to maintain, Agog found them to be quite insistent about tithing and finding the means to encourage it. He preferred the gods and goddesses of the woods and streams. They required nothing more than a simple word and the occasional burnt offering.

Before Agog lost his patience, the priests produced flaming torches, much to the delight of the assembled. With the brazier lit, the crowd threw in their sticks and charcoal. The flames grew until it was a fiery conflagration. Then to Agog's amazement, the huge red doors slowly swung open.

Agog could see no man pushing the doors. They seemed to have opened by magic. As the crowd shuffled into the temple, Agog followed.

Like the spitting soldier statue, Agog could see no markings or levers that moved the door. Miracles upon miracles these Alexandrians witnessed on a daily basis. Why they hadn't risen up and thrown off the yoke of their Roman masters perplexed him.

The crowd settled onto the chipped stone pews, whistling and calling liberally. Skins of wine could be seen passing down the rows.

A pale cloud of incense hung in the vaulted portion of the temple. Agog's eyes watered and he desired a beer from the café. Here on the edge of the southern sands, their beers were no better than camel piss, but the heat made them taste like the water of the gods.

Agog grabbed a skin of wine from the row in front, squirting the liquid in his mouth and spilling some across his chest. The worshipers around him swallowed their protests.

The crack of wood against wood turned the heads of the faithful and as they did, Agog spied a vulture-headed priest in violet robes stepping from a hidden alcove into the middle of the temple, standing before a massive black marble statue of the goddess Nekhbet.

When the faithful turned back, surprise lifted easily from their tongues, but it quickly turned to taunting jeers. They had not come for simple trickery. The high priest with the vulture head hesitated, bringing down more insults.

The clearly drunk and rowdy crowd would not be subdued easily. The high priest raised his arms decisively and shouted an incantation in a tongue Agog did not recognize. The languages south of the Mediterranean were mostly unknown to him. Only a smattering of the Egyptian words were familiar to his ears and the high priest's words were none of them.

But the tone and pace were familiar. In the beginning, the priest spoke simply, gathering momentum like a shepherd gathering his flock upon a grassy hillside. The vulture-headed priest captured their interest for a time.

Agog drank from the wine skin, examining each member of the crowd for one that could be Heron. He cursed himself that he hadn't gotten a description from the old man, though the task of finding him, he thought, should be easy.

Agog found it odd that he would find a person such as Heron in the temple at all. Most of the crowd were common folk and merchants. Given the size of the workshop, three times the buildings around it, Heron had to be wealthy, even accounting for bad luck.

Maybe cursed, he came to the temple for favor. Agog hoped not, for he cared not for those who expected the gods to weasel them through each task.

The vulture-headed priest had lost the crowd, Agog decided. He'd lectured too long, or asked too stridently about coinage before properly lubricating the masses, though lubricating they had done much on their own.

"*Hazz'em ler agresseum!*" screamed the priest, clearly cutting right to the expected show. He pumped his hands up above his head in two fists.

It seemed like the priest had expected something to happen, because he checked back over his shoulder and repeated the fist pumping.

The second time, a loud thud and sparks erupted from the peak of the Nekhbet statue. From the white cloud after the sparks, an ebony vulture screamed out, flying the length of the temple with wings spread.

Agog expected the vulture to crash into the back wall when another loud bang from the front of the temple, at the offering well, turned the crowd's heads. Warned to the trickery from the priest, Agog watched as the vulture completed its flight by being pulled up into a trap door in the ceiling.

To the great surprise and delight of the crowd, and by the urging of the priest as he lifted his arms repeatedly in flight, the statue of Nekhbet rose an arm's length from the floor. The crowd ducked in unison and Agog followed this time, witnessing that the statue was actually floating above the floor with no supports.

Agog didn't have long to consider how the miracle was being performed when the statue moved forward. The priest stayed ahead, flapping his arms quite ridiculously while the statue moved forward. The crowd seemed suitably awed by the miracle and cheered with aplomb.

The vulture-headed priest in violet robes, even beneath his mask could be seen buoyant with the fever of the crowd. Feverishly flapping his arms, he began to move faster down the aisle between the pews.

The statue kept pace with the priest, which Agog found odd. The second thing which was odd to him occurred right after the first and before the third and mostly terribly odd thing to happen in the Temple of Nekhbet.

As the priest began to run down the aisle, the massive stone statue began wobbling behind him like an ox cart and Agog heard a female screaming from high above, clearly and in Greek: "Slow down, you imbecile!"

Agog glanced up, signaled by a sudden change, and in much the same way he read the flow of battle, he sensed the impending disaster.  The statue seemed to be moving much faster now, even more than the priest.

Then Agog realized as he watched the events unfold, idly drinking from the borrowed wine skin, that the statue was tipping.  Observing the descent of the statue, he knew its marbled head would crash through the back of the temple, bringing the whole structure around their heads, and there was nothing he could do to stop it.

# 4

Heron hoped to speak to Plutarch and assess the progress on the miracle before the temple hierarchy knew she had arrived. She stepped through the umber curtain, glancing down the curved hallway.

"We aren't paying you to sleep," said Ghet, the temple high priest, surprising her from the opposite direction.

He squinted at her through his mass of black ringlets, tilting his head back in obvious disdain, tapping his long fingernails against his chin. The fingernails were long claws that scraped and clicked as he moved his hand across his violet robes.

"The miracle will be ready on time," said Heron, cursing that she'd run out of lotus powder. Doubly so, since the Temple of Nekhbet reeked of burnt cinnamon.

"We have no patience for failure, even from *Michanikos* himself," said Ghet, evoking the nickname she was called by the poor of the city. It meant Machine Man.

"Do you have some purpose other than to obstruct me from mine?" she said, carefully treading the line between outrage and insolence.

"As the high priest, I am in charge of its finances, and currently its finances are invested in an obscenely verbose Grecian with ill manners," said Ghet, pawing her shoulder with his long fingernails.

Heron pushed past. The high priest followed her with his hands entwined at his midsection, the nails forming a pale fan.

"It's fortunate you are not a farmer or your oxen would be dead from the rod," she said, leading him into the acolyte's chamber, only to stop in frustration.

The room was stuffed full of pulleys and ropes like a web spun haphazardly from a drunken spider. Her foreman, Plutarch, was arguing with a lesser priest over an ornate table spilled onto its side.

When Plutarch saw her, his hands took flight like a pair of doves. "Heron! I cannot work like this. They keep making demands that cannot be met!"

Plutarch's hands settled around his mouth, fluttering like baby birds. He was a slight, reed-like man, with delicate features and a subtle air in his words.

The lesser priest indicated the fallen table with ink stained hands. "We must have a place for the sacramental ointments."

Heron thought it odd that a priest used ink. She knew from her dealing with the temples that most were illiterate. Especially the lesser ones.

Plutarch, clearly tired of the priest's arguments, turned on him. "You don't *need* a place for the sacramental ointments. At least not here. I was given this room in its entirety, and I have already made four adjustments to the design based on previous requests."

He waved his hand at a section of tangled pulleys next to a wooden cabinet painted with ceremonial designs. Heron could see that Plutarch had tried to satisfy their placement of the cabinet by constructing a counterpulley system, but the table had clearly upset the whole thing and it had unraveled into a tangle.

Heron spun on Ghet. "My instructions with the temple were very clear. We were to have our own room to setup your miracle. If you cannot abide by our agreement then this miracle will not work and if it cannot work, we shall take our equipment back to the workshop this very day."

Ghet spat into his hand and slapped them together, setting the nails to quiver obscenely. "For Nekhbet! You cannot! The crowd already gathers and if you take you wares back during the daylight, they will see the implements of your miracle."

"Then remove these..." she shook her hand at the cabinet and table, "pieces out of this room so we can do our job."

Ghet pointed a long fingernail at her. It hung limply between them. "I've heard rumors of the debts you owe Lysimachus. You would not dare. You need our coin or he will put you to the rack in the market square."

Heron squared her shoulders at him. "Rumors are like rats in this city. Kill one and five more take its place, so the only way to deal is to ignore them."

Ghet slanted his eyes at her, splaying his fingers. "What I hear is more than rumor. The Temple of Nekhbet is an ancient order with well placed friends throughout the city, even in the Alabarch's house."

The Temple of Nekhbet was ancient, going far back into the histories of Egypt, and Heron knew they had friends. But the temple was also stiff with tradition, and run through with cracks and rot, and Heron knew this.

"Even the collector of customs, this city's dear Alexander

Lysimachus cannot know all," she said, treading carefully, since anything she said could make it back to him. "Otherwise, he would not need his network of spies and thugs to ferret out coin from its residents."

She paused, and Ghet attempted to speak, but Heron cut off the high priest. It was clear that Ghet was an informer for Lys, and she had a message for him.

"Ghet, high priest of the Temple of Nekhbet. Know that I, Heron of Alexandria, respect your ancient temple and wish it to continue as a member of this region's honored pantheon."

She wandered over to the fallen table and ran her finger across the molding.

"But as you know, your coffers are growing empty and you need a miracle to bring back your followers. There are," she said, raising an eyebrow, "more exciting temples in the City and new ones being formed every day."

Stroking the tangled ropes, she glanced over her shoulder at the high priest.

"So if you do not get these hunks of wood out from our pulley system, we will not be able to perform your miracle. Therefore, it would be better to just pack up and take our things back to my workshop, before they are ruined by catastrophe."

She gripped the leg of the ornate table and gave it a tug.

"And if we do that, you will cease to be a temple in the City of Miracles, and we will sell our wonders to a more worthy temple."

Heron finished by ripping the leg from the table and handing it to the high priest.

"So remove this table before I remove it myself, and stay out of our way until the miracle is complete," she finished.

Ghet contained his fury, barely, nodding tersely to his acolyte before storming from the room. After the lesser priest removed the table and cabinet, both Plutarch and Heron sighed.

"You're playing a dangerous game," whispered Plutarch, "and though in dire need of new finances, the temple is still a dangerous foe."

"Did I have a choice?  Fools wonder why they can't draw coin when they interfere with the very people they hired to help them," she said.

Plutarch nodded and began restringing the pulleys to their original formation.

Heron shook her head.  "The old temples are the worst. History has given them an arrogance that they are right no matter what they do.  I long for a day when I'm not a slave to their miracles."

The pulleys, tangled as they were, would not free themselves with simple tugging.  Plutarch placed his hands behind his back and surveyed the mess.

"Then why do you labor for them?" asked Plutarch.  "Your inventions have made you modest coin.  The self-trimming oil lamp is a wonder to behold."

"But modest coin does not pay the heavy debts I am burdened with," she said, making sure no one was lurking nearby.  "Only the miracles can do that."

Heron tapped her foreman on the shoulder and pointed to a knot in the web.  When he shrugged, she reached out and pulled a seemingly unimportant rope and the whole web sprung into its original formation, a structured cross with pulleys at each end.  Now the system seemed orderly and purposeful, rather than one strung up by a child.

Plutarch shook his head in wonder.  "And that is why you are the *Michanikos*, and I am just your foreman."

"And the best foreman in the city," she said, patting him on the shoulder.

They continued their work, tightening the pulleys and

fitting the ropes snugly.

"Couldn't you invent more of your amazing devices and sell them, rather than perform these miracles?" Plutarch asked again.

"My inventions are novelties when it is cheaper to purchase a slave to keep your house running efficiently," she lamented. "And without slaves, the nobles cannot feel their power, as a domicile stuffed full with gadgets does not make them thrum with arrogance."

Plutarch nodded, knowing the truth of her words.

Once the pulley system had been fixed, Plutarch went in search of the other workers. Heron wandered into the basement of the temple where the automation door mechanism was housed, raising a lantern to see.

The doors were still closed and the water bucket was suspended against the ceiling. The frequent splashing of water left mold and sludge growing against the stone surfaces. Heron held her tunic to her nose to block the fumes. Holding the lantern high, she thought she saw a rat's tail shuffle out of sight.

Content that the door mechanism would work when the time came, she returned to the chamber. Plutarch directed two workers in cleaning up.

"Are we ready?" she asked.

Plutarch nodded. "The priests are going to light the brazier now."

"What about the priest in charge of the ceremony?" she asked.

"He's ready," said Plutarch. "Nervous and a little drunk, but he's waiting in the hidden chamber beneath the statue."

"Drunk?" Heron shook her head. "I don't like this already."

Plutarch squeezed her shoulder. "Our string of bad luck

can't continue."

Heron ignored him and asked. "Are the mirrors ready? The illusion of levitation doesn't work if they're not properly set."

Plutarch nodded again. "Everything is ready. We just have to manage the lifting mechanism and we'll get through it."

The sounds of laughing and cheering erupted in the main chamber of the temple. Heron and Plutarch shared nervous glances and then went their separate ways.

Heron climbed up the stairs to the observation room. Peering through a modest hole in the ceiling, she could watch the miracle unfold.

The incense smoke was thick near the hole and made her eyes water, but it was necessary to hide the ropes the vulture would fly upon.

After the priest appeared from his hidden spot, he made a hash of his part, but Plutarch adjusted accordingly. The temple's patrons were rowdy and drunk, which helped the illusion work. When the ropes lifted the statue, the crowd cheered.

Heron sighed, knowing the most difficult part was over. As long as the priest moved at a moderate pace, they would float the statue across the temple floor, safely and without incident. She could almost feel the crushing debts ease from her back.

As she watched the priest lead the statue down the aisle, and the temple followers reveled in its wonder, Heron noticed a strange man in the pews.

His black hair was flecked with gray and had been cinched into a knot on his head. Even from her angle, she could see he stood at least a head taller than the others. He wore ratty furs that marked him as a barbarian of the northern Germanic tribes and despite the wine skin in his hands, he seemed infinitely more alert than the temple followers surrounding him. But she couldn't figure out why he would be in the Temple of Nekhbet in Alexandria.

Her thoughts were interrupted when she noticed the statue wobbling slightly. The priest was leading the statue too quickly. He had a thin metal cord attached to a girdle around his waist that linked him to the bottom of the statue.

While the pulley system kept the statue suspended, and rollers helped it move across the floor, hidden by the mirrors; the priest's forward movement was required to get it to the other side of the temple.

Heron yelled, "Slow down, you imbecile!"

The priest did not slow, and in fact, sped up—buoyed by the cheering of the crowd. Even before the statue began to tip, Heron knew what was going to happen.

She sprinted down the stairs to the acolyte chamber, summoning the configuration of the pulleys into her mind, so she could cut the right one when she arrived.

The pulley system was not in the formation she expected as she slid to a stop. The cross was lopsided with one pulley pulled out of place, but she quickly made adjustments to her plan. She also briefly considered that the ropes had been tampered with, but she had no time to investigate.

The ropes strained and the pulleys groaned against the load of the statue. When the statue fell, it would tear the room and anyone in it apart.

She hoped Plutarch recognized the danger at the lifting mechanism. The stone blocks would likely be thrown from the tower.

Heron pulled a hidden knife from her tunic and sliced a slack rope decisively. She grabbed the end and ran down the stairs to the basement.

She'd forgotten to grab a lantern but didn't have time to

go back and get one. The screaming from the temple above her goaded her to hurry.

Heron splashed through the muck, using the faint light from the stairs to guide her way. She stepped on what she thought was a rat as she reached the bucket, which was now full of water from opening the door.

Hitching a quick knot, she sawed through the thick rope as she heard the screams reach a crescendo. Without the bucket to hold it down, the counterweight pulled her rope, falling into a deep well beneath the basement.

As the counterweight fell, pulling against the statue's pulley, the whole building shook and muck and water fell from the ceiling, dousing her. Heron was knocked to her knees from the impact. As she struggled to her feet, she tested the rope with her hand, finding it pulled taut, indicating that it now held the weight of the statue.

Heron ran back up to survey the damage. Peering around a hidden alcove, she could see the statue had fallen into, but hadn't broken through, the temple wall, thanks to her counterweight.

However, the interior of the temple was ruined and small fires had broken out when candles and braziers had been scattered. She doubted that Ghet would complete the payment to her, no matter how much she argued that it was the temple's fault. The image of the tampered pulley stayed firmly pressed into her mind.

Heron slipped from the temple, avoiding the crowds streaming towards the partial destruction. It wouldn't be long before Lys heard about the disaster and would come calling for her debts, knowing she couldn't pay.

Fire brigades and city guards blocked her way. She would have to go around the Museum to reach her workshop. It would take longer but she would make sure she didn't get pressed into service putting out the fires.

She pushed through the crowd, going the opposite way, already planning the supplies they would need for their journey. She wasn't sure if they would head south or east, but either way, they would have to flee Alexandria.

# 5

The foundry fires had dimmed by the time Heron burst through the courtyard gate, using the hidden lever to open it from the outside.

The sun had set, leaving a pink haze in the sky. Torches had sprung up throughout the city. Heron moved through the near darkness of the foundry, slamming her foot against obstacles more than once in her rush.

In a pile of black sand, broken from the mold, faintly glowing pieces of broken egg shell, or at least that's what they appeared to be, lay scattered. Heron couldn't remember what job Punt had been working on.

"Master Heron?" A gruff voice rumbled through the darkness.

Punt stood away from the fire, something clutched in his hand. He appeared confused or conflicted. She couldn't tell in the dim light.

"Another fine pour," she said, noticing the thinness of the castings.

"Pour?" Punt hesitated, clearly lost in thoughts. "Oh. Thank you, Master Heron." His voice was as steady and emotionless as his mannerisms. Sudden movements did not make for a foundryman that lived long and no better foundryman existed in the whole of Alexandria, and maybe not in the whole of the known world. At least he would find work again easily, she thought.

"In truth, I thought them egg shells of some great bird, so skillful your craft," she said.

Punt mumbled.

"But I'm sorry to say they will progress no further in this workshop," she said. "Sepharia and I must flee the city ahead of our debts."

Heron expected Punt to offer condolences or frustration, or say nothing at all, as his thoughts usually ran deep.

"A man came to the gate a little while ago," said Punt.

Her heart constricted.

"Was it Lysimachus?" she asked.

Punt shook his head, while staring at the small bag in his hand.

"A northerner by his garb and massive, even accounting for my size." Punt stood a head shorter than Heron. He was not a dwarf, but he was not much taller than one.

Heron knew that it had to be the same northerner she'd seen in the Temple of Nekhbet. The man stuck out like a botched equation in a number sieve.

She didn't know much about northern customs. Maybe he was coming to collect damages since he'd been in the temple during the near collapse.

"I have no time for him now," she said. "I'm certain I will not get a chance to conclude proper goodbyes with Plutarch and the others. Would you give them my heartfelt thanks for such exemplary service in my workshop?"

Heron left Punt in the foundry, fumbling for his words. If she'd waited for him to get them out, it would give Lys more time to come calling.

Sepharia was hunched over a table with her goggles fastened on her head, working under the light of a half-burnt candle, delicately tapping a miniature brass hammer against a tiny chain.

"Sepharia," Heron said gravely.

Her niece burst into tears as soon as she turned.

"Gather your things," said Heron. "We must flee this night."

"But this is our home." The tears streaked down Sepharia's face, smearing the dirt.

"No time for tears," said Heron, wondering if she should have kept her niece so protected all these years. Now she would have to face the cruel world outside the workshop walls.

A heavy banging on the front door startled them both.

"Blow out your candle," Heron whispered through gritted teeth.

Someone banged again, and Heron heard a familiar voice calling out. Heron snuck up to the entryway while the banging continued.

"Open this door or I'll have my men break it down and then I won't be so forgiving," said Lysimachus.

Heron began backing away slowly. They would have to flee without any of their things.

"And if you're thinking about escaping out the back, I have guards posted there as well," yelled Lysimachus.

Heron closed her eyes and took a deep breath. Guards meant rough men with clubs and not a hint of mercy. She wouldn't be able to avoid this encounter.

"Just a moment," she yelled out.

Heron collected herself before she opened the door.

Outside, Lysimachus waited with four thugs. His opulent attire contrasted to their rough tunics and dirty feet.

"Alabarch Lysimachus, so pleased to have you visit my humble workshop," said Heron, bowing slightly.

"If by humble you mean poor, then by all means," sneered Lysimachus. "When I heard about the Temple of Nekhbet, I thought I should make sure you didn't think about fleeing the city."

"I have other jobs," she said. "I will pay my debts."

The Alabarch brushed aside an errant curl and smiled wistfully. "Oh, but I'm sure they will dry up, as sure as the great desert, when they hear of this disaster. I'm beginning to believe all the talk about you being cursed."

Heron blew hot breath from her lips. "The fault lies squarely at the foot of the temple's high priest Ghet. He'd tampered with my designs and caused the statue's fall. I intend to take him to court."

Lysimachus made an amused sound. "The result, win or lose, will leave you still far short of the customers required to pay your debts. Who wants to do business with someone who's always suing their way out of their mistakes?"

Heron had nothing to say, because the customs man was right. But she hadn't really intended to sue, because she was going to flee the city. Lysimachus saw right through her.

"So there you have it. A miracle worker whose miracles are frowned upon by the gods." The Alabarch had wandered inside the entryway, pushing his way past, two of the thugs followed, while the other two stayed outside.

"To be honest," said Lysimachus. "I believe more in the might of arms and coin, rather than the fickle whims of the gods. I might as well be tossing bones to understand them."

Lysimachus straightened his crimson chlamys, pursing his lips while he did.

"But I truly wonder about this curse thing. I might be doing you a favor by shutting you down and selling you to pay your debts," he said.

The two thugs moved near Heron. She felt they were going to grab her at any moment.

"And maybe it is the gods who divine your fate," he said. "For this morning I saw a vision, standing in this very room. One that I did not know existed until today."

Heron steeled her face, knowing he spoke of Sepharia. "What vision do you speak of?"

Lysimachus moved close to Heron, putting a hand on her shoulder. "Why, your daughter. And I can see why you've been hiding her all these years. She could make Helen of Troy jealous."

"I have no daughter," said Heron. "That girl works for me."

Lysimachus laughed, his pot belly shaking. Even his thugs chuckled along with their master.

"I'm no fool, so don't play me as one," said Lysimachus. "That girl is as much your daughter as the Governor likes boys, and I should know, I've sold him a fair share."

It was common knowledge that Governor Flaccus purchased boys for his amusement, but saying such things out loud could be dangerous. That Lysimachus said it so easily showed Heron how much power the customs man had gathered.

"Don't be so glum, dear Heron," said Lysimachus, squinting and giving a rueful smile as if he'd just said the most entertaining thing. "That daughter might be proof that the gods haven't cursed you."

Heron held her tongue, as nothing she could say would help her cause.

"I'd be willing to forgive some of—" Lysimachus was cut

short when Punt appeared suddenly.

The four thugs reacted swiftly to his presence, two moving to defend the Alabarch, and two moving to intercept Punt. Though considerably shorter than the thugs, his arms were as big as their legs and littered with scars from the foundry. Punt had been able to sneak up so easily because his skin, already a deep bronze, was covered in soot, making him nearly invisible in the dark.

Heron moved to stop Punt from attacking Lysimachus, thinking that was his intent. Punt surprised them all by tossing a small object at the customs man.

She knew what it was the moment it hit Lysimachus' hands, but not how he had acquired it. The bag made a heavy *chink*—the sound of coins.

"Apologies, Alabarch and Master Heron for interrupting," said Punt in his gruff emotionless tone.

Heron sensed by the way that Lysimachus weighed the bag in his hand that the sum was sizable. She wanted to pepper Punt with questions, but doing so would risk whatever stratagem he was invoking.

"Payment for one of our other jobs just came in," said Punt.

Lysimachus' mood soured as he peeked into the bag. His thugs seemed thoroughly confused by the change in events, visibly hesitating on their way to accost Punt.

"Stand down," said Lysimachus and the thugs backed off.

Punt glanced stone-faced at Heron. "It was the northerner that had come in earlier. I forgot to give you the payment in my haste to break my molds before they had cooled too much. Apologies for my inattentiveness."

Heron kept her face calm, as she knew of no job they had contracted for the northerner. "Apologies accepted Punt, but do make sure that it doesn't happen again. We should not challenge our guests with surprises."

She nodded and Punt left the entry room. One of the thugs tried to keep him from leaving by putting out his arm, but Punt walked right through it. Heron knew well enough from bumping into Punt that he was built from granite.

"Cursed or favored, the gods can't seem to make up their mind," said Lysimachus coldly. "Either way, this payment only covers your interest for the turn of another moon. I will expect another payment equal to this, plus a sizable dent in your principle at that time, equal to forty talents."

Heron nearly choked on the amount.

Lysimachus tucked the coin purse into his silver belt and prepared to leave. As he crossed the threshold of her entryway, he paused and said over his shoulder: "I would be happy to take a loss on my debts for the company of a certain young lady, regardless if she is your daughter or not."

"I would sell myself first," said Heron.

"It may come to that." Lysimachus snorted and motioned for his thugs to follow. Spinning around and walking backwards, the Alabarch yelled back to her with arms raised. "And don't even think of running. I'll be giving all the gate guards your descriptions and offering hefty rewards should you dare to run."

The Alabarch turned back around, laughing, tending his curls bouncing on his head and straightening his chlamys.

Heron sunk to her heels and put a hand to her mouth. She heard a soft footfall behind her and spun around to find Sepharia lurking in the darkness.

Her niece made a tiny yelp and scurried off. There was no doubt that Sepharia had heard the Alabarch's threats and his interest in her.

Heron's head thrummed with the implications of an impending migraine. Tiny spots formed before her eyes and her stomach roiled in nausea. Before the migraine could claim her completely, Heron stumbled to her quarters and crashed onto the cot, letting the pain consume her.

# 6

Plutarch announced his entrance with a dutiful cough. Heron was hunched over the drafting desk with an ink tipped quill clutched in her hand. Errant ink smears littered her tunic. Sheaves of parchment marked with neat lines, cylinders and other geometric shapes, annotated with tiny lettering, lay across the surface haphazardly. An ornate box filled with a pale violet powder sat on the corner of the desk.

The workshop foreman waited at the doorway and adjusted his tunic, waiting for Heron to notice. He coughed again and her head bobbed up.

"Apologies, Master Heron," said Plutarch. "You have a visitor. He says his name is Agog."

Plutarch stepped aside and the northerner ducked through the doorway into the workshop.

Lost in the designs of the moment, Heron couldn't remember why he was important. Then she recalled the coins, nodding to Plutarch to leave the barbarian with her.

The foreman stepped close to her and whispered, "Can I

bring you a meal or drink? The dark circles around your eyes are worse than normal."

Plutarch glanced at the ornate box. Heron frowned.

"The gods be damned, you know well I do not eat or drink while I'm working. Go be a wet nurse to someone else and leave me be," said Heron.

Plutarch paled and left swiftly, glancing again at the box. Heron regretted her words after he was gone, but she dared not show weakness before a client and Plutarch knew that. She would apologize later.

Heron tried to focus on the barbarian, but spots formed across her eyes. Stiff-legged, she leaned against the desk and lifted a small silver spoon from the box and placed it against her nose, inhaling the lotus powder.

The spots retreated, and she could once again focus on the barbarian in her workshop.

From the spy hole in the temple, his size had been evident, but standing in the same room with him, she appreciated his presence even more. Even though he carried no weapons, Heron could imagine Agog with a great two-handed sword in his hands, hewing his enemies in half with ease.

Heron was familiar with the hair knot tied on his head, but she couldn't recall the name for it. The knot reminded her of the tails on the Persian horses, except his was black and flecked with gray rather than brown.

As she studied him, he studied her with his impenetrable green eyes. She was not at all surprised when he spoke in fluent Greek.

"What is that powder?" said Agog. He ended his words with a click of the tongue, punctuating his question.

"Medicine," she answered, putting the spoon back into the box and closing the lid. "Your coin made the most fortunate and awkward entrance last night."

"I wanted to ensure I acquired the services of the best miracle worker in Alexandria," he said.

The lotus powder made itself known with a shiver zipping up her spine. Her face flushed with fever.

Heron indicated the workshop behind her with a sweep of her hand. "You've acquired all the talents my humble workshop can offer."

Agog stepped forward, clearly reviewing the contents of the grand workshop for the first time. He bent his neck at the half-finished falcon head on heavy timber scaffolding.

"That will go to the Temple of Horus when it's complete," she said smiling, even though word had come that morning that the Horus Temple had pulled its contract. The down payment, and more, had already been spent on materials.

"Those orange lights through the archway are the fires from our foundry. Punt, our blacksmith, knows no equal," she explained.

Agog nodded, studying the Horus' head intently. "Have you made war machines before?"

Heron turned to hide her disappointment. "Why, yes, we have made palintonon stone-throwers and cheirobalistras. Trifling easy to make, though we do get orders now and then from the Roman army."

Agog ignored her comment and went over to a two-wheeled cart with a box on it. The back of the box was open, revealing a series of connecting sprockets.

"What is this?" he asked, clicking his tongue again.

"An odometer," she said. "It tells the distance it has traveled. I improved on an idea first presented by Archimedes in his later writings."

Agog grunted. "The Claw of Archimedes. He was a worthy war engineer."

"Archimedes    did    much    more    than    make    war

machines, though in the end, it did little to protect him from being speared by a Roman soldier," she argued.

"Is it true he made a heat ray that could ignite ships with the reflected light of the sun?" Agog asked.

Heron swallowed the words she wanted to say. She wanted to denounce the barbarian and send him out of her workshop. While she could make devices for war, it was not what made her mind sing. But with the Alabarch's threat looming over her and Sepharia's heads, she had no choice but to engage the barbarian.

"His writings indicate as much, though I was unsure if he'd ever carried it out," Heron said.

The northerner moved to a separate table and indicated a bronze cast ball suspended above a pot. Two angled tubes jet from either side of it.

"An aeolipile," she said. "A toy that spins."

Agog spun the aeolipile lightly with his finger. It rotated a few times and then settled to a stop. "It seems more than a toy."

"Nothing I can determine," she said. "A remarkable toy, but its practical uses have escaped me."

The barbarian wandered around, poking the metal and wooden contraptions strewn across the workshop. She added explanations at times, but mostly stayed silent, glancing impatiently at the work on her desk.

"How did you make the statue lift in the air and move across the temple floor?" he asked.

Heron sighed. So this is why he had come to her, she thought.

"Simple physiks and sleight-of-hand," she said. "We were constrained by the architecture of the temple, or it would have been more spectacular."

Agog raised an eyebrow. "So you meant to bring the temple

down around their heads?"

She thought he was serious until a wry smile, lifted the corners of his lips.

"A meddling priest was the source of the disaster," she said.

"Not a god-sent curse?"

"So you've heard the rumors and still came to me for work?" she asked.

Agog nodded. "I find the gods less interested in our daily lives than we give them credit for. Mostly I find the priests are the ones interested in our daily lives."

Heron eyed the barbarian warily. "I've never met a northerner before. Are you all this philosophical?"

Agog ignored her comment, and indicated a table filled with stoppered vials and jars full of colored powders. "Are you an alchemist by chance?"

"I've dabbled," she said. "Nothing but wasted coin for my efforts."

The barbarian went to the table and shook a few vials. A detailed parchment lay underneath a ceramic plate. Agog moved it and began to study the writing.

"Just because you've paid me coin does not give you the right to poke through my things or writings," said Heron, pulling the parchment away from his view.

"So you've determined how to fool Archimedes' Principle?" said Agog.

Heron scoffed and tucked the parchment into a pile on her desk. "One cannot fool a Principle."

How the barbarian knew of such writings and interpreted her sketches so quickly baffled her. She steeled her face, lest she give away her concern.

"The story of Archimedes and the Golden Crown is a favorite of mine," he said. "I hope I can prove that clever, should I be assailed by a dishonest goldsmith, or at least have someone that clever in my employ."

"It's a good story," she said.

Heron moved to the ornate box and put her hand gently upon it. The formula of silver and lead she'd determined, in theory, could replace an equal weight of gold without upsetting its density, thus making it impervious to simple tests to verify its quality.

Heron had never attempted to test the formula and thought it would fail regardless. And the barbarian couldn't have memorized the formulas so quickly, so she felt her theory was safe.

"So about the war machines," he said.

"What about them? We haven't discussed any, save in passing reference," said Heron.

Agog put his hand to his chin thoughtfully. "I saw a statue of a Roman soldier that could move on its own and spit water from a sword. I would like to have an army of those, except the size of the Nekhbet statue and that could fight. I would pay you all the coin you need to accomplish this task."

If it weren't for the bag of coin she'd already taken from him and handed over to Lysimachus, she might have laughed in his face. After all the intelligent questioning and referencing of Archimedes and his Principle, she wasn't prepared for him to ask for an army of giant fighting automatons.

"What you ask is impossible," she said, shaking her head and trying to keep herself from shouting. "I can make statues move using a complex series of ropes and pulleys. I can make doors open and close as if by the whim of the gods. I can give life to a foundry's bellows with wind power. I can even count the number of lengths from here to Rome with unerring accuracy."

She spun the aeolipile toy. "But I cannot do that," she

said incredulously. "I would not even know how to start. You ask the impossible."

Agog not so much as blinked during her tirade. He smiled softly, almost gently, which Heron found unnerving because it seemed he was almost patronizing her. An absurdity, considering he was a northerner and she was the greatest inventor and mathematician of her time.

"The impossible stays impossible when one won't even try," he said.

Heron crossed her arms across her chest. "Next you'll be telling me the gods wish it so, so it will be done."

"The gods care nothing for my request," he said. "I ask only that you try and I will fund you generously if you do."

The northerner threw a small bag of coin onto her desk. Heron eyed it suspiciously.

"To get you started, since my last payment went toward your debts."

Heron turned away to hide her shame, leaning heavily against the desk. She had hoped to hide that from him. It worried her that he had contacts in the city already.

"Plato have pity, I don't even know where to start," she said. "I don't even know how I would power the damn thing, or how to get them to take orders."

Agog shrugged. "Start wherever the beginning is. Just as long as you start."

She grabbed her own hair and pulled lightly. The request was madness. She felt the fool for even thinking about taking it. But she had no choice if she wanted to keep Lysimachus away from Sepharia.

Heron picked up the bag of coin and when she turned around, the barbarian was gone. She never even heard him leave. Heron shuddered. Everything about the man made her wary.

# 7

The heat of the day drained out of Alexandria as the shadows rushed in. Even the foundry had cooled enough that the sweat didn't bead up on Punt's forehead each time he wiped it away.

The last of the day's work had been packed for shipment and the cupola fires had been spent. Punt ran his hand lovingly along the row of tools, touching each one as a mother touches her child. He would miss them while he was gone.

With a sack of supplies over his shoulder, Punt cut through the workshop so he could have one last word with Heron.

Candlelight dwindled around the hunched form at the desk. The quill, tip wet with ink, was still clutched in his hand. Heron snored lightly, almost like a cat purring.

His Master had been working day and night without sleep. The ornate box sat open near Heron's elbow, the pale violet dust almost gone. Punt sighed and flipped the lid closed.

The candle flame played softly across Heron's face,

exposing gaunt features and hollow eyes. Heron had been working feverously on some project for a week now.

Punt examined the parchments on the desk. Various designs of moving statues filled each one. He couldn't understand the coiled ropes or s-curved levers beneath the statues, but that wasn't why he'd worked for Heron as long as he'd been in the city.

Though Punt never bothered to ponder on it, he knew he was unmatched in his craft. Other inventors had tried to lure him away, but he had turned down every request, even when the salary was triple what he earned under Heron.

Punt had never failed in bringing to life the sketchings of Alexandria's greatest living engineer. When Heron had asked for iron castings as thin as a finger and wide as a fan, Punt had delivered. When the job required forgings as complex as a Roman army and delicate as a butterfly, he completed his task without error.

He'd never shied from a challenge, nor failed at one. Plutarch often joked that Punt had been forged in Hephaestus's fires.

So Punt had been struck dumb at the thought that Heron would send him on an errand that would require nothing of his blacksmithing skills.

Before leaving, Punt retrieved a blanket from a woven basket in the corner beneath unused scaffolding. A pair of adopted cats had been sleeping in the blanket, so Punt sniffed it for urine before draping it around Heron's shoulders.

Punt blew out the candles and left Heron asleep at his desk. He would have carried him to his quarters had he thought he could have done so without waking the man, but he knew if Heron awoke, he would return right away to his sketchings.

Bare-chested and coated with a light skim of sweat, the

night air refreshed Punt. The moon had hidden herself from the world, so the streets were dark. Only flickering candles from open windows or distant torch light gave him enough sight to avoid the sleeping dogs lying in doorways.

The faint rattle of his sack barely disturbed the near empty streets. Further away, hammers echoed like distant thunder. Punt traced the sound in his mind to Philo's foundry, lamenting that he himself was not still at work.

A hooded lantern came to life, showering him with light.

"Halt in the name of the Empire," said a rough voice in Latin.

"Ave," replied Punt, with the traditional Roman greeting.

Two soldiers dressed in walking gear, no shields but gladii at their sides, dark cloaks, and a leather breastplate stamped with the Roman seal, considered him warily.

"What business is yours to be wandering the streets at night?" said the first soldier.

Punt gripped the end of the sack, choking the fabric beneath his fingers.

The second soldier held the lantern higher. "Answer him, dung man."

Punt had heard this insult before, but never directed at him. It referenced the color of his skin and the propensity for Egyptians to burn dung fires. He flared his nostrils and flexed his massive arms in restraint. "I have labored long this day and seek my home to enjoy the company of my woman and break bread. And I did not know the streets were forbidden at night."

"Governor Flaccus has decreed that no non-Roman man shall walk the streets after dark unless that man has business of the Empire," said the first soldier.

Punt gripped the fabric tighter. "Apologies. The decree had not reached my ears this evening in the foundry."

The second soldier leaned closer, eyeing the bag suspiciously.

"What is the nature of the decree?" asked Punt, hoping to distract the soldiers.

"What do you mean 'the nature of the decree?'" asked the first soldier, clearly looking for a reason to be insulted.

Punt paused and thought through his answer carefully. He was not the skilled orator like Plutarch, who had been canvassing the city trying to lure new business to the shop. Nor could he think quickly like Heron, whose mind whirled faster than an aeolipile. Nor was his tongue as sharp as Sepharia, ever the viper, whose husband, should she ever choose to marry one, be pitied.

"Why does the honored Governor make this decree, so that I may determine if I am doing Roman business or not?" said Punt.

The two soldiers shared glances. Punt hoped they did not take his words as further insult.

The second soldier nodded. "With the influx of vermin outside the city, building ramshackles and lean-tos, thieves have been thick lately. And Flaccus wishes to make sure the city is well behaved ahead of the new taxes."

When the first soldier knocked the second in the arm, Punt seized his opportunity and spoke, "I do indeed labor this evening on the Empire's behalf."

"Speak, dung man, or feel the sword caress your belly," laughed the first soldier.

"I carry goods for Good Philo, my master, a great supporter of the Empire," said Punt, sliding a pair of coins from the pouch on his belt.

The soldier's eyes widened as Punt opened his hand revealing the two coins. Before the lantern light could fall upon them, Punt threw them high into the air, arcing over the two soldiers.

When the two soldiers spun around to catch the coins, Punt sprinted into the darkness, his short, thick legs carrying him away in powerful strides.

Cries of alarm could be heard behind him and the bullseye lantern flashed across the buildings, searching. Punt disappeared into an alley, cursing the bag he carried, for it clanked and rattled as he ran. Clutching it in his arms silenced the worst of the noise.

With the bag quieted, Punt evaded the soldiers though the advantage of darkness. After a good run through the city, he slipped inside a doorway in a cluster of buildings.

The scents of bread filled the small kitchen. A woman in a colorful robe crouched on the floor, stirring spices into a bowl of broth.

"You're early, good husband," said Astrela, peering over her shoulder. "And sweaty and out of breath. What is wrong?"

Astrela rose, and though she was no taller than Punt, and lithe, where he was built like a bull, she commanded the space like a general. His wife put her hand to her hip.

"There was no breeze tonight, so I made my own," said Punt cheerily, feeling flush with excitement for outwitting the soldiers.

Astrela narrowed her eyes and frowned. After studying Punt for a couple of breaths, she pointed to the backdoor. "Luckily for you, the bones told me much this evening, including that you would be early. A bucket of fresh water awaits. Food will be ready when you return," she said sternly.

Punt set the bag gently in the corner and went to the common courtyard in back. He washed himself silently, thinking about the encounter with the soldiers. Plutarch would be proud of his deception, throwing his disobedience to the halls of Heron's greatest rival, Philo.

His brief pride, however, faded when he thought of the new tax. Already the city groaned under the weight of oppressive taxes. How could the Romans dare add more?

When Punt returned, clay bowls and cups had been set upon the small table. Two bronze plates sat on either end. Punt breathed deeply, savoring the smells.

Astrela was pulling the bread from the oven. Punt snuck up behind her and grabbed her around the middle.

His wife squeaked and dropped the bread. "Ra's children! Do not startle me with such."

Astrela scooped the bread from the stone floor, dusting away the grit.

"Think of your foolishness when you bite into a pebble," Astrela lectured.

Punt took the bread gently from her hands and set it upon the table. He took her hands in his own, squeezing them reassuringly.

"I merely wished to hug my wife, for I missed her dearly," he said.

Astrela looked away before nodding once. Punt pulled her into his arms and embraced her, inhaling the light perfume in her hair.

"If you missed me dearly then why do you stay at the workshop so much?" she whispered into his neck.

Punt sighed. "Without fire and hammer, I am not a man, only a spirit haunting my own body. And working for Heron gives me hope for the world."

Astrela shuddered in his arms. "Why you work for that cursed man makes no sense when Philo has offered you triple to work for him." His wife pulled away, her face resuming its stern form. "And just this morning, the bones gave me grave news about your fortunes with Heron."

Punt put his fingers to Astrela's lips. "Do not speak this

way before we have eaten. Let us sup and then talk."

Astrela nodded and the two took their places around the table. They dined upon fresh bread and perch preserved in salt brine and tepenen spiced chuba; drinking wine in full, not watered down. The end of the meal brought dates soaked in honey and cinnamon.

Sucking the spices from his fingers, Punt asked, "Why do you ply me with such a grand meal? Is something wrong?"

Astrela took a long drink from her wine cup. "The bones," she said, simply, the stern face from before being replaced by a concerned one.

"Do not speak of bones," said Punt, finding his mood loosened by the wine. "They portend the future as much as a flock of geese."

"Ra's children! Do you mock me, husband?" said Astrela.

"I mean no insult, wife," he said. "But you're always speaking of bones and curses and boons and signs. It tires my mind to hear these things. A hammer bends metal when it is hot, this much I know."

"Which is why you should let me worry about these things," she said. "The ways of gods and spirits are too much for you. Especially after you've labored long in the cursed halls of Heron's workshop."

Punt slapped his hand on the table, shaking the empty dishes. "Good Heron is not cursed. Unlucky maybe, but not cursed. His time will come."

"The bones tell me otherwise," said Astrela.

Punt sighed and put his hand to his forehead. "Bones, bones, bones. Tell me of these bones so I may not have to hear of them again."

Instead of launching into her tale, Astrela cleaned up the table and poured more wine for them. Punt was used to pale watered down wine and the second cup was already going to his head.

Astrela took a sip before speaking. "When I gathered the bones in my hand, I knew it was an important throw because both my palms itched. That has happened only once before, on the day I first met you."

Astrela smiled, briefly, before turning grim and continued. "But this was not a happy throw as that one. The bones tumbled into the sign of the crow, crossed with a resurrection staff, which means terrible things. Had the staff come first, crossed with the crow, all would be different, as the staff is a powerful totem. But it was the crow that fell and the staff that followed."

She shook her head.

"Speak wife, what does it mean?" Punt said.

"At the moment of the throw, I asked how fared the house of Heron, knowing the ill-luck that has plagued the man and with it the fortunes of my husband," she said.

"Our fortunes are fine," said Punt. "We have purpose and food on the table."

Astrela ignored his comment. "I threw the bones two more times, as the weight of the first throw demanded it. I will not bore you with the details of those throws, just say that they gathered momentum towards a dark and terrible place. The bones told me there will be a great accident in the house of Heron and from that accident, the pillars of this great city will be shaken and shaken so violently, even Rome will feel it."

Punt couldn't help but laugh, though he regretted it by the slashing gaze he received from his wife.

"If that's what the bones say, then I guess we cannot avoid it," said Punt.

Astrela shook her head, taking her husband's hands within her own. "But you can. Tomorrow will be the feast of Osiris, the resurrected one. If you go to the workshop tomorrow, and burn an offering of barley, and sacrifice a goat, taking care not to let its blood fall upon any shadows. And beg coin from Master Heron, to pay the Sumerian priests to chant on his behalf, and tithe to the gods Saturn and Inanna and Nu-Gan, and purchase a hair shirt—"

Punt soured at his wife's words. "You speak madness. Heron would never do these things. He does not believe in the gods, only the power of ideas and men."

Astrela made a warding sign with her crossed fingers. "Then that is the source of his curse. The gods mock him for not believing in them."

She gripped his hands tightly, gazing into his eyes. "You do not believe as he does? That the gods do not exist?"

Punt's shoulders slumped. "No," he said quietly. "But I'm not sure what purpose they serve, nor what they want."

"It is not them who serve us, it is we that serve them," said Astrela. "We serve the gods in their whims as they divine higher purposes than we can understand. Just as you serve Master Heron, not truly knowing the purpose of his creations until they are made."

Astrela's eyes flit to the sack he'd left in the corner, reminding him of his business tomorrow. Her words hit him squarely in the gut. When Master Heron had told him what he wanted the blacksmith to do, he'd uncharacteristically argued. Punt's gifts were made for the foundry, not of the tongue. That was Plutarch's realm.

"You seem concerned about the contents of that bag, husband," said Astrela.

Punt rose and returned with the bag, pulling from it a brass lamp. A curved iron bar rose from the base in which a wick would be suspended. The clever mechanics were hidden inside the base along with the oil.

"Is that the self-trimming lamp? You've told me of its

creation before. Quite magical, I would say," she said.

Punt nodded. "I've made scores of these lamps in the last week."

"Scores? Then why did you bring home a bag full of them?" she asked.

Punt set the lamp on the table, rubbing the side absently. Astrela's words about not understanding her master's purpose were made even more true by the contents of the bag.

Punt spoke, though the words sounded to him as if they were coming from someone else. "Good Master Heron wants me to go from shop to shop and sell these lamps to the shop keepers. I am not to return until I have sold every lamp."

Astrela mumbled something that could have been, "Ra's children!" and gathered the dishes up to wash them in the courtyard.

Alone with his thoughts, Punt stared at the lamp trying to figure out why his master would send him on such a foolish and ill-conceived errand.

No answers came.

# 8

Heron set the quill next to the ink well and rubbed her temples. The silence of the workshop had become a distraction.

She opened the ornate box to find it empty again and her hand immediately dipped to the meager pouch at her side. The coins were far too few.

A plate of half-eaten waterfowl sat next to the ink well. Her stomach protested even the sight of it, so she drank deeply from the cup of wine instead.

Heron stood, and the world rotated around her. A heavy pounding echoed in her head. Too heavy, in fact, to be in her head, she realized. There was someone at the front door. She straightened her tunic and went to answer it before Sepharia got a foolish notion again.

Reaching the door, she hesitated, thinking about Lysimachus' henchmen and that no one else was at the workshop. The person at the door, pounded again, much too feebly to be thugs or the barbarian.

The door rattled lightly again, under the insistent pounding of her caller. Heron envisioned the weak fisted priest from the Temple of Nekhbet, standing on the other side. The high priest had sold all of her equipment to an opportunistic Philo to pay for their repairs.

She shook her head as the door rattled again. It couldn't be them. They'd been throwing dead rats over her courtyard gate since the disaster. If they truly had coin to spare, and were spiteful enough, they would have hired a Hittite assassin to take care of her.

Whatever her fate, she couldn't ignore it by not answering, she decided.

Sighing deeply, Heron opened the door to find a beggar in dirty, wine-soaked robes reaching out to hit the door. The old man had a gaping near-toothless mouth and reeked of urine and gutter wine.

Heron held her arm across her mouth. "Go away, old man. I'm not giving handouts here."

The beggar staggered on his frail, emaciated legs and Heron thought he might fall over dead on the spot. Then as if the clouds had parted and sunshine poured through, he opened his eyes and spoke in fluent Latin.

"Greetings, Heron of Alexandria. I bring a job for your hallowed halls," said the old man, holding his hands clasped together at his waist and swaying slightly.

"Hollowed would be more appropriate," said Heron. "I'm afraid all my workers are currently busy and cannot be pulled from their jobs for another."

Heron hated to lie to the old man, but she was sure he had no job to offer and was probably a lunatic trying to remove her of coin, though his Greek-accented Latin made her wonder. And he had made imitation of the oration styles used at the Great Library.

"This job would require only your great mind," said the

old man.

The request piqued her curiosity. She felt foolish for even considering the old man's request but she had to know.

"Speak your job so I can be rid of you," she said. "And if this is a foolish attempt to gain coin, I will call my guards on you."

The old man broke into a grin, revealing his few remaining teeth, as if he knew no one else was at the workshop.

"I would speak to you in the privacy of your entryway," said the old man. "For this job is for your ears only."

Heron crossed her arms, shaking her head. Maybe he really was an assassin? Could he be hiding a dagger under that urine soaked robe? She had heard of assassins with poison concealed in a glass tube that only had to be thrust into one's side. Even an old man could cut her with glass.

"Come in, beggar," she said. "But if you think to attack me, I will use my dagger."

The old man smiled again, mocking her bluff.

With the door closed, the old man reached inside his tattered robe. Heron stepped backwards, expecting a weapon to be revealed.

He pulled a coin purse from his robes and tossed it to her. Heron checked to find the amount modest, but it could pay for a few pressing needs.

"What is this job?" Heron asked, hoping to be rid of the beggar soon.

The old man coughed, spittle flinging from his lips. Heron stepped back again.

"To find who burned the Great Library during the reign of Gaius Julius Caesar," said the old man.

Heron laughed. "Where did you get this coin for such a foolish request? The Library burned a century ago and all clues vanished under the political coverings of the Roman

Empire."

She threw the coin purse back to the old man.

"Take your delusions somewhere else. You speak the madness of gods," said Heron. "No fee is large enough to anger the Roman Empire and I have enough problems of my own making."

The old man wavered on his feet, hesitating. Confusion wracked his form as his mouth opened and closed like a dying fish.

"You were sent by someone else on this errand, weren't you?" she asked.

The old man nodded.

"Who?" she asked.

"I am not to say, good master Heron," said the old man.

Heron blew hot breath. The world was full of mysteries and problems and strange visitors to her doors these days. Had she believed in the gods, she might have thought they were testing her.

She was familiar enough with all the religions, having made their miracles for them, that she knew their stories well. Each religion had its version of the *testing*. But typically, it was a believer that was tested. She believed nothing but what was observed, true to Aristotle's theory of universals. This *testing* was just coincidence.

"Then tell me why this person needs to know?" she asked. From the reason, she might deduce the requester. It had to be someone she knew. Maybe Philo wanting to trap her and finish her off for good.

"I cannot say," said the old man, tapping his finger to his grizzled chin in a searching manner.

Heron gave the old man a long look. "You once spoke in the Library? You are not familiar to me, but you carry its habits."

His eyes rolled in his head and then came back center, locked onto her.

"Once, yes," he said. "But no longer."

The old man glanced to the floor sheepishly, almost embarrassed with shame long past. It was mixed with confusion as he seemed to be searching for a word or phrase, lost in his wine-addled brain.

Heron decided she'd wasted enough time on the old man, even if he'd once graced the Great Library.

"Time to go," said Heron, putting her hand on his shoulder to turn him toward the door. Knowing that he was once a philosopher, calmed her concerns about him.

The old man stood firm, clearly still trying to remember.

"Take that coin back to your master and tell him that I am not interested, especially for a pittance," she said.

Her words sparked the memory in the old man, for he exclaimed and clapped his hands together. She could see the philosopher of old in that instant and smiled with him at his memory.

"That coin was only a token," he said. "The man who sent me seeks the truth of who started the fires of Alexandria. He priced that knowledge at the value of the Lighthouse."

Heron gasped. "Surely, he is mad, this benefactor of yours."

The old man grinned, rocking on his heels, visibly pleased he had remembered the whole of his speech.

"The Lighthouse was built on the treasury's of kings. Eight thousand talents did Sostratus spend to build such a wonder," she said. "No man could offer those rewards unless he was a wealthy king."

Heron paled at her own words. A king could have the funds to pay her and the motivation as well. Perhaps, relatives of the Ptolemies were plotting their revenge and sought knowledge of the fires to sway the Alexandrians.

Others had reason, as well. King Amantienmemide to the south had been beaten back by the Romans on multiple occasions and had ties to Egypt. The Parthian Kings, like Gondophares, were subject to Rome, but bristled under its watchful gaze.

Rome's potential enemies were so numerous she dared not solidify her thinking to one, lest she be wrong and it tainted her actions incorrectly.

But why send a beggar? It was a clue that she would have to unravel if she chose to follow through this insanity. Heron chuckled out loud as she realized she was considering it.

"Tell this benefactor of yours that if I am to take this job, I will need fifty talents to get started, for the appropriate bribes and research assistants," she said.

Fifty talents was a massive sum, not compared to the size of her debts, but considerable.

The old man nodded. "I will carry your message."

"I need the fifty talents by tomorrow," she said. "And that trifle of coin today, as a token, you said."

The old man nodded again and tossed back the coin bag before leaving. She weighed it in her hand, smiling and thinking of what she would purchase with the coin.

The fifty talents would not go towards bribes or research assistants as she had said. She would need the money to pay off Lysimachus. It wasn't the complete debt, but would keep him from pawing at Sepharia for another month, giving her time to come up with more money.

Maybe she could drag out the investigation, fifty talents at a time. That way she might keep Lysimachus off her until she could figure out how to make Agog's war machine and silence the debt forever.

Heron laughed. The non-existent gods were nothing

compared to opportunity, skill, and reason.

She left the workshop soon after, with the ornate box in her hand, buoyed by her good fortune. She would stop by the Library first, before moving on to other errands.

Walking briskly in the morning sun, cooled by breezes coming in from the sea, Heron couldn't help but glance repeatedly at the Lighthouse across the bay. The white marble structure climbed to a point, high in the sky, the statue of Poseidon resting on the dome above the fire lens.

Heron chuckled to herself. Solve the greatest mystery of Alexandria's past and receive a reward equal to the great wonder. With that coin, she would transform the city to a place worthy of the title of the City of Miracles.

And not the miracles of the temples. Real, practical miracles that would change people's lives and free them from the tyranny of the gods.

Under her care, she would put to work every workshop and transform it into the greatest city on the Earth, making Rome and its Senate pale under the glory of the Alexandria. A City of Wonder, perhaps.

The heat of the day felt strangely buoyant, and Heron reached the Library proper in good spirits. Heron entered a side courtyard, hoping to avoid the crowds near the front. A lesser fellow of the Library recognized Heron, marking a greeting with a hearty nod.

Other patrons recognized her as she slipped through the many hallways and they called out greetings.

"—good Heron, it has been far too long."

"—the Library misses your airs, Heron."

"—were you planning on waiting until the last days of earth had come before gracing us again?"

"—Ave, Heron!"

"—see Levictus, I told you Heron would come back. He's

probably been creating whole new schools of learning for us to study while he's been gone."

The well wishes and genuine greetings warmed her heart. She'd been away too long from the Great Library. She wished, as some had suggested, that she was working on a new tome of learning. The last one she'd presented as a gift was *Geometrica*.

Instead, she'd been busy trying to dig from the mountains of debt her twin had left her. The constant failures of her miracles hadn't helped, either.

A scribbler with ink stained hands and an armload of scrolls passed her on his way to the deeper halls. She thought she recognized the man, though she couldn't remember where. A hint of burnt cinnamon followed him.

Heron passed through a narthex filled with musty scrolls in piles on a table, waiting for delivery to the storage rooms. An apprentice scurried in and scooped up an armful to disappear into a hallway behind her.

The Inner Antechamber lay beyond the narthex, after a long walk through a narrow hall, passing through a chamber filled with sycamore trees bound in marble pots with benches between, so one could sit and quietly think.

The space was less an antechamber and more a cathedral to light. Ebony columns circled the great chamber, surrounding a central, circular pool, sparkling in the sun shining in from above. On one side, a fresco of painted stones climbed the wall, revealing the god Apollo in his entirety, clutching a book in his hand and firing sunbeams down to earth.

If one walked the circumference of the room, glancing at the pillars, they appeared as black trees in a sunlit forest. Only the hard marble floor, alternating tiles of gilded diamonds and black moons, gave away the true nature of the room.

Heron ran her hand across the rough surface of the pillar, feeling the breeze swirling from the opening in the high ceiling.

When it rained, she liked to come to the Antechamber and listen to the falling rain play music on the surface of the pool.

"Greetings, Heron. Giving up paying off your debts to fair Lysimachus?" The voice cut through the calming air of the antechamber, slicing her across the back.

"If you paid me a tenth of the fees you received for the works stolen from my designs, I would be free and clear long ago," said Heron.

Philo strolled between the pillars to stand across from Heron. Her rival fancied himself a cultured citizen of Rome, dressing in the fashions of the Empire, which was at the moment, a verdant toga of silk, bound with golden edges. His hair had been powdered with a substance that made it appear thicker and darker.

"Jealousy of my elegant designs will get you nowhere, except under the Alabarch's rack," said Philo. "Though it looks by the thinness, he's been starving you."

Heron ignored the later comment, and said, "Then why did you purchase my equipment from the Temple of Nekhbet? I'm sure you'll trot out the floating statue trick soon enough."

"The Na-gun's loved my floating statue, but that was weeks ago. I had come up with the idea all on my own before," he said, glancing peevishly. "And I was just saving the temple from the ruin of your disaster, by buying up your broken things."

"Careful, Philo. If the Alabarch runs me out of town, your muse will dry up," she said, running her hand along the pillar, using the touch to calm her urge to punch him. Heron was thankful she'd arrived at the Library in good spirits, or she might have strangled Philo before his fifth word had reached her ear.

Philo snorted. "Lob your insults all you want. Just remember in the records of history they will remember me as the greatest to have roamed the Great Library, and you will only be remembered as a failed debtor."

Philo sauntered away from her, taking a different passage from the room. She hadn't come to banter with Philo, though it confirmed what she'd suspected, that he'd bought her Nekhbet designs to create a miracle of his own.

He'd been the benefactor of her misfortune so many times, she wondered if he'd had a hand in them somehow, but she'd never been able to detect a trace.

Heron made for the bowels of the Library, the places filled with the remnants of the fires. It hadn't been the Library itself that had burnt during the battle with Caesar, but the warehouses that housed the many tomes and scrolls that couldn't be kept in the main buildings.

The few that had been salvaged, only a fraction of the whole, had been brought to the Mausoleum. Heron nodded to the attendant as she entered. Her time spent teaching and her gifts of knowledge gave her access to the whole Library without restraint.

"May I see the *List of Accounting*?" she asked.

The attendant nodded and disappeared into the dim light, carrying a covered candelabra, revealing swirling dust motes hanging amid the shelves of burnt books. The narrow shelves crowded the busy room.

Minutes later, the glow from the attendant's candelabra returned, and with it, a bound book, marked with the Library's seal.

Heron accepted the book, careful not to damage the edge. The tome listed the known works to have been destroyed. Either from the memory of its scribes and scholar, or by investigating the fiery remnants.

She set the book under the candelabra, running her finger along the listing, turning each page at a pace of one per breath.

The attendant watched her carefully, not because she might damage the book, but because, she assumed, he'd heard of her famed memory.

After paging through the book, she closed it and handed it back. The wide-eyed attendant opened the book cursorily as if he didn't expect the words to be there anymore.

Heron smiled and left the way she came, the images of the words dancing in her head. She would copy them down at the workshop later when she had time and study the results. If she was to figure out who started the fires, or at least acquire enough information to keep the coin coming, she needed information about the catastrophe.

The list would give her an idea of what was lost during the fires. It wasn't the complete accounting, but it offered the best estimate.

Heron was familiar enough with the story of the fires to know that holes were missing in the official version.

The facts of the battle were clear. Caesar had come to subdue Egypt and ally himself with Ptolemy XIII, but had on the basis of an evening in Cleopatra's arms, instead closed ranks with her.

Escaping the Egyptian army, Caesar led his small force and took the island of Pharos, the location of the Lighthouse. As the Egyptians rallied to their ships, Caesar, ever the opportunist, seized his chance when the east winds blew, and set fire to his enemy's fleet.

The fire quickly spread through the harbor, leaping into the warehouses on the wharves, ending in a conflagration that claimed over four hundred thousand papyrus scrolls by the Library historian's accounting. Only a scant remainder made the list, but from the titles alone, Heron could guess at the magnitude of the loss.

While the facts were clear: the fleet's fire, the battle

with Caesar and what was lost; the rumors and untruths that erupted from the ribbons of flame and billowing smoke obfuscated the source of the destruction.

Written accounts of the fire starting long before the fleet fire reached the land were numerous. Though, they were not well kept as they proved an unpopular opinion in Alexandria. No one liked to think that someone from the city had started the fires.

Most residents assumed that Caesar had sent saboteurs into the city to start the fires and distract its citizens from the battle, giving them a choice between fighting him and saving the Library. Rome had also been long known to harbor ill will towards Alexandria's place on the world stage. If Caesar removed the Library's influence, then Rome was free to continue its dominance.

Other reasons surfaced over the decades that passed. The last remaining Carthaginians burnt down the Library in spite to keep it out of Rome's hands. The Egyptian god Ra, jealous of the Library, started the blaze with a sunbeam. The temples in the city feared the influence of the Library on its followers and had it destroyed. Or even that it had been Archimedes' heat ray, smuggled into the Lighthouse by Syracuse dissenters.

The last one had made Heron chuckle the first time she'd heard it. The heat ray made from reflected sunlight had been a tale that even she couldn't believe. Of course, she'd performed small scale experiments that proved it wasn't true, but that didn't keep people from speculating. It was often the most outrageous idea that traveled the furthest.

Heron sighed, holding up her arm to block the midday sun. Her eyes hadn't adjusted from the dim corridors of the Great Library, so she did not see the men until they had grabbed her by the arms.

# 9

Heron recognized the men as thugs of the Alabarch. Fingers dug into her arms as they steered her through the crowd. While they kept to the center of the main streets, Heron played along. If they veered away towards an alley or a doorway, she would fight them.

The thug on her right had the breath of a dung beetle and a jagged scar on his chin. It appeared that something with powerful jaws had bit him long ago.

Lefty, as she began thinking of him, dragged his leg slightly at each step. If she had to get away from them, she'd only need to outrun dung breath.

They were broken men, but useful to one such as the Alabarch. Hired muscle was cheap in the city, only one step above slave.

She assumed they derived pleasure from their actions. Lefty leered at her venomously, the intent of what he would do with her in a dark, secluded room was apparent on his scruffy face. She doubted he would care the nature of her sex, only pausing with an amused snort when he ripped off the molded genitalia before assaulting her.

As they reached the square near Pompey's Pillar, the feeling in her arms had given way to needles. A crowd had gathered on the cobble stones, pushing each other around a hastily built stage.

The moment she saw the man and woman on the stage, Heron knew the reason she'd been brought. The pair lay on their backs chained to a box with unsupported limbs hanging over the edge. A second box, heavy by the size of it, rested on their chests.

The woman moaned a high keening wail like a babe crying for milk. The man was visibly trying to stifle a cough. When he finally did, it set off convulsions and a second round of coughing. Even above the crowd, Heron could hear his whimpering.

"They own the Spinning Wheel trading company, though for not much longer if they can't pay their debts," said a familiar voice.

The thugs spun her around to face Lysimachus. The Alabarch had dyed his bouncy curls the color of gold. His pot belly was hidden beneath a chlamys of maroon silk and his many perfumes overcame even dung breath's stench, making her want to retch. He held his ring encrusted hand to Heron.

"You can release him, I only wish to talk, this time," said Lysimachus.

The thugs milled nearby, keeping hands on the daggers at their belts.

"Escaping to the Library isn't going to get my coin back," said Lysimachus.

"I had a question for an old friend," said Heron. "A problem I was stuck on."

Lysimachus laughed, holding his hands out as if he were

giving a speech on a stage. "The *Michanikos* going to ask for help? You lie poorly."

Heron rubbed her arms, trying to get the feeling back.

"Why were you really at the Library?" said Lysimachus. "I should get to know what my investment is doing, right?"

"I thought you were the customs collector for the City," she said, goading him into changing the subject.

Lysimachus held his arms high, letting the silk sleeves fall to his shoulders. "Why Heron, I *am* the City. For whoever controls the coin, controls the city. Even Flaccus, that dreadfully boorish fop dares not oppose me. I keep him supplied in boys and he does not bother to open his beady little Roman eyes."

The woman on the stage broke into a soul wrenching scream that faded into more crying.

"These two fools thought they could escape the city and their debts," said Lysimachus. "But as I am a vengeful Alabarch, I am also merciful, so when their three days are complete, I will let them return to their business so they may work off their debts."

The crowd seemed bored by the continued anguish of the couple and dispersed, flowing back into the city or outside to the camps.

"In your case, I could be even more merciful, forgiving the whole of your debt for one small favor," grinned Lysimachus.

The Alabarch held his hand to Heron's face, pressing a ring into her nose. The effluence of perfumes made her eyes water.

The ring had two golden claws on the sides of a ruby. Heron held her ground, not even flinching as the claws bit into her flesh. "I would treat her fairly, of course," he said, speaking of Sepharia. "Assuming she did everything I commanded."

Lysimachus pulled his hand away and wiped it on Lefty's

leg.

"We both know that women are the dull half of the species." Lysimachus winked. "If it weren't for their wet thighs and warm wombs, what need of them would we have?"

The Alabarch smirked and patted Heron on the shoulder. "And the Governor doesn't need them at all does he?"

The thugs both laughed while Lysimachus kept his hand on Heron's shoulder.

"Staying silent isn't going to protect your daughter," he said.

"She's not my daughter," said Heron, truthfully.

"Fine," he shrugged. "Call her what you want. Staying silent isn't going to protect that girl that lives in your home. Be she your daughter or some common whore."

Lysimachus and Heron matched gazes until the Alabarch finally broke away.

"'No,' is the answer it seems," said Lysimachus, gritting his jaw. He poked a finger into Heron's shoulder. "It seems your debts are coming due earlier than planned. I will stop by tomorrow at dusk for sixty talents, or I will be taking the girl with me."

Heron kept her gaze level.

"I will be keeping a close watch on the workshop. Don't think about running. You're much too well known to make it far." He tilted his head, looking her up and down. "And eat something, you look like a long discarded mummy."

The Alabarch put his face up to hers, waiting for a reaction. When she didn't move, he punched her in the gut, doubling her over.

"*Lex talionis*," he whispered, leaving her kneeling in the dust. The two thugs left with the Alabarch.

"*Lex talionis*," she replied. The phrase was Latin for: "eye for an eye, tooth for a tooth."

Heron stood and dusted off her knees, checking to make sure the thugs hadn't taken her coin purse when they'd dragged her through the city. She would have to figure out how to get another ten talents later, but for now, this close to the outskirts of the city, she had an errand.

Heron, clutching her stomach, weaved through the tents and improvised buildings. A pack of camels, lashed together, stomped dust into a brown cloud. One reached toward her and snapped its teeth.

"See Amenemope!" said the camel herder to another man, wrapped in layered, dusty coverings. "I told you that camel was dumber than a Roman soldier. It tried to bite that stick of a man."

The two men laughed abruptly, at the camel as much at her. Heron ignored them, slipping between two tents.

The mass of humanity piled on top of itself outside the City walls made the heat stifling and the dust ever present. She held an arm to her mouth to breathe through the fabric.

Heron passed a squad of Persian mercenaries: loose-fitting garments reinforced with iron guards around their torsos, nicked bronze helms with wings fitting comfortably on their heads, and availability for hire announced with crimson knots on swords.

She overheard them mumbling and pointing at her, referencing Roman scum, so she casually changed her direction to not pass by them. Two mercenaries started to follow her, but she ducked under a pavilion, startling a woman breast feeding a babe, and ran out the opening.

With a little distance between her and the mercenaries, she slowed. The temporary road that circled through the camps to the front gates blocked her way. A major trade caravan rumbled past, kicking dust up from wagon wheels, feet, and hooves.

A great, silken covered pavilion on a cart, pulled by a train of horses, riding on a dozen gilded wheels, towered over its surroundings. Male and female slaves, dressed only from the waist down, worked huge feathered fans, blowing air across the great merchant perched on his sedan chair.

Carts followed the massive structure, loaded down with goods from across the known world: yaka timber from the deep jungles south, bundles of ivory tusks from Ethiopia, and richly-stamped Babylonian brick. Heron recognized the trade markings of Chorasmia, Ionia, Sindh, and Arachosia, among other foreign and fantastic places.

She assumed the trader made two or three year circuits, traveling far east to the lands of the gaja-vimana. At the rear of the caravan - after the wagons filled with precious stones, silver, gold and spices had passed - was a large troop of slaves, chained to posts on wheeled platforms.

Heron recognized men of Sardian, east of Thracia, who were prized for their stonecutting skills. It was said the stone-wisdom of the Sardis had helped Sostratus construct the Lighthouse of Pharos.

Other nationalities were bound to the posts, ready to be sold in the flesh markets of Alexandria, and possibly further north in Rome, for this great caravan must make stops in all the great cities.

"Wasteful," was all she remarked before resuming her trek into the camps outside of Alexandria.

Avoiding further trouble, she found her way to a small tent surrounded by the markings of the Mazda. A simple stone brazier smoldered outside of a dusty azure tent where a withered old man with a brown stub at the end of one leg sat and rocked and gummed a soft willow branch.

His eyes widened in recognition and he peeled back the tent flap for her to enter. Heron ducked through, where the heady incense and lack of a recent meal made her lightheaded.

"May Ahura Mazda fill you with his purity," said the priest.

He huddled over a small fire in the center of the tent, while smoke drifted out through a hole in the top. He wore white robes smudged gray with time.

Heron took the spot across from the priest. She pulled the coin purse that had been given to her that morning and weighed it briefly before tossing it to him.

The priest gave her a warm smile tinged with concern. "While my gifts will sustain you for long periods, they will not sustain you indefinitely."

Heron held her hand out impatiently. The priest sighed, picked up the coin purse that had landed in his lap and peered in.

"I suppose it will do," he said.

The priest pulled up the corner of the woven mat he sat upon, revealing a box in a hole. He pulled the box out and rummaged through it, until he pulled out a coin purse similar in size to the one she'd thrown him. He tossed it to her.

Heron nodded reverently and prepared to get up.

"Before you go," he said. "I have words for you."

She hesitated, wanting to get back to the workshop. She sighed and nodded.

"A dream I had, two nights ago." The priest's eyes grew hazy and dim, like he'd returned to his faraway dream.

"You were the principle actor, with a circlet of silver upon your head. Though hair fuller, and longer, and different." He seemed to rest upon this thought, unsure what it meant, and then continued.

"In your hand was a blur. A strange apparatus I could not lay my sight upon, for it must have been veiled by the Ahura Mazda," he said. "And from this device, the world shook, and a crack formed traveling north, and then floodwaters,

floodwaters roiling with turbulent foam, came down the crack and its fury scattered men and women like seeds."

The priest's breathing had gone shallow, and his voice tempered with worry.

"There was more. Beyond the floodwaters, but my mind could not hold onto it, or I am not meant to know it, except down in the deeps where Ahura Mazda blesses me," said the priest. "But I have had this dream for three nights straight, and that portends."

And then he looked into her eyes with the haze now gone and his deep brown eyes, like the thick yaka woods of the jungle, poured into her. He opened his mouth to speak, to possibly explain what the dream might have meant.

But she left, ignoring the cackle of the stump-footed man outside and rushed back toward the city and her workshop. For if there were gods and goddesses, she did not abide by them, nor honor their rituals, except when it served her purposes.

Stepping over a sleeping goat, she tucked the bag into her belt, securing it from thieves. The oppressive sun warmed her back, as she'd felt strangely chilled in the priest's tent.

But now outside, it quickly turned to sweat, so she wiped her brow, smearing dust. The path to the tent had seemed tortuous and winding, but now with her purchase securely acquired, she whipped time back to the city.

Passing the Roman guards at the gates, she saw Lysimachus' coin reflected in their eyes. Her return to the city would be known by the Alabarch before she reached the workshop.

The matter of the ten talents and her niece would have to be dealt with when she returned home. Her work on Agog's business would have to wait. She just hoped the Fires payment would arrive before Lysimachus did.

Heron rubbed her temple with one hand, mind wheeling with plans for Lysimachus, as her other hand covered the pouch on her belt obsessively. Time, ever the enemy, had cast its stones against her.

# 10

Agog banged on the front door. Shadows had piled up in the entryway, hiding it from the morning sun.

He sensed an ominous quiet from the workshop. It should be a place of metal clanging, fires crackling, and hammers ringing. Joyful noise in the service of creation. Not the pit of silence it now was, surrounded by a city already awake.

The door was unlocked, so he went in. Metal junk was piled around the entryway. Agog didn't know if there'd been a struggle or Heron was unkempt. He recalled the work area before had been neater with metal rods kept in barrels.

He crept through the lower level, until he entered the area he had spoken to her last. Dim light from a high window filtered in, exposing dust mote, and providing enough light for Agog to review the papyrus sketchings on the desk.

The figures on the sheet appeared to be soldiers, or at least armored men. It was hard to tell, since they were metal, except the base provided no mobility and they were wrapped with gears and bound with coiled ropes. They were not the war machines he'd hoped that Heron would make. It appeared the level of usefulness was only slightly above the toy that shot water from a sword in the square.

Agog searched around for other documents, but found none except a box of papyrus sheets scrawled with the names of books. The stack was at least one hundred sheets high and had forty names on each. Agog searched through a few documents before throwing the papyrus back into the box, silently deriding scholars and their propensity for useless lists.

His eyes had adjusted enough that he could view the workshop for signs of progress on his war machines. Nothing indicated the statues from the drawings, nor did there appear to be weapons of any kind amid the clutter. At least none that he could discern.

Agog picked up the spinning toy and gave it a whirl, slowly clicking his tongue in thought as he watched it. Once it had stopped spinning, he set it back down on a wagon, punctuating it with a click of finality. The end of the wagon snapped closed, startling the northerner and spilling the toy across the stones. Water began to leak from its ends.

Examining the wagon, he realized it was a box, but when he knocked on it, the wood echoed dully, despite the knowledge that he'd just closed it.

The smooth wood revealed no latches or hidden compartments and crawling beneath it gave him no new clues to how to open it. He tried prying the end with his fingers, but nothing moved.

He slammed his fist into the wood, considering for the first time since he'd entered Heron's workshop, that the miracle maker had fled Alexandria ahead of his debts. The fires from the foundry had been quenched and no workers toiled in the great room.

The loss of coin wasn't the problem. The knowledge

in Heron's head was. He'd been in the city long enough to hear the whispers that Philo's designs were regurgitations of Heron's, so that made Philo redundant.

The constant failures smacked of sabotage with Philo the most likely suspect. Heron was brilliant with machines, but absent when it came to good business sense. If the inventor came back, he would keep better watch on his investment.

A high, soft voice awakened him from his thoughts. "The opening latch is on the hitch."

The boy stood at the edge of a beam of light cast down from above. The tunic hung loosely on his willowy frame. Agog had heard the boy approach, with soft shuffles, like a dainty dancer. Nothing in the sounds had suggested danger enough to interrupt his thoughts.

"The hitch?" asked Agog.

Stepping into the light, the boy cleared his throat and said, this time in a forced deeper voice: "The box opens from the outside by way of a piston hidden in the hitch."

Agog chuckled and said, "Show me."

The boy moved to the long beam jutting from the front of the wagon, grabbed the spike that attached to the harness, and pushed it. The back of the box raised, clicked into a fixed position, and revealed a long steel pole attached to a swivel. The box had enough room for a smaller person, a child or perhaps a slight woman.

"What's your name?" asked Agog.

The boy hesitated as if he'd forgotten it. "Sada," he said finally.

"Strange," said Agog. "An Egyptian name on a Greek boy dressed in Roman styles."

Sada stammered, glancing back the way he'd come. The boy was hiding something, that was plain for even an idiot to see, but Agog was too concerned about his missing miracle worker and decided not to question the boy further on that subject. But on Heron, he had to know.

"Where is Master Heron?" he asked.

With the focus off Sada, the boy stepped forward.

"Upstairs in his study room," said Sada. "He goes there to think."

"Take me there," commanded Agog.

After ascending an iron spiral staircase, narrow enough that Agog had to turn sideways, he entered a darkened room. Sunlight had been banished from the room with thick curtains.

Perched on an apparatus made of coiled springs and stuffed leather pillows, Heron rocked slow as the ocean. The ornate box was cradled in his hands, delicate silver spoon dipped into the powder.

Agog couldn't tell if the miracle worker was asleep, though he couldn't imagine staying atop the apparatus very long if he was.

The northerner crossed his arms and cleared his throat, taking a deep breath to fill up as much space as possible. Sada lurked at the top of the spiral staircase. Agog could feel the boy's eyes bouncing between Heron and himself.

"I need another twenty talents." Heron opened his eyes. Despite the darkness and the sunkenness of them, they burned as an eclipse.

The miracle worker's request punched him right in the gut. "For what?" he answered. "Your designs are immobile and lack cunning. I'm wasting money on toys."

Heron's eyes drifted to the boy Sada. Agog watched Heron's moment of confusion pass to recognition. Sada retreated from the room, rattling the metal stairs in escape.

Agog noted the currents between the master and the boy. Sada had surprised Heron, and that in turn, surprised Agog. The northerner decided he would need to pay more attention.

With a subtle nod, Heron appeared to accept that the boy had retreated beyond listening range.

"Those designs on my workbench are not for your war machines," said Heron.

For the first time since they'd met, maybe sparked by the servant boy, Agog realized how high and melodic the miracle maker's voice lilted. It was strong and filled with the comfortable authority of a person that gave orders all day, and even had the volume to carry, despite its musical quality.

Agog prized a voice that carried authority in his captains and Heron's was imbued with that quality. Captains also had to understand tactics, but if they couldn't get their men to follow orders, knowledge of tactics was useless.

The two maintained eye contact in the dim light. It was a war of wills that Agog was comfortable letting fall as he casually wandered to the window and flung open the dark curtain.

He admired the view of the Lighthouse from the window, shining white against the pale blue sky, while speaking over his shoulder. "Then where are the plans for my war machines?"

Heron sighed reluctantly. "In my head."

"Then how can your workers build them?" asked Agog.

Heron glanced at the box. "The designs aren't finished." Then added after a brief pause. "I haven't determined the power source, nor how to mobilize them."

"Then why are you sulking in the dark?" said Agog, bellowing his voice. "Get up and get to work."

Heron moved like silk to the window and closed the curtains. "I am working."

Agog slapped his heavy hand against the wall. The madness of miracle workers enraged him. "You call this working? There should be men in the workshop, hammering. And fires burning in the foundry."

Heron ignored his outburst and returned to his perch on

the strange stool. With a practiced scoop, he lifted the silver spoon to his nose and snorted. Heron's whole body shuddered and the blissful expression was all Agog needed to know about the effects of the dust.

Madness.    It was madness to trust his revenge to a decidedly cursed and distracted drug addict.

"I need another twenty talents," said Heron.

"Enough with the twenty talents. Your request for more grates on my nerve," said Agog. "Without progress, or proof, I cannot dare give you another twenty talents."

Agog opened the curtains again. "I must be able to see progress. And then I might give you twenty talents."

"If you want to see men hammering and fires burning, I will need fifty talents," said Heron.

The northerner stared out the window at the Lighthouse of Pharos and how it stood against the sky as a monument of man's mastery of the elements. In the room was such a man that could deliver miracles in the shape of floating statues and automata war machines. His was the mastery he sought and no other lay under the sun.

While the coinage wasn't an issue, the speed at which Heron devoured it concerned him. He couldn't maintain the pace, given the secondary project he was funding. Given that one had similar issues of reliability, he might be building his plans on sand.

Agog pulled his coin purse out, weighing it idly in his palm. He dumped out fifty talents worth onto the floor. "I need to see progress."

Heron ignored the coins. "You commanded hammering and fires. I cannot guarantee progress on your war machines beyond that."

Through gritted teeth, Agog said, "Give me something so I can know my coin is not wasted." He restrained the urge to shake Heron.

Heron closed his eyes solemnly, resting his wrists on crossed legs.

"Aurinia save me if I am wrong," said Agog under his breath, then to Heron: "I will be coming by each day to confirm our agreement."

Agog hovered over the inventor, expecting a response, but when none came, he stormed from the study, clanging down the spiral staircase.

"Dreadfully difficult miracle worker," muttered Agog. "I'd swear I was dealing with a woman."

About to leave the workshop, Agog sensed the boy, Sada, lurking in the shadows.

"Where is your home, Northman?" asked Sada.

"The lands of cold waters, warm women, and great beasts." He grinned in the dim light.

The boy, face full of curiosity, stepped forward. "What kind of beasts?"

"The kinds full of darkness and death. All horns and claws and teeth," said Agog. "Many a pelt have I harvested in the dark forests of the North."

Rather than show excitement and ask for more description, as most boys were prone to do when he told stories of his exploits, Sada surprised him with a narrow squinting of his eyes.

"I've heard all Northmen were liars."

"Bold words for an untested youth," said Agog, right after.

Sada visibly reacted as if he'd said too much. Curious happenings in the house of Heron.

Quick to follow up on Sada's unease, Agog followed with: "What more can you tell me about Master Heron? I wish to know more about where my money goes."

Sada shrunk into the shadows.

Agog sighed. "Coin for your troubles."

Sada shrunk further into the shadows, nearly disappearing down the hall. The boy had loyalty for his master.

"I don't wish to know anything private about your master," he said. "Just enough so I can help. I'm funding his debt."

Sada hesitated, and Agog saw opportunity.

"Where did Master Heron learn to make such miracles?" And when Sada opened his mouth, halfway, "There's no harm in knowing this? Surely, that cannot be a dreadful secret?"

"For a Northman, you speak too well," said Sada, as the boy disappeared.

Shaking his head, Agog left the workshop, pushing into the morning crowd now flowing through the streets.

A closer watch on Heron's progress would serve his purposes, Agog decided, or his revenge might disappear into the desert sands along with all his former fortunes.

A thick bull of a man with a scruffy beard rammed his shoulder in Agog's chest as he passed. The man recoiled, wild eyes surveying him as an opponent, but quickly realizing Agog was an elephant to his bull.

Such glances were common to the northerner, though the man's looks had lingered longer than most. Agog watched the man limp away, his left leg clearly damaged by a long ago wound. The man had once been a warrior, Agog detected in his movement, though not a good one. Probably rushed into battle relying on his strength and was felled by a savvier opponent, who dropped low and struck at his left leg.

Agog resumed his progress, quickly forgetting about the man. While the man he'd bumped into clearly had thuggish intent on his brow, whatever business he had was no business of his. But whoever was on the other end was not going to have a good day.

# 11

Heron shuffled through the lists of books she'd scrawled in a marathon session the previous night. Even the fraction of information represented by her meager list had been a major blow to the world.

While her innovations had been her own, they'd been built upon the knowledge of previous great thinkers. How could she have written *Pnuematica* without the treatise of Archimedes? *On Automata* would not exist but for Strabo.

What might she achieve with the whole Library at her disposal? Her automata would sing and dance like flesh and blood, rather than stumble and jerk like drunken statues. The tyranny of slavery would be broken by the power of machines!

Heron flung the papers back into the bin. Whoever had instigated the tragedy of the Library deserved a fate akin to the crime. A thousand years under the cruel hands of Lysimachus would not be enough.

How might she have raised the city to be a clockwork marvel for the world to imitate? Instead of the poor shuffling, mass chained and bound by distracted masters, beating each other in the alleys for scraps of food, or selling themselves in the slums outside the city.

But no clues surfaced from the lists of destroyed papyrus. No specific pattern of books lost could be seen scrawled in ink. Only a madman wanting to shutter the world in ignorance would gain anything by the burning.

The most likely reason was an accidental burning, though from whose hands? Caesar had started the fires in the fleet, that was written in his histories, recorded by his hand. But that didn't mean he wanted the Library burned.

Evidence would suggest the contrary. Caesar had thrown his lot in with Cleopatra, and she would have never condoned the burning of her ancestors' most precious gift to the world. So if he'd caused it, he would have covered it up immediately.

Heron rubbed her temples. One hand reflexively snaked toward the ornate box, but she yanked it back, scolding it with her eyes for disobeying.

Without clues to go on, she would call in a favor from an old friend. She knew what Hortio would ask for in return for access to his private library, and the thought made her shudder. But he had papyrus from before the fires, and some written around those times. If there were clues to be found, they would be found in Hortio's library.

Heron sighed and poked the fat purse on the desk. The coin from Agog would appease Lys for the moment, assuming the remainder arrived from her source requesting the fires investigation.

She surveyed the quiet workshop. The half finished head of Horus stared ominously at her. She wanted to be done making miracles for the temples. Their ways subverted her goals for the city, but she had no other way to gain significant coinage.

The cold shadow consuming her heart lifted slightly with the thoughts that it was time for her workers to begin new works. She'd sent messages for them to return the next day.

How she missed Plutarch and Punt, and the others, dusty and doused in sweat creating monuments to man's creativity.

Heron ran a finger along the ink filled papyrus on the desk. The designs were not complete, but she had enough that they could fire the cupola. Plutarch and Punt often contributed during the creation process. She would need their ideas more than ever.

She glanced at the wagon, wondering where Sepharia had gotten to. The disguise worried her. Had Sepharia been sneaking into the city? Heron wouldn't be surprised. She'd done the same as a youth and the stories she'd told Sepharia had probably emboldened her niece.

A rattling crash that came from the front of the building startled Heron. It could have been one of the cats that had adopted them, or the old man bringing coin for the investigation. Though she didn't remember leaving the door open.

Heron investigated and found a bronze tube lying in the middle of the entryway. She circled around, trying to remember which pile it'd come from.

The cats liked to play with objects like the tube, pawing it until it rolled away and then pouncing before it stopped. Heron had thought about building an automatic cat toy that would drag a colorful rope in a looping pattern, but the winding mechanism would require too much energy and make the whole structure top-heavy. She would have to refine the idea before building it, but not while more important - and paying - projects loomed on her horizon.

Heron leaned over to replace the bronze tube on its pile, when she heard a shuffling gait behind her. As she spun, her vision was consumed by a fist. Her consciousness fled right after.

§

The slab of stone was cold and sucked the heat from her body. Heron shivered, pulling her arms that had been hanging from the sides to her chest.

*At least my clothes are still on*, she thought, sitting up in the cell. Heron checked her molded genitalia, to confirm her ruse was still intact.

Almost the moment she sat vertically, a flickering torch light lit up the hallway outside. Keys rattled in a lock.

"Follow me," said Lysimachus, holding his torch high so the flames licked at the stone ceiling.

Heron crossed her arms and followed. Thoughts of attacking the Alabarch were squashed when she saw Lefty waiting outside the door. He had the eager grin of a Sobek crocodile waiting for a sacrificial hen.

The room beyond the stone cell was a sepulcher adorned with crypt entrances along the opposing walls. Lysimachus shoved his torch into a groove in the wall and brought a goblet of dark liquid to Heron.

While drinking from his own, Lysimachus indicated with a nod that she should drink. Heron swirled the liquid, bringing the scent of fermented grapes to her nose.

Lysimachus set his goblet on the stone. "Do you think you're fooling me?"

"About what?"

"Your daughter." He raised his eyebrows.

"I'm not in the mood for this game again," she said. "I

have the monies for my debts this month, as requested."

The coin pouch appeared in the Alabarch's hand. He shook it mockingly. "This one?"

"Yes, that one."

"Shame. Shame." Lysimachus threw the pouch to Lefty. "It's not the full sixty talents."

"I have the rest back at the workshop. If you would have asked instead of sneaking into my place and clubbing me over the head, I could have given it to you," she said.

She didn't have the full amount yet, but it was to have arrived before dusk.

Lysimachus approached her with a smile on his face, eyes darting to Lefty.

"Heron, that fee won't be good enough now."

"You can't keep changing the game. I'll get the monies for you."

He shook his head. "But you violated my clearly stated rules. I said there would be no escaping and my sources clearly saw someone sneaking out of the workshop the other night."

Heron sucked in a breath.

"I see you know about this."

Heron shook her head. "No."

"Tsk. Tsk. You lie poorly." Lysimachus nodded toward Lefty.

Rough hands grabbed her by the shoulders.

"Wait." Heron held up her hand.

Lysimachus waved her on. She sighed, showing she would listen to him. The hands left her shoulders.

"Make any deal you want, but the girl can't be a part of it," said Heron.

The Alabarch's face soured into a grimace. He punched her in the gut. Lefty grabbed her as she doubled over, cinching his arm around her neck and dragging her backwards.

Heron struggled against his massive arms. He smelled like dried blood.

She tried kicking backwards into his groin, but he held her firmly. A small amount of air was making it past his choking grip.

Heron looked up to see Lysimachus kicking her between the legs. His foot contacted partially between the molded genitalia and her leg. Heron realized her mistake when he glared at her questioningly for her lack of reaction.

Before she could fake the pain, Lefty threw her backwards, cracking her head against stone. Ropes burned into her wrists as she was tied to a sarcophagus. On her back, she could see Lefty's eyes, coldly observing her.

"You really need to start listening to me," said Lysimachus. "I'm going to have to teach you why this is so important."

He reached down to the ground and handed a long object to Lefty. She couldn't make out what it was in the flickering light.

"And when I find your daughter, she's going to join my household as my body slave," he said. "And if the payments on your debts don't keep coming, I'll take it out on her."

Lysimachus nodded to Lefty and he raised the axe handle above his head. Right before he swung, Lysimachus stuffed a cloth covered in mildew in her mouth.

The impact exploded her knee, sending white-hot shards of pain into her head. She blacked out, twice. Spots rotated in her vision.

As she came to, she heard Lefty shuffling to the other side. Lysimachus leaned over and spit in her face. She choked on the cloth, trying to catch her breath.

Lefty swung three more times.

# 12

Punt hefted the sack over his shoulder, sighing regrettably. He'd only sold a third of the self-trimming lamps that Heron had given him. The coin in his pouch felt thin, like watered down soup.

Astrela lay in her bed. He dare not wake her after their arguments the night before. When the message had come to return to Heron's workshop, she begged him not to go, citing signs from her bones.

Furious at his wife already, Punt had shouted her down. In their sixteen years of marriage, he'd never done that before. But she'd been negotiating with Philo on his behalf without his knowledge.

Punt didn't want to work for the snake Philo. He would rather toil for a trinket merchant making children's toys than lend his strength and knowledge to Heron's greatest rival.

Punt spit into the dirt. It was painful to even consider that Philo was a rival. The man had clawed his way to the tops of the workshops through deceptions and bribery. His designs were clearly stolen from Heron.

Swinging the bag to the other shoulder, Punt jostled through the crowd. An errant elbow caught him in the ribs and someone stepped on his foot.

"Excuse me," mumbled Punt.

On the way to the workshop, Punt was stopped by a crowd too thick to pass through. Sliding around the side, he came upon a scene.

A minor trader from the deep southern lands, wearing colorful robes and a head scarf of golden fabric, had his arms waving in the air.

"I will not pay!" yelled the trader. "I cannot make profit this way."

The merchant shrugged. "Flaccus decrees, so I must collect. If I do not, he will shut me down."

The colorful trader stomped his feet in the dust. A young boy nearby, probably the trader's son, held the reins on a camel loaded with bags.

"This Flaccus cannot have my coin," said the trader. He spit in his hand and held it out. "We trade southern way, man to man. Not Roman one, like vulture on a carcass."

Gasps traveled through the crowd. A pair of Roman soldiers pushed their way through, until they came face to face with the trader. The merchant faded into the shadows of his awning.

"What were you saying about Romans?" sneered the first soldier.

The trader proudly held his ground. "I cannot pay tax. It too much. I will take trade east."

The first soldier glanced at the second. "Not paying taxes? Well, then...we can't have that on Roman soil." They moved toward the trader with one hand on their swords.

The trader stepped back once, his eyes wide. "No. No.

We have no trade. No tax to take."

The soldier shook his head. "That's not what I heard. I heard that you weren't going to pay the coin owed to the generous Roman Empire that keeps your roads open so you may trade freely."

The second nodded agreeably. "That's what I heard, too."

The trader looked like he wanted to run, but as he glanced at his son, he stayed. The soldiers grabbed the trader and led him away. When he began to struggle, they tripped him and beat him with their fists.

The crowd faded away from the scene, not wanting to be there in case more soldiers joined.

As Punt left, he noticed the trader's son, holding onto the reins of the camel, pull a knife from a pack. Punt made eye contact and shook his head. The boy narrowed his eyes and returned the knife to its hidden location.

The scene he'd left was not unfamiliar. The taxes cut cruelly into the population. Those subsisting on meager earnings sipping root soup, now found themselves with empty bellies most days.

The tax had prompted his wife to push for Philo's employment, but Punt hadn't wanted to hear any of it.

Dusty winds from the south brought heat almost as oppressive as the taxes, quickly dispersing the crowds. Punt wrapped a scarf around his face and leaned into the biting wind.

The rotating wind wheels above Heron's workshop brought a smile to his face, even though it meant gritty sand blowing into his mouth. Black smoke announced that the cupola had been fired. Shimmering heat wafted over the roofs, obfuscating the gleaming white Lighthouse in the distance.

Punt followed a load of timbers being carried into the courtyard in back. He returned smiles to familiar faces. It'd been a month since he'd been in the workshop. The sharp tang of burning metal put a hurry into his step.

Weaving through the warehouse, Punt noticed the head of Horus had been removed. Other projects they'd been working on before the Nekhbet disaster were missing, as well.

Then Punt realized the workers all had weapons hanging by their sides. He increased his gait to reach Heron sooner. The implications worried him.

The first thing Punt saw when he neared his master's work area was the Northman. He reminded Punt of a great bear, seen in sketchings from the Library.

The Northman seemed to be supervising the workers, bellowing his voice at them to move barrels and tables. Already, construction on a project had begun. Punt wondered why Plutarch wasn't directing the workers.

Punt was so focused on the Northman, he didn't notice the contraption that Heron was strapped to, until he reached the desk.

"Master Heron—," Punt gasped.

Heron was bound to a vertical table. Bandages covered his knees and ankles. Punt hurried to his side.

"What happened?" he whispered.

"The Alabarch."

Punt found it hard to meet Heron's gaze. A mixture of pain and fury formed a potent cocktail in his master's eyes. A chill trickled down his spine.

Looking down, Punt surveyed the damage. The bandages weren't bloody, but the flesh beneath seemed swollen.

"How fared your task?" asked Heron.

Punt had forgotten about the sack on his shoulder and set it on the ground, letting his eyes fall downcast.

"I'm sorry, Master Heron, I failed you," said Punt. "I only sold a third of the lamps."

Heron laughed. A weak and broken laugh, but a laugh none the less. Agog's deep baritone joined his, and Punt followed, not understanding why.

"A third? Your dedication to every task honors me, friend Punt," said Heron. "Maybe I should put Plutarch in the foundry and you can be our mouthpiece."

"Oh, no! Please, I prefer the foundry," said Punt.

Heron smiled. "I jest. Plutarch would make me nothing but slag and I know it makes your heart sing to swing a hammer."

"Where is Plutarch?" asked Punt, still worried about his absence.

"On errands." Heron shared a glance with Agog and the Northman nodded.

Punt was surprised by the Northman's involvement. He'd been distant before. Had the attack from Lys convinced him to be more involved? Punt didn't mind the Northman, but he knew nothing about him, either. They'd been betrayed once too often for him to trust anyone new.

"I have two favors to ask," said Heron.

Punt bowed at the waist. Though Heron was a slight, erudite Greek and Punt deeply Egyptian, who made a living with his hands, he loved Heron like a brother.

"The first is that I need to send a package to your house for safe keeping," said Heron. "The second is that I need you to make me some legs that I can use once the swelling goes down."

"Make legs?"

Heron handed him a papyrus with sketches of a leg harness on them. The apparatus attached to the knee had interlocking gears and a rod between the two lengths, appearing to provide support.

"What does this part do?" asked Punt. "This is a new

design."

Heron rubbed his temples, probably warding off his frequent headaches.

"While laying in the entryway after Lefty dumped me there and before Sepharia found me, I saw in the depths of my pain, that design," said Heron. "I guess I have that much to thank Lys. I'd been racking my brain about a way to provide locomotion to automata and the Alabarch, through hobbling me, gave me the spark."

When Heron saw that Punt still didn't understand, he continued, "The round connection interlocks and allows the two rods to move freely, while the small rod to the side slides in and out of a sleeve, providing support and locomotion."

Punt stared at the papyrus until he understood.

"Making the interlocks rotate freely will be difficult," said Punt.

"Yes, I was stuck on that too, until our Northman friend suggested using sand to polish them smooth. We can bond sand to a stone and utilize the wind sail on the roof for power," said Heron.

Agog lifted a heavy timber as if he were wielding a stick. "If water can wear away a beach, then sand can wear metal." He flipped the timber easily in his hand. "And we use sand to knock the rust from our weapons."

Punt nodded, and left the bag of coins from his sales on the desk. He went to the foundry to begin work on the leg harnesses when he realized Agog had followed him. The big man had a light step and he had not heard him at first.

"I wish to watch the god of iron and fire work his trade," said Agog, bowing nimbly. It was unnatural that a man that big could move that delicately.

Punt squinted, drawing his lips thin.

"And I make an excellent assistant," said Agog.

The Northman had the strength to work the foundry, but he wasn't sure he wanted the help.

"Why?" Punt asked, simply.

"I'm making a great investment in the halls of Heron. After the attack, I decided I needed to take a more hands-on approach to his safety," he said.

"So the weapons were your doing?" asked Punt.

"Yes, though Plutarch agreed. Otherwise, your master would have ignored the suggestion." Agog's eyes sparkled with import. "I think we all know that not everyone in the city wishes for Heron's success."

"You suspect sabotage?" asked Punt.

"Better than the curse that supposedly hangs over his head."

"You don't believe in curses?"

Agog flexed his powerful arms, cracking his knuckles by squeezing his thumbs across his fingers. "I prefer dealing with men. They're easier to kill. Gods are a troublesome lot."

Punt agreed with the Northman's practical wisdom. "My wife counsels with bones that tell her the gods are affronted by Master Heron's reliance on human knowledge."

"And you believe her?"

Punt shook his head, picking up his smithing hammer. The weight felt comfortable in his hand.

"I believe in Master Heron."

Agog patted the smithy on the shoulder. "I do, too." The Northman hefted his bulk on top of a pile of timbers. For a big man, he was as graceful as the wind.

"I had other ideas for protecting the workshop and Master Heron, but he waved them off, saying he had other plans in the works," said Agog.

Punt could see where Agog was leading him. He hated to go against his master's wishes, but seeing Heron strapped to the table with useless legs burned at his heart.

"What are these ideas?" asked Punt.

Agog grinned and leapt down, sending up puffs of dust as he landed. He wrapped his arm around Punt's shoulder. Punt felt like the Northman's smile was going to engulf him.

"Have I got some ideas for you."

# 13

The light burning through the curtains reminded Heron that she'd slept too long. She rubbed her eyes and grabbed a water pouch, groaning audibly as she rolled over.

Her thirst sated, Heron stared at the two serpents on the box next to her bed. She desired to lift the lid and mine the powder within. But eating needed to come first. Once she took the lotus powder, her hunger would fade.

The harnesses that Punt had made for her lay in a pile. Heron maneuvered around until her legs lay parallel with them. Each jarring movement shot pain up her thighs. The swelling had reduced in the weeks since the attack, but every day was a new lesson in agony.

Heron cursed repeatedly as she fit the harnesses over her legs and strapped them in. Climbing to her feet required use of two poles, the wall, and tricky maneuvering like a newborn foal. The day before, she'd fallen the moment she'd made it upright.

Heron desired the powder as she leaned on her poles,

sweating from the effort, but she couldn't reach. She took a few feeble swipes at the box and gave up. After taking a deep breath, she made her way down the spiral staircase.

Eventually, she made it to her desk in the workshop and settled on the pedestal they'd made for her. Exhausted and out of breath, Heron surveyed progress.

The reddish-orange glow of liquid iron being poured into molds reflected across Punt's chest. Sparks erupted from the pour like a delicate fountain of light.

In the main warehouse, workers scurried over scaffolding. Plutarch's high, lilting voice carried above the hammering and sawing, keeping them ever in motion. Her workshop had never housed so many projects at once, including a few she didn't recognize.

Sepharia appeared by her side. "You weren't supposed to be awake yet."

"I've slept long enough. There's work to do," said Heron.

Sepharia hugged her and squeezed her hand. "You need rest. This pace is killing you."

Heron smoothed the hair away from her niece's face. "Better to die in the workshop working than at the hands of Lysimachus."

Sepharia bit her lower lip and her eyes grew glassy and liquid.

"I think it's time we got you safely away from the workshop," said Heron.

"No!" cried Sepharia. "I want to help. There's so much you need me to do. Please. Especially with your legs."

At mention of Heron's legs, Sepharia recoiled her hands to cover her mouth.

"You'll help me by not being here. The game has grown too dangerous. Lysimachus has been hiring more men and the spies are doubling each week. I'm tempted to have the workers stay here. We have the work to do, and they're in danger each time they leave the workshop."

Sepharia kneaded Heron's arm with her fingers, pleading with her eyes to stay. Heron could practically feel her saying that her twin would have let her stay. It was an argument she'd thrown in her face a thousand times before.

"There's no use arguing. I've made up my mind," said Heron.

The girl squeaked in frustration and ran from the room.

Heron stared after her niece. No matter what she did for her, she'd never accepted her as a surrogate parent.

Heron sighed and turned her thoughts back to the problem. The tricky part would be getting her out of the workshop unseen. The best opportunity would come when they were delivering her current project.

After mulling the options, she turned back to the desk, finding Agog looming like a thunderhead. Plato have pity, that man is quiet, she thought.

Heron sensed his disappointment even before he spoke.

"When do you begin progress on the war machines?"

Heron ignored the northerner and straightened the papyrus on her desk, placing smooth stones on the four corners to hold it down.

"Preparations are in progress."

Agog extended his great arm toward the workshop, indicating a row of metal soldiers on a platform being loaded onto carts by a trio of workers. Pulleys hanging from the ceiling reduced the weight, while it rolled over thin rods onto the wagon.

"Those are toys, not an army!"

The Northman paced around the desk, as much talking to himself as to Heron.

"I'm throwing away coin, expecting an army and only

getting toys to amuse children," he ranted.   A few workers glanced in their direction, clearly worried by Agog's shouting.

Agog picked up the aeolipile and spun the toy.  "I might as well fight a war with these, they do me as much good."

Heron watched Agog the whole time, quietly following him with her eyes.  Patiently waiting.

When he had expended his energy and stood over her, glaring with intensity, she calmly responded, "Are you done?"

Her measured response deflated him and he uncrossed his arms and wandered away from her, only to come back when Sepharia entered the room with a rolled papyrus in her hands.

"A messenger delivered this," said Sepharia, as she handed the papyrus to Heron.

Heron broke the seal, letting the stamped wax fall to the floor, and opened the scroll.  She'd been expecting the answer for days.

Sepharia picked up the wax.  "It's from the Library."

Heron ignored Agog and Sepharia, who watched expectantly, and read the document.

It was from Levictus, a scholar of the works on Caesar. She had delicately sent him a request about circumstance of the fires.

She read the papyrus:

*Ave Heron,*

*Words find you well.  The summer swoons upon us with a great horde of rats.  I do hope dear Flaccus sweeps them away.  Your request is well received in my heart, but my hands would be robbing my own pockets, so I must busy myself with trivialities instead.*

*Signed, your dearest friend, Levictus.*

His response made it clear he knew exactly what she was asking, but gave nothing she could use and worded in a way to warn her of making further requests. The topic of the fires would be taboo to a scholar of Caesar. He would lose access to Roman records if he was seen to be pursuing that path.

Heron put the edge of the paper into the candle and dropped it onto the floor, watching it burst into flame and consume the message.

With no other avenues forward, her deal with Hortio was the only way out of the dead end. She shuddered visibly.

While she'd been reading the papyrus, Agog had been studying her. When she looked up, he raised an eyebrow to her in question.

Sepharia waited silently at the edge of the room, cautiously wringing her hands. None of Heron's plans could move forward while her twin's daughter was in danger.

Heron made a grunt of finality.

Sepharia asked, "What?"

"We're moving you tonight."

§

Heron snapped the reins, advancing the cart through the crowd. The streets were overfull. Rumors of free bread had brought hordes from the outer city. At least two fights had broken out since she and Punt had left the workshop.

She was glad for the high wagon and horses to keep the people at bay, and Punt to keep her company, quiet as he was.

She steered the horses around an old woman hobbling across the street. Heron grimaced as her knees erupted in agony, only to have to pull the horses up when another fight broke out right in her path.

Three men argued with a meat pot merchant, claiming he was to be giving away his food free today, by order of Governor Flaccus. The merchant screamed at them, cursing in a multitude of languages, only half of which Heron recognized.

The merchant had latched onto his pot, which normally cost a few pennies or a meat trade to draw a ladle from. Heron guessed more than a few rats made up the meat portion of the pot.

The three men were trying to drag the pot away, but the merchant had wrapped his legs around it and was wailing at the top of his lungs.

If it weren't for the crushing crowds, Roman soldiers would have been on the scene already, breaking it up. Heron imagined the soldiers were busy with other fights around the city.

Attentive to the action in front of her, Heron didn't notice the old woman with only one eye until she'd grabbed onto her leg, eliciting a cry of pain.

"Get off me, old hag," she grimaced, trying to kick her from her leg, but the pain kept her rigid.

Punt reached across to pry the hag's fingers from Heron's leg, but woman had a tight grip. She climbed onto the step, and put her face up to Heron's.

The fetid smells of rotting teeth emanated from the hag's mouth.

"The fires..." the old hag said.

"What?" The word tumbled out of Heron's mouth as her body snapped straight, even though the pain threatened to make her pass out.

"The fires can only be found within the hidden waters of Ammon."

Then, the old hag released her hold and dropped from the wagon, disappearing into the crowd so quickly it almost seemed she just evaporated.

"What did she say?" Punt asked.

Heron shrugged him off. Not because she hadn't heard,

but because the way was opening up in front of them.

The struggle for the meat pot resulted in it being spilled. Greedy hands snatched the meat in a frenzy, leaving the merchant crying, straddling the pot in the mud of his former soup.

Heron wanted to take some meaning from the hag's mention of fires, but knew that fortune tellers and mystics, just like the temples, used vague wordings to lure weak minds.

And likely, the mention of fires was merely coincidence. Heron struck the hag's words from her thoughts.

"You should have let me drive," said Punt on the bench next to her. He crossed his arms and scowled.

Heron laughed with tears in her eyes, rubbing her legs. "You look like a child refusing to eat ankut root."

"Steering the cart is injuring your legs as much as that woman did," said Punt. "You should be resting them."

"You'd make a horrible mother, Punt. I can poke fifteen holes in your feeble argument."

Punt scowled deeper and shifted so he was facing away from her.

Heron was enjoying picking on her blacksmith. Since the attack, the whole crew had been treating her like a child. Only the barbarian pulled no punches.

Thinking of Agog as "the barbarian" struck her wrong. The man knew at least four languages and had working knowledge of her favorite thinkers. She couldn't let her guard down around that one.

They approached Punt's abode from rear. A courtyard would give them opportunity to unload the crates without scrutiny. Heron slowed the wagon to bring it around, glancing at the wagon and wondering how her cargo fared.

A familiar voice cut through the crowd noise, making her cringe before she recognized it.

"Ave, Heron. Might we talk a spell?"

Astride a pepper gray stallion, Lysimachus rode up with Lefty and Blackfinger trailing behind on foot. The Alabarch wore a verdant silk tunic with a gold belt. His pot belly rested comfortably before the pommel.

"No horse for your underlings?" asked Heron.

Lysimachus piloted his horse next to the cart, leering at her legs. Lefty and Blackfinger bent over at the knees a few lengths back, heaving breaths.

"The exercise is good for them. Keeps their legs in shape." Lysimachus chuckled.

Heron left the reins across her lap, and put a gentle hand on Punt's arm. The blacksmith seemed ready to leap from the bench. While she was certain Punt could kill Lysimachus before Lefty and Blackfinger could get to him, they would both be hung before sundown.

Lysimachus spurred his horse to prance, pulling the reins and cackling softly. Heron wished the Alabarch would leave so they could finish their work. Part of her feared that someone had tipped Lysimachus off to their purpose.

"I haven't seen your daughter around," said Lysimachus, grinning.

Heron squeezed Punt's arm, reminding him not to take the bait.

"I don't know who you're talking about," replied Heron.

Lysimachus laughed and glanced at the wagon. "Quite a cargo there. Strange to see the *Michanikos* out on a delivery."

"With my legs in their current state, I'm not much use otherwise."

"Interesting."

Lefty and Blackfinger, partially rested from their run, staggered to the wagon.

"Is this the one, Alabarch?" said Blackfinger, pointing his

dead, black finger at the wagon.

A chill burst down Heron's spine. She thought about driving the cart away, but knew that was a foolish notion. Lysimachus only had to ride along and call for guards and they would stop her.

"You're ruining all my fun," said Lysimachus.

Heron whispered under her breath. "Don't do anything rash, Punt."

Lefty reached up and grabbed the reins from her lap. The man glared like a feral dog, baring his teeth.

"Go ahead, open it up," said Lysimachus.

Blackfinger nodded and climbed between the wagon and the horses. He started fumbling around the hitch, pushing and pulling on it.

"Problems?" asked Heron, keeping her face neutral, despite the underlying rage.

Alexandrians began to crowd around the scene, staying a distance away from the wagon. They eyed Lysimachus with excitement.

Lysimachus grinned possessively. "Routine check up. Can't have a poorly connected hitch injure a defenseless horse." The Alabarch seemed so positively in control, he barely bothered to give a credible excuse.

Blackfinger looked about ready to give up, when he punched the hitch and the hidden compartment under the wagon swung open with a huge clang. A triumphant grin burst onto Lysimachus' face.

Both Lefty and Blackfinger hurried to the back of the wagon, as if they expected something to burst from it. Their immediate confusion cast doubt on the Alabarch's face. He steered his horse around to see the contents of the hidden compartment.

"Expected to find something there?" Heron asked.

Lysimachus kicked his horse, which sidled around knocking up puffs of dust.

"Why do you have a hidden compartment on that wagon?" demanded Lysimachus.

"To hide valuables from thieves, of course," she said. "Isn't it obvious?"

Lysimachus rode his horse up to her, until the stallion's head hung over her legs. The stallion bumped into her harnesses. Heron steeled her face not to react even though it felt like her bones were being ground to dust.

"Where are you taking these crates?" asked Lysimachus.

"Why, right here," she answered in a mocking tone, hoping to keep him off balance. "Punt, unload them please."

Punt nodded and hopped off the wagon, pushing past Lefty and Blackfinger to close the hidden compartment.

"What's in them?" asked Lysimachus suspiciously.

"Show them, Punt."

Punt climbed into the back of the wagon and opened the nearest crate. It was half as tall as Punt, and equal on all sides. After lifting the lid, he produced a self-trimming lamp. Punt threw it to Lysimachus, who had to scramble to catch it.

"Consider it a gift for all the trouble I've caused you," said Heron, holding the grin between her teeth.

Lysimachus stared at the lamp incredulously.

"But why are you delivering them here?" he asked.

Heron shrugged. "Punt has shown himself to be quite the lamp salesman. He offered that his wife might peddle them during the day. All proceeds going to pay my debts, of course."

Lysimachus scowled, clearly unhappy with the turn of events. The crowd seemed disappointed by the results, and murmuring could be heard throughout.

The Alabarch glanced at the people watching, and narrowed his eyes. "Why don't you two help our good friend

Heron with his crates? With his legs so tragically mangled in the unfortunate accident, he can't help his blacksmith unload the crates."

The two henchmen didn't look happy to have been volunteered for manual labor.

"Thank you, Alexander. That is most generous of you," said Heron, bowing slightly for the crowd's benefit. With the potential showdown being turned into a simple job, the crowd dispersed.

Punt grabbed the first crate, the one he'd opened, and carried it through the courtyard into the back of his house. Lefty and Blackfinger awkwardly carried the second crate to the threshold and deposited it there.

With the crates unloaded, Heron waved to Lysimachus. "I must be getting back, miracles await."

Heron snapped the reins and brought the wagon around. Lefty and Blackfinger stared dumbfounded, while Lysimachus looked like he'd eaten a bag of wasps.

Safely up the street, Heron allowed herself to take a deep and cleansing breath. The encounter with the Alabarch had been too close. If it wouldn't be improper and give Agog the wrong idea, she might hug him for the suggestion to move Sepharia from the hidden compartment to the crate next time she saw him.

The Northman had been right in his concerns that there was a spy in the workshop. Lysimachus had gone right for the wagon. Only someone with knowledge of its design could have found the hidden lever and even with that knowledge, it'd taken Blackfinger a while to activate it.

At least Sepharia was now safely in Punt's house.

Heron snapped the reins again, feeling the cold ache in her legs. All her plans would be in jeopardy while a spy was in the workshop. The spy had probably been the source of her "curse" as well.

She shook her head, thinking of each of her workers. No one stood out.

Heron snapped the reins harder, driving the horses recklessly through the street. Alexandrians scattered out of her way. A few yelled insults at her back.

Without the identity of the spy, they couldn't work on any more projects, lest Lysimachus find out. But if she didn't make progress, she wouldn't have the coin to pay the Alabarch.

Heron shook her head. She needed to uncover the identity of the spy tonight or all her plans would be sunk.

# 14

The guards beneath the gilded arch refused Agog entry into the gathering, nervously touching their swords. Heron had asked him to attend the evening's festivities at House Hortio, but now the guards weren't cooperating.

"I am expected by the master of the house and his guest of honor," grumbled Agog.

The soldier glanced to the unrolled papyrus in his hand. "You're not on the list."

"Yes—," he said through gritted teeth. "I've told you that already. I was to be added, verbally, I assume."

The guard with the papyrus raised an eyebrow to his fellow guard. "Were you told anything?"

He shook his head and shrugged. "I took over for Legtis right before you got here."

Agog squeezed his hands, cracking knuckles loudly. The two guards took a step back and gripped their hilts. "Consider that your fellow guards did not pass along the message and one of you run off and confirm my attendance."

Agog silently cursed his decision to consult Gnaeus on the proper attire for a gathering of this kind. The acquisition of a Roman tunic of his size had proved more difficult than he thought possible.

He'd convinced the alchemist to shit gold with that trick of Heron's faster than it'd taken one Agog-sized tunic to be made. The delay had made him late. His only solace was the friendly attentions of the bath attendants while he waited for the tunic.

Neither guard had moved and Agog considered taking their weapons from them and knocking them out, but decided that would be a poor introduction to this friend of Heron's. He just wasn't used to waiting outside like a common peasant.

Before he could talk himself out of pummeling a guard, Plutarch appeared in a soft blue toga.

His eyes flickered with amusement at seeing the barbarian in the tunic, making Agog regret listening to Gnaeus once again.

"We've been wondering where you've been," said Plutarch, as he put a gentle hand on the guard's shoulder. They parted.

"For the sake of those guards, it's a good thing you showed up when you did," said Agog.

Plutarch tittered and led Agog to the rest of the party. The contrast to Heron's workshop was as an ox pulling a plow to a zebra dressed in silks.

The stone floors of the workshop had been made for dropping heavy objects, chipped and worn from the abuse. Soot burns along the walls made strange ideograms, marking it as a place of fire and steel and muscle.

In contrast, the crimson and gold interconnected tiles of Hortio's dwelling formed a pattern around the shallow pool in the middle, flaunting the decadence of a wealthy man. Rose petals floated in the pool, while half-naked slaves of both genders carried trays of indulgences. The sounds of the party were soft and curved like the gentle wings of doves.

The attendees represented the Alexandrian upper class, though he'd overheard back in the workshop, they all had a distinct dislike for Rome and its Governor Flaccus. A useful group with which to rub elbows.

Agog wrestled with the black belt holding his tunic. Every step he took hitched the fabric around his stomach. He had no idea how they wore such confining garments.

Plutarch, whom Agog saw as a competent and efficient foreman in the workshop, had taken on a different air as he led him through the party. The foreman floated ahead of him, slipping through the crowd like a whimsical ribbon.

For him, the party guests staggered away when he tried to pass, stunned by his size. The Roman tunic failed to hide his origins.

Plutarch slipped next to him and reading his thoughts, whispered, "It's your mane of hair. No proper Alexandrian wears such a dreadful mess, nor a knot on their heads."

Agog put a hand to the Suebian knot holding his unruly black hair and grunted. Gnaeus would pay for his ill-suited advice.

Holding court between two marble statues, Heron was recounting a tale to an enraptured audience including a man Agog first mistook to be a woman.

Agog quickly realized the effeminate man was Hortio based on his jeweled and sparkling attire. No Alexandrian would wear that many valuables that they would have to transport across the city after the party was over. Plus the crimson and gold theme matched the silks and banners of the party. It had to be the owner of the house.

His conclusion was rewarded when Plutarch sidled next to Hortio and whispered a few words. Heron had also noticed his arrival, but was in the middle of explaining a story about his experience with a Thracian whore.

Agog had seen no evidence of a social life for Heron, so he doubted the story had any truth to it. But the crowd gathered around, clutching golden cups of wine and wearing the finest garb in Alexandria, were so enthralled by his tale, they did not detect the falseness.

Once the climax of the story had been reached, in words and in past deeds, laughter erupted.

"Enough, you sycophants! Shoo! Shoo!" Hortio laughed and swept away the crowd with gentle limp-wristed motions.

As Heron's eyes fell upon him, Agog sensed a deeper emotion, but unlike the lies about the whore, he couldn't determine their source.

Hortio spread his arms wide, smiling and shaking his long blonde hair, distracting Agog from his insights about Heron. "This must be the dreaded barbarian from the North, disguised in the local attire."

The remaining members of the circle appraised him with interest as if he were an animal in a cage. Hortio pushed them away until it was only the four of them.

Agog bowed, putting one fist over his chest in a traditional salute. "Greetings."

"Oh! A custom of your people." Hortio widened his eyes in mock excitement. "We'll all be doing it before the week is out, if I have anything to say about it."

Agog wasn't sure if the host wasn't making sport of him, until he caught the glance from Heron.

Hortio hooked his braceleted arm around Plutarch's and Agog finally understood the change in the foreman. Plutarch ran his fingers through Hortio's hair and the two men shared intimate smiles.

Such men lived in the North, so Agog was accustomed to their ways and made no outward indication when the two kissed. Heron shrugged again, which was about all the man could do with his poles and leg harnesses.

When the two men were done kissing, Heron asked, "Have you decided if you can lend me those books?"

Hortio made an exaggerated sigh and wrinkled his nose distastefully. "Always business with you. When will I ever see Heron the whore slayer?"

Hortio, along with Plutarch, who'd taken on a very subdued role compared to his normal commanding presence in the workshop, laughed like naughty children.

"After the play," said Hortio. "If you've pleased me with your mechanics, then I will consider it."

Heron nodded solemnly. "Then I should go inform Punt that we'll be starting soon."

He limped away on his poles and harnesses. Agog was reminded of the creature they called the giraffe, when he'd seen one in a cage in Antioch.

Agog moved along side of Heron. "Why is Punt working it? Have your workers run off on you?"

Heron shook his head. "I had to send them away."

Agog staggered to a stop, putting his hand on Heron's pole. "Send them away? Then how will you complete my war machines?"

He said it louder than he had intended, drawing more stares than he'd already enjoyed.

"Hush," said Heron, whispering. "I had to. One of them is a spy, but since I do not know which, I had to send them all away. I haven't determined the power source in any case."

Agog put his hand to his temple. The troubles of his home land seemed simple compared to his dealings with Heron.

"How will any work get done?" he asked.

"I don't know," said Heron, shaking his head again. "But I couldn't let Lysimachus know what our plans are."

Agog grunted. "I could have *questioned* your workers for you and found the spy. I can be quite persuasive."

"I could not let you do that to them. I'm sure the one who is spying is only doing so because the Alabarch has blackmailed them or is threatening their family," said Heron.

"You're so naïve," growled Agog. "The tax man broke your legs, threatens your daughter, and is preparing to destroy all your hard work and you're letting your workers go without questioning them?"

"I have plans in the works," said Heron.

Before Agog could rebut, they came upon a curtained stage. Agog hadn't seen the statues in action, but given their immobility, he was prepared to be unimpressed.

Punt crawled from beneath the stage, sweat rolling from his bald head. Agog offered a hand and helped him to his feet.

"That you should be crawling beneath these wooden planks like a common worker is a crime," said Agog. "If you were in my country, your skills at the forge would have you revered as a god."

Punt looked embarrassed as he wrapped a rope around a pulley on the back of the stage.

"Are we ready?" asked Heron.

Punt nodded. "I double checked the connections. A wire was severed beneath the main actor, but I cobbled together a fix."

Heron nodded. "Seems I was right in sending all the workers away. I should have paid more attention to this curse business."

"The well pulleys need checking," mumbled Punt as he shuffled away.

"The well?" Agog raised an eyebrow in question.

"The play is powered by a heavy stone falling down a well, yanking a series of pulleys," Heron explained.

"A play?"

Heron indicated for Agog to return to the main room.

Heron climbed upon a bench and cleared his throat loudly. "Good citizens of Alexandria! May I have your attention?"

The gentle clatter of the party quieted to a murmur. Once they had assembled before him, Heron began to speak again.

"Tonight we gather together to witness my newest mechanical play," said Heron to a light applause, who waited until it died down before continuing again. "But this time I did not script the actors."

A point of surprise carried through the assembled, whispering guesses as to who might be the author. Heron waited until their lots had been cast.

"I am pleased to announce that your gracious host, Hortio, did the honors!"

The party goers cheered, holding up their goblets of wine, whistling and clapping as Hortio ran to the front of the crowd, holding up his hands like a victor of a gladiatorial match. Hortio bowed deeply, exaggerating the flip of his blonde hair upon returning upright.

Heron carefully climbed off the bench and signaled for Hortio to pull the golden tasseled rope that hung from the edge of the stage.

Hortio gathered Plutarch into his arms, giving him a gentle kiss before skipping to the rope, eliciting much laughter from the crowd.

Everyone's faces were lit like sunbeams, shining at their host, who stood poised before them, ready to start the mechanical play.

Everyone but Heron.

Agog had been intrigued by the idea of a mechanical play. During the long sunless winters, his soldiers and their women amused themselves in his great hall, telling tales and acting them out before a blazing fire.

But Heron looked as if he were attending a funeral.

The pull of the golden rope elicited a great thunderclap. The crowd shrieked.

Trickles of laughter came after, especially when Hortio yelled, "I told him to put that in!"

Agog's eyes were drawn to the stage immediately to determine the source of Heron's concern. Upon the platform were four bronze statues, clearly Roman senators by their elaborate dress togas.

A fifth statue sat on a great throne on the left side of the stage with a laurelled head and a great receding hairline. Whispers of Caesar's name carried through the room.

On the right side of the stage was a miniature Lighthouse of Pharos. The top of the Lighthouse flared with an internal fire for which Agog could determine no source.

The four senators began moving back and forth, bowing and raising their hands in adulation. The movements were smoother and suggested the human form more than Philo's water spitting statue in the square.

Caesar seemed to be waiting, his head bobbing listlessly, almost bored by the senators. Though the play was silent, minus the thunderclap to announce the beginning, Agog found himself drawn in by the lifelike movements.

The only portion of the statues that did not evoke humanness were the bases, thick poles that moved in slots upon the stage.

As the play continued, Caesar slammed his hand on the arm of his throne and the senators grew more agitated.

Agog sensed the mood of the story by the reaction of the party goers. Caesar was clearly a hated figure. Agog himself admired the man, even though he'd killed his forbearers upon the fields of Elyusia.

As Caesar began to react more violently to the approach of the senators, the Lighthouse flared in return. Agog checked for Heron, only to find the man at the back of the crowd, as if he were planning on leaving.

Agog needed to talk to Heron, but wanted to watch the conclusion of the play. Agog edged around while keeping his eyes on the stage.

A steady drumbeat rumbled up from beneath the stage. The attendees surged forward, drawn by the escalating performance.

When the play seemed to be approaching a climax, the Lighthouse flashed red, three times. As the senators slinked closer to Caesar, he raised his fist skyward. With all eyes on Caesar, no one saw the front of the Lighthouse open up, no one but Agog, for his agile eyes never missed a thing.

Their excited screams were immaculate as the figure of Alexander the Great strutted across the stage on two mechanical legs to stab Caesar with his spear.

When the curtains came down around the stage, the audience cheered wildly and lifted Hortio onto their shoulders. Agog followed Heron easily, due to his condition, into a wide room filled with scrolls and books on every side.

# 15

Heron pulled a book from the shelf, admiring the soft beechwood cover and compact design. She favored the searchability of the book rather than the scrolls that kept most of the knowledge of their world.

She also enjoyed that Hortio had transferred his favorite scrolls into the tomes, so the ones she sought were easy to find among his massive private library.

Heron traced her finger across the title: *The Taming of Caesar.* She desperately wanted to open the cover and begin reading, but she needed to find the other books first.

Cocking an ear, she could still hear the wild raucous of the post-play party. Heron grimaced, thinking of the stones she'd loosed by doing that play for Hortio.

"Miracle worker, whore slayer, and now a book thief," said the baritone voice of the barbarian Agog, finishing his sentence with a satisfied click of the tongue.

*Damn that man is silent*, she cursed under her breath.

"What makes you think I'm going to steal them?" she asked.

Agog raised one eyebrow in a taunting salute. "I consider myself student in the nature of intention. It's kept me alive in battle and outside of it."

"Fine," said Heron. "Grab that sack and put this book in it...carefully..." she said as he took it from her.

Agog frowned at her admonishment. The Northman was clearly unaccustomed to taking orders.

Listening for the state of the party, Heron limped around the room, pulling another three books and two scrolls from the walls. She silently thanked Hortio for having a sense of organization. She'd been in other private libraries that had more in common with a rubbish heap.

Agog followed her around the room, taking each book and putting it in the sack, not gently enough for her tastes, but she didn't want to delay them longer.

"Come now," she said, noticing a slight bristling at her command. He really didn't like to be told what to do. She filed that away for later use.

They left Hortio's dwelling, nodding to the guards on the way out. The taller guard eyed Agog's sack suspiciously, but her presence was enough to stay any questions. She doubted Hortio would even notice the books were gone for months.

Away from the flickering torches of the party, they made their way through the streets. Though they weren't far, already the harnesses rubbed against her leg and the poles dug into her hands.

"Why steal those books? Wouldn't Hortio have given them to you for your play?" Agog asked as he marched next to her.

Heron glanced up at the Northman, noticing for the first time flecks of gray streaking through his hair knot, highlighted by the gibbous moon.

"Hortio is a prickly man. He'll promise the stars and the sun, but in the end, hand you a bucket of dung and call it even," she said. "Which is why I have long hesitated to create that mechanical play for him, given that the material could inflame tensions in the city."

Agog nodded, listening attentively. "Alexandria would throw off Rome's yoke?" he asked after a time.

"If it could," she replied. "But Rome's armies are too great and we have no leader to rally around. With the ending of the Ptolemies, and Old Egypt rotting and fractious, no one could take the throne."

Agog made some sign, for which Heron didn't recognize. A warding sign from the North, she supposed. His casual nature from their book thieving seemed to have changed to a more serious tone.

As Heron was about to question her financier more, he asked a question, almost, as she guessed, to cut off her line of thinking. "Why did you tell the lies about the Thracian whore?"

Her pole caught a dent in the street and nearly caused her to tumble. "How did you know?"

"When would you have time for whores? When you're not sketching new designs, barking orders at your workers, or scribbling in books, you're brooding in the darkness of your upstairs room, sniffing lotus powder and reimagining the world," said Agog.

Heron opened her mouth to speak, when a clutch of boys scrambled out of the darkness, nearly bumping into them. They were playing a game of sorts and paused, as if deciding whether or not to cause mischief, when they took in the size of her companion and disappeared into the darkness.

"So why lie?" he asked after the boys were gone.

The stray barking of dogs echoed through the street

behind them, chasing a rodent probably.

"Because it's useful for the upper class of Alexandria to think of me in that way," she said. "They spend their time fucking their slaves, drowning themselves in wine, and spending their coin on the latest fashions."

She paused and adjusted the harness on her leg. "If they see me only as an inventor, then they will guard their coin jealously. If I am one of them, the coin will flow."

Agog grunted in agreement. "A worthy plan."

"If only they used their coin in more productive ways. I could remake the city as a beacon for the world," she said.

"Is it not already?" Agog asked with true interest in his eyes.

"It is the City of Miracles, yes. A city dancing on the purse strings of the temples. But it could be so much more. A City of Wonders. Unbeholden to the gods. A citadel of man to forge a path to a wondrous future," she said, almost out of breath in her excitement.

"Some call it the Clockwork City, but a few statues and waterclocks do not make it so. If I had the funds, I would free the slaves and replace them with clockwork servants."

Heron paused, realizing she'd said too much. She glanced sideways at the Northman, to gauge his reaction. His white teeth glinted in the moonlight, grinning.

"You think me a fool," she said.

"I would not dare," he said. "Your statue of Alexander the Great ran across the stage on two mechanical legs to kill Caesar."

"Guided by wires and powered by ropes," she said. "He would have fallen over otherwise. Not a miracle, just a trick."

Agog shrugged. "Even battle strategies are just tricks. And countries are won and lost on them. But the world changes upon them. Didn't your Cleopatra conceal herself in a carpet?  That sounds like a trick to me."

The Northman paused, cocking his head in thought.  "Who knows?  Maybe the world will change upon that little spinning toy in your shop.  What's it called?"

"The aeolipile."  A cold shudder went through Heron.

She hadn't realized she'd stopped until she looked up to see Agog steps ahead, looking back at her with head tilted.

"Did I say something wrong?"

Heron shook her head.  The aeolipile.  The spinning toy danced through her head.  It was important, but she couldn't figure out how.  She needed to see it.

She glanced around trying to remember where they were.  "How far to my workshop?"

"We're past the Paneum.  A third of the journey," he said.

Heron hurried her pace, ignoring the rubbing harness.  The palm of her hand had blistered from the poles.  She hadn't walked so far before.

Visions of the aeolipile spinning, spitting out steam as it rotated filled her head.  The two escape pipes were pointed in opposite directions on the rotating ball, so when the central chamber was heated by fire, steam escaped, spinning the ball in tight revolutions.

She didn't know what it meant, but she knew enough that when she had strong feelings about an object or an idea, to study it closely to let her mind finish its work.  She wanted to get home quickly and see the aeolipile in action so she didn't lose the connection.

"Talk to me," said Heron.

"About what?" he asked.

"Anything.  I need to keep my mind from focusing on the aeolipile until I can get home and see it.  I've been missing something about its nature, but I can't place my finger on it," she said.

They traveled a few more steps before Agog started talking. "In the North, the days are weaker. Clouds vie for attention with the sun, blotting it and leaving us in a smothering gray twilight..."

Heron let the aeolipile remain in her mind, but focused on the baritone of the Northman, letting it soothe away her anxiousness and allowing her deep mind to work on the problem.

"...the forests flourish under the constant rains and so do the beasts within their depths. When I was a young man, and wanting to make a name for myself, I sought out the greatest beast in the surrounding area."

"There was a great black bear. The mother of all black bears, who towered over the trees and whose teeth could be made into pale white boats that would fit forty men."

"Like an avatar of the forest, she'd slain the warriors who had come for her pelt. Swiping the flesh from their bones as easily as we swat flies."

"In preparation for the hunt, I took the tallest tree in our village and cut it down to make a spear that could get past her long claws. But when I made it, I realized I was not strong enough to carry it to her lair, nor wield it in battle."

"I was a smaller man then. So I started by cutting down smaller trees in the village and carrying them around at all times. The men laughed at me, openly mocking me while I circled the village with the tree on my shoulder."

"The women mocked me too, but behind snickering hands and downcast eyes. As I cut down bigger and bigger trees that winter, circling the village and enduring their laughter, I knew that once I killed the great black bear, I would never return."

"Once I was able to carry around the largest tree, the one I had fashioned into a spear, I went to visit the Witch of the Wood in her walking house..."

Agog's voice trailed off, waking Heron from her trance. The aeolipile still spun in her head like an hourglass falling over and over itself, steam spitting out in puffs.

She realized then why Agog had stopped. A group of men wandered out of the darkness, at least six of them.

Heron thought they might have just chanced upon travelers making their way through the city to their homes, but then she heard her name on their lips.

Steel whispered out of sheaths and the glint of swords reflected the moonlight as the men approached. Despite the danger, Heron still saw the aeolipile rotating in her head.

Agog handed her the bag of books and stepped forward to confront the thugs.

Heron saw what they saw. A large, but unarmed man, in a Roman tunic and a strange hairstyle.

They spread out and encircled him, laughing as one might at a child pretending in his father's armor.

Heron hobbled to a spot against a wall, leaning on her poles and trying to snap the vision of the spinning toy out of her head. These men had been sent to do her harm, but yet she couldn't stop thinking of the aeolipile.

The men attacked.

The first thug leapt, bringing his sword down in a deadly arc at Agog.

The Northman nimbly side-stepped and connected a fist to the man's face, dropping him to his knees.

He'd moved faster than she thought possible.

The other thugs saw that as well and as a group, they hesitated. The first man stood, holding a hand to a bloody nose.

Then they realized they were six and armed, and he was one and unarmed, and advanced again.

This time they moved in two at a time.

Agog moved like a snake.  Sinfully quick for such a big man.

The swords sung through the moonlit air, shining blades.

Heron heard the impact before she saw it.  Agog had deftly moved past the sword thrust, grabbing the man's arm and using him as a shield for the other.

She could see how outmatched his opponents were, even unarmed as he was.

The Northman seemed to be stalking through them.  She swore he was relishing the fight.

Agog took the sword from the fallen man.

The sharp kiss of sword on sword gave voice to the silent battle.

Agog stepped through them like a dancer.

Their footfalls were heavy, grunting with effort.  His steps were a maiden's touch upon the hip.

He used his hilt to break a nose.

The four remaining men attacked from all sides.

Agog spun around, slicing his sword in a downward motion, creating a shield of whirling steel.

The image of the Northman and his blade married with the aeolipile in her head.

Heron felt on the edge of a great abyss.  She could see the spinning toy puffing steam and the sword connected to the arm on top of it.  The images meant something but she couldn't figure it out.

Why would she care about the bent arm with the aeolipile?

A kicked shuffle woke her from her vision.

A man with a sword over his head was approaching fast.  The Northman had slain two more of the thugs and was finishing the third, but the last had escaped to attack her.

Heron tried to bring her poles up, but her mind was so enthralled with her vision, she felt mesmerized by the approaching man.

The thug stumbled a few steps from her and dropped to his knees.

A sword tip was sticking from his chest.

He whispered, "Heretic..." before dying.

Agog stood a few paces back, his hand empty of sword, the thugs lying in a scattered pile around him.

Barking dogs sounded around them, woken by the clanging steel. Torch light flickered rapidly toward them. She could hear the clanging armor of approaching guards.

Agog appeared at her side and lifted her on his shoulder, handing her the bag of books.

"I'll get us to the workshop," he said.

And as he sprinted away, his heavy shoulder banging into her gut, the vision of the spinning toy and the swinging sword came together in her mind.

She knew what it meant.

Her whole body shuddered with the implications.

# 16

Heron closed the book she'd stolen from Hortio, having read it for the fifth time. Each time, she gleaned nothing new, save hints and shadings that lent nothing to her investigation about the fires.

The other books hadn't done much either, except convince her that the facts about the fires were incomplete and the truth buried in the ashes of that day.

Her benefactor, the one supplying coin for the investigation, had come the day before, leaving another pouch of coin. She'd told the old man to bring lotus powder next time and where to find it in the out-skirts of the city.

These days it was too dangerous for her to leave the workshop, nor did her hobbled legs provide the ease to make the journey.

Heron glanced at her scribbled notes as a lone hammer rang softly from the foundry.

— *Caesar*

— *Rome*

— *Ptolemies*

— *Temples (too many to list)*

— *Old Egypt*

— *Accident*

— *Carthaginians*

— *Parthians*

Caesar still ranked among her suspects, though only by the nature of his presence during the fires. Still, the facts did not support him burning the Library.

He was busy fighting a battle for his life and had lit the ships in the harbor to protect himself. And having Cleopatra as a lover only reinforced his desires not to burn the Library. Why anger your bed companion by burning the jewel of her family's legacy?

The Roman Senate had cause, jealousy of Alexandria's stature in the world, but the opportunity to strike at that exact moment seemed ludicrous in its probability. Heron dismissed it out of hand.

A cheer from the foundry silenced her thoughts for a moment. Through the archway, Agog's broad back could be seen leaning over a cart. The northerner had volunteered his help when she'd sent away her workers. Now the workshop consisted of Plutarch, Punt, herself, and Agog.

They seemed to be making progress on her latest project. Heron turned back to her desk to focus on the list of suspects.

While she placed the Ptolemies on the list, she did so only to make it complete. Like Cleopatra, another Ptolemy, she did not believe they would harm their greatest asset even as brother and sister fought over control of the city.

Granted, it'd been widely known that her brother, much younger than his sister, was under the thrall of his three ministers. But they had little to gain from the fires and much to lose.

In fact, their side had been bolstered during the fires by the efforts that they took to put them out. She left the name on her list should new facts arise, but mentally crossed them out.

The temples had a strange bond with the city. Some openly disparaged the "truths" of the Library, citing conflicts with their particular god. Yet they relied on the gifts of the Library to supply the miracles that placated their followers and loosened their purse strings.

The other point that bothered her was the last word of the dying man. "Heretic," he had said. It implied that she'd been attacked for reasons of religion, though she knew of no way they would have known about her investigation.

She hadn't mentioned that to Agog, who still believed the thugs were hired by Lysimachus. And they still could have been. The man may have harbored individual prejudices against her. She wasn't much loved by the temples, regardless of her work for them. The disaster at Nekhbet had only solidified their thinking that the gods had cursed her and that she should be shunned.

No temple would give her business now, not that she minded. Except for the crushing debt, and the threat of Lysimachus hanging over her head, the parting with the temples had been liberating.

So while the temples as a collective still remained on her list, she attributed recent events to her local influence rather than anything to do with the fires.

Old Egypt, the next suspect on her list, was a nebulous one at best. The Ptolemies had been in the region long enough to insinuate themselves into the local consciousness, but some ill-thoughts were harbored long.

The only reason the Egyptians had welcomed a Macedonian king named Alexander the Great into their realm, was because of his visit to Siwa—the Oracle of Ammon.

There, Alexander had learned he was the son of the god Ammon.  An unlikely story, as much as the gods performed their miracles in the temples, but it had served Alexander well. The oft bending knees of the Egyptians prostrated themselves once more before a god-king from another country.

There was much for Old Egypt to hate about that story. The country had been a theocracy for millennia: a stretch of time that Heron found staggering.

The next item on the list seemed the most likely at first glance.  The ship fires could have sent fiery ashes into the air to slip into an open window in the storage warehouses and set them alight.

Old papyrus was dry and flammable.  The Library had strict rules for flame in its halls.  That it was an accident seemed plausible.

Except that the Library had another enemy: water.

That the Library would leave seaward windows open, letting in moisture that would lead to mildew and rot was a poorly conceived cause.  In all Heron's time in the papyrus storage rooms, not once had she seen an open window.  She wasn't sure if any even had a window.

The eye witness accounts were clear in the books she'd stolen from Hortio that the flames had been inside of the warehouses, not burning from without.

The last two, Carthaginians and the Parthians, like the temples, could be a bigger entry as Rome had developed many enemies over the centuries of its rule.  In their haste for revenge, they might have set the fires to rob Rome of the new jewel in its crown.

But like the Roman hypothesis, they might have had

reason, but not opportunity. Heron didn't cross them out either, but they seemed unlikely.

The three men were rolling a cart from the foundry, laughing and clapping each other on the back, so Heron rolled up the parchment with the list and shoved it in a cubby on her desk.

She didn't want them to know about her other project. Besides its secrecy, it felt ludicrous to be investigating a crime one hundred years old.

The cart stopped before her desk. Upon the small platform was an aeolipile suspended over an unlit container of lamp oil. On the other side was a miniature bellows and between the two were connecting rods like her leg harness. The whole contraption was about the size of a dog.

Plutarch bowed with a giddy, lunatic grin on his face, born of days without sleep, and swept his arm overtop the cart. "We had to make a few modifications to make the connections fit, but your design worked perfectly."

Her blacksmith nodded in his normal stoic manner, but he'd worked long enough for her to see the pride in his pulled back shoulders, despite his exhaustion from working through the night.

Agog stood to the side, watching. His hands were blackened from helping in the foundry, but he didn't share the elation of the other two. Heron guessed he was trying to figure out how the contraption would help his yet unmade war machines.

"Let me see it work," she said.

Plutarch lit the oil with a small flame he'd brought from the foundry and stared greedily at the suspended aeolipile like a hungry child.

Heron let the grin rise to her lips. "I haven't seen you having this much fun since I left you in Hortio's arms the other night."

"What I do in service for the Good Master," said Plutarch, grinning.

Agog's head bobbed up, as if a wind had goosed him. "You were with Hortio upon command?"

Heron let her grin deepen to taunt the North man. "Just now figuring that one out?"

Plutarch answered, "A command I was *more* than willing to carry out. Hortio has been trying to get into my toga for quite some time. That it served the needs of the workshop made it more enjoyable."

"You Alexandrians are a duplicitous lot," said Agog dryly.

"A skill of survival, nothing more," said Heron. "We do not play the game for the sport alone, unlike the Romans."

"It was a compliment," said Agog with an eyebrow raised.

The conversation halted when the aeolipile began to spit steam. Everyone stared at it, waiting for the arms to move. When they did, slowly at first, Heron felt her heart thrum.

She knew it would work, but seeing it in action was almost more than she could bear.

The aeolipile began to speed up, overcoming the resistance of the pistons. As they moved back and forth, the motion was converted into a lever, pressing on the bellows. As the first piston stroke hit, the bellows heaved a breath, knocking the dust off a nearby table.

Once the aeolipile had gathered enough speed, the bellows were chugging away like a hyperventilating mother giving birth.

"I can harness the heat from the furnace to stoke the bellows," said Punt.

"Yes," said Plutarch. "We could begin hooking it up today."

Heron stared at the spinning aeolipile. "No." She shook her head. "We're not doing that."

The three men exchanged glances. Plutarch opened his

mouth, but Heron cut him off.

"We need a bigger one."

She pulled the designs from her desk and handed them to Plutarch, who stared opened mouthed at the new paper in his hands.

"By tomorrow morning."

The three of them had worked for two days making the small contraption and now she'd asked them to repeat the feat on a larger scale in a fourth of the time.

Punt and Plutarch returned to the workshop to begin work, while Agog hung back.

"You're pushing them very hard," he said.

Heron nodded.

"The next payment to Lysimachus comes in five days," she said.

Agog sighed. "No need to be dramatic about it. I can fund your debts another month."

Heron shook her head.

"I don't think he's coming for coin this time."

Agog stared back at Heron for a long moment and nodded as though he saw something he liked.

He walked away and she slumped in her chair, wondering if her feeble plans would work, but content to know that either way, she would be free of Lysimachus, through victory or death.

# 17

Sepharia could still hear Astrela's snoring even though she'd stuffed tufts of cotton in her ears. She thought about taking her work table into the courtyard in back, but she was forbidden to leave the house.

No wonder Punt stayed at the foundry for long hours, she thought.

Sepharia hadn't heard much news from the foundry. Since her aunt had been maimed by the tax collector, and she'd been shipped off to hide at Punt's house, Sepharia had been kept in the dark.

She blew her hair out of her face and readjusted the shaping tool to get a better grip. She leaned over the piece of brass and set the curved tool into the ridge.

After raising the small hammer, she leaned back to review the sketching before she struck the tool. Aunt Ada's notes had been clear: if the teeth didn't fit exactly, it would be useless.

Sepharia tapped gently, scraping away the soft metal. After a cleansing breath, she picked up the companion piece and set it into the notch.

When the pieces fit snugly, she blew out the breath she'd been holding and sat back. She was about to congratulate herself when she noticed the notes at the bottom of the sheet.

*"...the fitting between the two sides must be no tighter OR looser than a human hair..."*

Sepharia frowned and plucked a hair from the back of her head, grimacing slightly at the deed. She had to take one from the back to find one long enough.

Taking the two ends in her fingertips, she slipped the hair between the two pieces. It didn't want to go at first, but with a little pulling, slid around three-quarters of the way. On the last leg, the hair got stuck and she couldn't put it through.

Sighing, Sepharia pulled them apart and felt around the offending area with her finger tip. A small raised portion would have to be shaved off for the two pieces to fit perfectly.

She set the piece back into the catch, picked up her hammer and chisel, and set it against the bump. With a few light taps, she removed enough material, that to the eye anyway, would make them fit.

A quick test with the hair proved her intuition and she set the tools down and rubbed the bridge of her nose. She only had one tooth done and she'd been at it for hours.

Finishing the piece would require seven more fittings and if she made a mistake on any of them, it would require a complete redo.

Aunt Ada had given her until midday to complete the job. She wasn't going to get any sleep tonight.

Sepharia shook her head. Her father's twin had asked her to stop calling her that.

It was hard to remember. Each time she called Ada by her father's name, she felt like she was betraying his memory, erasing him from the world.

She'd never understood why Ada hadn't taken one of the many suitors in Greece that had offered. If Ada had, then Sepharia's life might have been a normal one.

She missed her father, not that she knew him, other than faded memories of him bent over at his work desk or when he returned drunk after losing his money on gladiator fights.

Sepharia pulled the clothes she'd brought with her out from under her mat. They were the clothes she'd used to disguise herself as Sada. She shook her head. She'd been so foolish not to have already picked a name when the Northman had asked her.

Luckily, it'd been dark and his mind had been on other things. At least she didn't have to worry about the chest bindings. Her budding chest was barely noticeable.

Yet the tax collector had noticed her. Sepharia shivered. She'd overheard what he'd said. She had no interest in a man with a pot belly. Especially one so much older than she.

Sepharia fingered the tunic and wandered to the doorway, tentatively peeking out at the night sky, being careful to stay hidden in the darkness.

The waning moon cast a silver light across the ground. Across the courtyard, a little brown dog with a paw missing lay curled up in a doorway.

"Get away from that doorway," whispered a voice menacingly from behind her.

Sepharia squeaked, holding the tunic to her chest.

Astrela hobbled out of the darkness behind her, squinting and scratching her matted hair.

"The absence of your hammering woke me. You know you're not supposed to be near a doorway. If the Alabarch finds you here, he'll take you and rape you and you'll never see your father again," said Astrela.

"Don't say that," whispered Sepharia.

"The truth? Why not?" she asked. "My life is at stake too because my pride-filled husband couldn't convince your father to beg the gods for forgiveness."

"The gods don't care about us," said Sepharia.

Astrela made a crossing sign with her fingers and spit into her palms before rubbing them together.

"The gods watch us every moment. Judging us." Astrela poked split fingers at Sepharia. "Don't you forget that."

Sepharia tucked the tunic behind her back. "If it helps you sleep, I'll get back to my work. I'll be up all night anyway, I really should get back to it. I just needed to stretch," said Sepharia.

Drawn by the motion to put the tunic behind her, Astrela stalked up to Sepharia and yanked it from her fingers.

"What's this?" she asked, shaking it.

Sepharia clamped her mouth shut and glared at the old woman.

Astrela unbunched the tunic and smoothed it out, holding it to the faint moonlight slipping through the doorway.

"A man's tunic? Why would you have such a thing?" she asked.

"I was cold."

Sepharia flinched, regretting her words instantly. She should have said that she used it as a rag or a pillow or anything but wearing it.

Astrela's gaze went from the tunic to her short hair and back again.

"You've been sneaking out?" she accused.

"Ah—No..." whispered Sepharia.

Normally she had witty comebacks for Punt or Plutarch or one of the workers, but standing in front of Astrela, who glared at her with the tunic clutched in her hands, all she could do was stammer.

Astrela grabbed her by the ear and dragged her into the kitchen. Then she pulled a small leather bag from beneath the wrap that hid her wrinkled body. The bag was suspended from her neck by a cord.

She loosened the bindings and shook the contents into her hand. The bones shone ghostly white, reflecting the moon even though they did not sit beneath its gaze.

"Your breath," said Astrela.

"Wha—?" stuttered Sepharia.

"Breathe on it for Ra's sake," she said.

When Sepharia hesitated, Astrela shoved her face into the bones.

"That's good enough."

Astrela cupped the bones between her hands, shaking them vigorously and mumbling to herself. The words were sharp and menacing, almost that each utterance was a curse in itself.

Astrela's eyes rolled back into her head until only the white remained. Then, before Sepharia could blink, Astrela cast the bones upon the table. The two short bones crossed each other while the curved bone with a flat blade on it sat to the side.

Astrela hovered over the bones, searching across the table, whispering to herself. When she made a satisfied grunt, Sepharia's gut twisted like a rope.

"The bones are wise," said Astrela, clearly waiting for her to ask what they said.

Sepharia bit her lip and resisted the urge. She hadn't yet decided if the gods were real, but such thoughts were heresy in the sands of Egypt.

But she also knew that once Astrela had grabbed for her bag of bones, the results wouldn't be in her favor. Ada's stories about the priests of the temples told her that much. Too often the "oracles" they made for the temples were manipulated by the priests so they could maximize their profits.

When she realized that Astrela was content to wait all night for her to ask, she muttered in her smallest voice, "What did they say?"

Astrela smiled, and Sepharia despised her for that grin. Even that Punt, her husband, was like a favorite uncle to her, wasn't enough to contain her hatred.

"Great pain awaits you outside these walls for the gender thief. If you dare sneak out before the words of your father have blessed your return, death by the jaws of Horus will be your fate," said Astrela.

Sepharia wanted to tell her that Ada wasn't her father, so her bones had to be a lie, but she didn't dare, so she plopped back onto her chair, signaling to Astrela that she needed to work.

Astrela smirked and left the room, tucking the tunic under her arm.

Sepharia picked up the tiny hammer and sighed heavily, staring at the papyrus, even though her mind was not on her work.

That little act wasn't going to scare her into staying in the house, Sepharia thought. In fact, it had practically guaranteed she would escape, just as soon as she could get her tunic back.

After a long spell of sulking and thinking about how much she hated Astrela and wanted to strangle her, Sepharia huffed and cleared her mind.

She needed to get back to work.

If she didn't get the brass connecting device shaped by the next day, Aunt Ada would strangle her first.

# 18

"Where is the Northman? We're ready for the test," said Plutarch with a touch of impatience as he paced.

Heron pulled an hourglass out of her desk and flipped it over, starting the sands to fall. "If he's not back in a quarter hour, we'll start the test without him."

Heron eyed her foreman Plutarch, covered in soot and grime. The sweet blue tunic he'd been wearing when he first arrived three days ago was blackened, ripped, and burnt.

Plutarch hated to get dirty, which was why he was such an excellent foreman. He never did what he could get others to do.

Heron threw him a rag. "Wipe your face. You're beginning to look like Punt."

Punt grinned and continued drinking from his mug of water. While Plutarch hated dirt, Punt reveled in it like a pig in the mud.

The last few days had been a whirlwind of activity. Heron couldn't believe how much the four of them had accomplished. Actually three, considering she couldn't lift a hammer without falling down.

She tapped on the hourglass. Lysimachus wasn't going to wait for her.

"Plato have pity, let's put fire to our plans."

"Oh thank the gods," said Plutarch. "Let's get this done. I'm dying for a bath. Even if it's just a bucket of rainwater dumped on my head."

"My nose would be better for it," quipped Punt uncharacteristically.

When Plutarch turned on the blacksmith, he just shrugged his shoulders and shot Heron a grin.

They made their way into the workshop, Heron limping along with her harnesses and poles.

On a heavy timber platform, an aeolipile the size of her head was suspended over a brazier. Like the smaller version, the spinning toy was connected to a pair of pistons similar to her leg harness.

The pistons were hooked to a rotating disc by the brass device she'd had Sepharia make for her. The disc was wound with rope that was connected to a heavy door.

Punt grabbed a torch and shoved it into the charcoal filled brazier beneath the aeolipile. Not long after, he had a small fire burning.

"Now we wait for steam," she said.

Agog arrived with a wrapped cloth in his hand.

"Couldn't wait for me, could you?" grinned Agog.

As he grinned, Heron got the impression he was a great bear, sizing her up for a meal.

"What did you learn from your source?" she asked.

Agog narrowed his eyes. "Lysimachus has hired a group

of mercs to make an assault on the workshop. He got the worst of the worst from the dregs outside the city walls."

Heron nodded. She'd been expecting this. He wouldn't let her hide Sepharia forever and without his spies in the workshop, he had no other way to find out where she was.

"When will they do it?" she asked, hoping they'd have a couple more days to prepare.

Agog glanced up at the roof. "Tonight. When all is dark. Two tens of mercenaries. Worst of the worst. Not prone to breaking easily at the first sign of failure."

"Plato have pity, that gives us no time."

Punt and Plutarch looked deflated, so Heron willed herself to be optimistic. She straightened her shoulders, took a deep breath and asked Agog a question.

"How sure are you of this information? Might your source just be trying to scare us?"

The Northman smirked and looked at the cloth in his hand, clicking his tongue once. Heron interpreted the noise as amusement.

He slowly unraveled it, drawing even Punt and Plutarch's attention, who had been previously staring at the dirt floor.

When he was done, he threw the object within onto the floor between them. A small black rod the length of a finger lay in the dirt. And then Heron realized what it was.

It *was* a finger.

And she knew whose it was, too.

She felt Agog's gaze on her. He was studying her. Seeing what she would say about his act of brutality.

She met his hardened eyes with her own intensity until he seemed to accept her willingness with a nod. She checked with Plutarch, who nodded and Punt as well.

Heron detected that they'd passed some sort of test and that worried her more than the finger.

She was about to ask a question when the aeolipile began to spin. Steam wheezed out the two ends and like the smaller version, it took a while to gain enough momentum to move the piston.

Pretty soon, the pistons were winding the disc which pulled on the rope connected to the door. The heavy door swung closed and as it slammed shut, a clever hitch on the disc grabbed the rope the other way and pulled it open.

Once it got going, the door was banging between open and closed every couple of seconds. The aeolipile was spinning like a hell-bent chariot wheel.

A grin bubbled up to her face, replacing the dark mood brought on by the rotten finger. Almost like a madman shifting feverously between one emotion and the next.

Either the lack of sleep or the steady banging of the door, which was proof of her invention, had made her light with laughter, but it started rolling out of her lips.

The others began laughing with her: Plutarch's high and willowy, Punt's silently shaking his body, and Agog's deep baritone rumbling like a herd of oxen.

Heron shared a moment with Agog, that through the steady banging, seemed like he saw through her disguise, as his eyes twinkled with devious mirth.

And then everything started to go wrong.

At first, a steady counterpoint to the rhythm developed.

The motion of the pistons developed a slight ticking.

Then the ticking turned to tapping, which turned to thumping.

The contraption began to shake and the rope banged the door more violently with each swing.

Heron saw the problem immediately. The aeolipile was spinning impossibly fast, more than she'd calculated in her designs, and creating force on the pistons. So much that the pistons couldn't handle the load and rocked back and forth to disperse the energy.

The whole thing was going on like an unbalanced wagon down a mountainside.

"Is there any way to stop this damned thing?" Plutarch shouted above the banging. The other two looked as worried as her foreman.

Heron regretted not making the brazier beneath the aeolipile movable.

"When it runs out of water," she shrugged.

When the pistons began to whine, everyone backed away.

"Run!" she screamed, limping away from the device as fast as she could go.

Agog appeared at her side, practically dragging her through the workshop.

When the whine hit a high screech and then a heavy thud, she pulled Agog to the ground.

The contraption exploded when one piston came loose and the rod crossed over the other. The spinning aeolipile provided the momentum and slung pieces all over the workshop.

The force of the pistons knocked the whole thing off the heavy timbers and as the tubes on the aeolipile grabbed the earth, it ripped itself free and rocketed towards the wall that separated the workshop and the foundry.

Heron watched all of it from the floor, holding her arm across her face cautiously in case something was thrown her way.

The runaway aeolipile hit the wall with the force of a battering ram, exploding into shrapnel and sending a cloud of dust from the ceiling.

The coals were spread across the workshop and fires sprung up where they could. Punt began putting them out using tarp he yanked off the Horus head.

Agog brought in the rain barrel, handling it easy in his massive arms and put out the fires that the other two couldn't handle.

Once the fires were under control, they wandered to the hole in the wall. It looked like a giant had punched through the stone with a heavy fist.

Plutarch had a hand on his head. His eyes were wide with fear. "We needed that for Lysimachus, didn't we?"

Heron nodded. Her mind was whirling faster than an aeolipile and it was all she could manage.

"Dear me," said Plutarch. "Dear me."

Punt had his arms crossed, shaking his head.

Agog kept studying the hole and then tracing the destruction back through the workshop. The spinning object had left quite the trail.

Timbers had been ripped in half. Metal sheeting had been torn like paper. The stone floor looked chewed upon. Half the projects in the room had been destroyed or damaged. There was even a few fist sized holes in the ceiling.

The silence was damning as to the extent of the destruction, so they were all surprised when it was Punt that spoke first.

"It's all my fault," he said simply.

# 19

"It's all my fault," Punt said again, feeling his heart wanting to burst in his chest. He'd failed Heron.

"What are you talking about?" Heron asked, gaze passing over him dismissively.

He let his head sink low.

"The pistons, Master Heron. I knew there was a slight bend in the one, but there wasn't enough time to get it out," said Punt. "I should have never put it on."

He felt a warm hand on his shoulder. "It wasn't you," said Plutarch softly. "The distance between the aeolipile and the connecting device was too short, binding the pistons. I'd bound them to the platform a half a digit from true, causing the problem."

Heron made an agitated noise. "Would you—"

"No, Plutarch." He turned toward the foreman, crossing his arms again. "It was my mistake. The connectors were forged wrong. Too much slag metal made them weak. The fault is mine."

"There's no—"

Plutarch cut Heron off and responded with penance flooding his voice. "The fault is clearly mine. I deviated from Master Heron's drawings in my haste to complete the device."

Punt was shaky from exhaustion and woozy from a lack of sleep, but he knew he'd been at fault. He raised his voice slightly in his response.

"Look. The damned thing is destroyed now, just let me have the blame and let's get on with it," he said, his voice rising in volume as he spoke.

Plutarch wiped his face with a rag, leaning heavily on a broken beam. "I will not let you have the blame. Master Heron must know who caused it so he can make sure we don't make the same mistake again."

The two squared off.

Then Heron shouted in a much higher voice than normal, "Will you two silence your bleating!"

"May Poseidon drown you in puddle. You two are arguing about nothing while we have a workshop to rebuild," said Heron exasperated.

Heron's face was blotchy and red and he was clenching his fists. Then he pointed a finger at his chest, while balancing with one pole. "I. Me." He paused to let the words sink in. "I was the source of the failure."

Heron looked back and forth between them, eyes scolding. "I calculated the speed of the rotation incorrectly. The number was off by at least a double. So it was my fault the workshop was destroyed."

When Punt caught Plutarch's gaze, the foreman raised an eyebrow impishly.

"Yes, Master Heron. It was all, clearly, your fault," said Plutarch with a straight face.

Punt nodded. "I do agree. I was mistaken in taking the

blame."

Punt felt the grin rising to his face. While Plutarch kept his face neutral, Punt couldn't help but let the smile tease the corner of his lips upward.

Heron eyed them both, lips in a thin white line, until he cracked as well and the three of them began laughing in earnest.

Agog stood off to the side. "It is said that those that can laugh in the thick of battle have the strongest hearts." The big man looked to each of them. "And if this isn't the first skirmish of our coming battle, I don't know what is."

The Northman snapped his head back and began heaving great belly laughs, his whole body was shaking, even the hair knot on his head.

When at last the laughter died down, Heron motioned for them to come closer.

Then, he glanced up at the holes in the ceiling, from which sunlight streamed through. It was the top of the day and though the heat was peaking, Punt barely felt it.

"First. We need to make a new..." Heron paused and scratched his head. "A new what? What are we calling this thing?"

Punt shrugged, while Plutarch spoke for the both of them. "You've always named your creations. We call them what you call them."

Heron adopted a thoughtful pose and said after a few moments, "We'll call it a steam mechanical. For now. Until we determine a better name."

Then Heron asked, "How quickly can we make another steam mechanical? Do we have another aeolipile of that size?"

"Yes, but it has flaws in the metal and the steam could cause it to explode," said Punt.

"No worries. The steam is escaping and so the pressure

on the vessel is minimal. We'll just have to trust the metal," said Heron. "The rest I know we have duplicates of except for what Sepharia made."

Agog wandered away from them and quickly returned with the bronze connector. He threw it to Heron who nearly fell trying to catch it.

Heron shot Agog a spiteful look before he examined the bronze fittings. He gave a heavy sigh before pronouncing it functional. "If it wasn't okay, we'd be hung before we started. There are a few nicks, but I can buff those out while you recreate the steam mechanical."

Back at his desk, Heron pulled out a papyrus, unrolled it and set it on the floor. They hovered around it. Punt recalled that the design didn't look like anything they'd ever made before.

He wiped the sweat from his bald head. He couldn't understand why Heron was showing them this new design. They didn't have time to try new things.

"It's a map of the workshop," said Agog after a while.

"Very good," said Heron.

"But what is it for?" asked Plutarch and Punt nodded along with him, the foreman speaking his thoughts as well.

Heron looked to Agog, so the Northman spoke, "For our defenses tonight."

"Have you two been scheming this when we haven't been watching?" accused Plutarch.

"The maps we use for warfare are similar," said Agog. "Though I'll admit we've never used them to defend a building. But the idea is the same, so it was easy to see the purpose."

Heron gave a quick rundown of the layout they would have to assemble. Punt shook his head. Rebuilding the steam mechanical and moving around the layout for the defenses wasn't going to be possible with the three of them.

"Impossible," said Punt finally, when he couldn't stand it anymore. "There isn't enough time. Not unless we call back some of the workers."

"We can't do that," said Plutarch. "As much as it pains me, we can't trust them. We can only trust ourselves."

Punt pointed to the half-finished Horus head. "The layout shows that over in this corner, *with* modifications. It would take me the rest of the day to do just that." He threw his arms in the air. "And there are at least another ten jobs like that!"

Surprised at the volume of his own voice, Punt put a hand up to indicate his apology.

Heron accepted it with a gesture of his own, but otherwise remained clear eyed and aloof, not rising to the discussion.

Agog scratched his head and adjusted his top knot. As he smoothed the tail of hair through his fingers, Punt was surprised by the streaks of gray within.

"And your defenses require two more people to properly function," said Agog, pointing to various places on the map. "We can't be in more than one place at the same time."

"You are absolutely right," Heron said slowly and deliberately, pointing his pole at Punt. "There is no way we can get all of that done with just the four of us. Three since you can't count me."

Punt kept his mouth shut. He knew when Heron was in a mood. The grim lips and mischievous sparkle to his eyes were warning enough.

Usually when the Master got like that, they were struggling to get a miracle to work and had been arguing amongst themselves. Heron would step up, with that look firmly planted on his face, and draw just enough of the solution that they had to figure the rest out themselves.

But that was for a miracle that would be performed in a temple, under ideal conditions. With the threat of Lys looming over them, Heron's expression took on a darker meaning.

Heron turned to Plutarch indicating him with the pole. "And you are right, too. We can't bring in any of the workers. We can't trust them."

Heron faced Agog. "Northman," he said simply, bowing slightly toward him with only his head. "You deduce our defenses correctly. We require six to defend as I have laid out."

Punt, along with Plutarch and Agog, stared at Heron questioningly. He couldn't figure out what Heron was getting at, though it wouldn't be the first time. Nor would it be the last, providing they got through the night.

Heron looked up to the holes in the ceiling and clapped his hands. Clouds had moved in from the sea, dimming the workshop, and bringing with them the threat of rain.

"Plato have pity, it seems the gods do favor us after all," said Heron.

Punt almost fell over from shock. "But—You...you don't believe in the gods?"

Heron shrugged in a playful manner. "Maybe they believe in me."

And though all odds seemed arrayed against them, and nothing made sense, Punt saw the lightness in Heron's demeanor and decided that everything would be all right, even if he didn't understand.

Heron glanced once more at the holes in the ceiling. "Plato have pity, no more room to explain. Plutarch, begin construction on the new steam mechanic. Punt, I'll need you to start on the Horus head. Agog, I'll need you for a special favor."

Punt spoke up before Heron could get too far. "But—Master Heron?"

"Yes," said Heron over his shoulder.

"It'll take me all day just to do the Horus head," he

explained.

Heron thought a moment and said simply. "Then I guess you'd better get it done in a fourth of that time." After a pause, Heron continued. "Don't worry, Punt. You'll think of something. You always do."

Heron let a small smile light his face. One that spoke of warmth and friendship. And then he turned and wandered off with Agog. The two began conferring in hushed tones and he overheard Heron speaking of vinegar and chicken's blood before they moved out of hearing range.

Punt examined the papyrus, rubbing his head and thinking about how he was going to accomplish what Heron requested. It seemed impossible, but he'd trusted Heron in the past. Why shouldn't he continue to trust the man?

Feeling the weight of his eyelids, he shook his head. He hadn't slept in days nor seen his wife in a week, except for a brief stop to pick up the bronze connector from Sepharia.

Punt let his gaze linger on Heron's ornate box. He dared not start down that path. Sheer will would have to do.

Looking over the papyrus, he noticed his name written to the side. Beneath it was a note in Greek. He could barely read Greek, but the words were familiar enough he could decipher the message.

"*When they reach Horus, make the crow fly over until they stumble into the staff.*"

Punt visibly shuddered as the words of his wife's reading came back to him. She had seen the signs of the *crow* and *staff*, and had said that after a great accident in the workshop, that the very walls of Rome would be shaken.

The destruction from the steam mechanic had to be the great accident she spoke of. The holes in the wall and ceiling were terrible and they'd almost all been killed when it had fallen apart.

But he didn't know how it shook the walls of Rome. It'd shaken their walls. Put holes in them, in fact.

Stranger things had happened under the watchful gaze of the gods. Punt shook his head trying to dislodge the thought. They were his wife's words, not his, spoken time and again.

But he wasn't sure, either.

Were the gods watching them? Punt had never been religious. He assumed his wife was religious enough for the both of them.

Astrela claimed that Heron was routinely punished because he mocked the gods. Just as he'd done once again just moments ago.

Before, Punt had been buoyed by Heron's surety and calm. The Master of Miracles seemed poised to bring forth another miracle, this time saving them from Lys the Cruel.

Now with his wife's premonition rolling through his head, Punt wondered if she was right and that the gods would seek retribution for being mocked.

The two thoughts warred in his head until at last, Punt shook them both off. What was he thinking? He was not a man of gods or philosophy. He was a blacksmith. A practical man who used his fists and his thoughts to bring form out of the earth.

Punt stood, dusted himself off, and got to work. Either way, in a battle between Heron and the gods, or Heron and the Alabarch, he was on Heron's side. And that was enough for him.

# 20

The walls of Punt's house constricted around Sepharia, squeezing the breath from her lungs. She sat in the dark, staring out the back door into the courtyard, even though she couldn't see much more than shades of night.

The three-footed dog that was normally a fixture in the far doorway was only a blotch of slightly lighter darkness.

A rare batch of cloud cover had moved in during the afternoon and as night had fallen, the streets had been dipped in ink.

She glanced at her work on the table. Another bronze connecting device. Punt had asked her to make another when he'd picked up the first.

She'd barely cut two teeth.

Punt refused to tell her news of the workshop, no matter how she begged. He just stood in the doorway, rubbing the edge of his leather apron absentmindedly.

Once the request had been given and the bronze device taken, Punt had left, with only a brief hug for his wife.

Sepharia fingered the shaving tool, letting the sharp edge scrape her at skin. She considered jabbing it into the palm of her hand just to feel something. She'd been trapped in the house for weeks. Astrela was unpleasant enough in small doses. But long exposure had brought on a form of madness in Sepharia.

Thoughts of the workshop were warm and inviting. Punt had been silent about the conflict with Lysimachus, but since she was at risk, she wanted to be part of the solution.

Her real father would have let her help. Ada was doing more than stealing her brother's identity, Ada was squashing her neice's identity by keeping her locked up with Punt's crazy wife.

She could probably sneak out on her own in the covering darkness, but if a guard caught her, they would arrest her for being on the streets unchaperoned at night. If she were a man, she could at least try to bluff her way through.

She knew where her Roman tunic was, at least. She'd watched Astrela tuck it under the head of her mat to keep Sepharia from using it and to add a little padding to her slumber.

Not that she needed it. The woman snored like a thunderstorm.

Aunt Ada...Heron. She. She could help her, even though she'd been the one to send her away. Sepharia blew hot breath from her lips.

Did her aunt get confused by her own gender? How did she hide her interest in men? Or was she interested at all?

Maybe she didn't have room in her head for those thoughts. Too busy with her inventions and miracles.

Sepharia had them. She wanted to experience the world and taste its fruits.

But right now, she couldn't even enjoy the workshop,

spend time with gruff Punt learning to turn precious metals into rings and pendants, or weave through the warehouse, watching Plutarch assemble miracles piece by piece like a puzzle that only existed for him.

Sepharia huffed and crept to the edge of Astrela's room. The woman lay snoring on her back. The leather bag containing her bones could be seen peeking from the place between her breasts.

The barest edge of her tunic had slipped from beneath the mat. Sepharia had to squelch the desire to run into the room and rip the tunic out from under, before disappearing into the night. If she did it fast enough, Astrela wouldn't even know what had happened.

But she didn't even want Astrela to know. A plan was forming in her mind.

She would sneak out to the workshop and survey the situation. If it seemed safe, she would sneak in and reveal herself. If not, she could disappear into the night and return to bed. Punt and Plutarch would protect her from her aunt's wrath.

She just needed the tunic first so she could move through the streets. Her disguise had fooled the sharp-eyed barbarian, so she knew it would fool the Roman guards.

Her thoughts lingered on Agog a little longer. When she'd first met him, she thought he was a dull brute using his pillaged funds to buy war machines for some far off war.

Heron had treated him as such in the beginning. But over time, Sepharia had noticed how Heron spoke to him with ever increasing respect. And not just because she was taking more and more of his coinage.

Sepharia didn't know what Agog's standing was in his country, and though he was a barbarian, he had a stately aura.

As she thought more about Agog, a kernel of frustration

lodged itself in her mind. How could Heron trust a barbarian of the North with the secrets of her workshop, while she sent her own niece away?

The kernel grew into a full fledged aggravation and before any logical arguments could dissuade her, she'd convinced herself to steal the tunic back and sneak into the workshop.

Astrela had proved to be a light sleeper before, so Sepharia took care as she stepped into the room. Dogs barking in the distance startled her and she scuffed a foot.

Astrela reacted with an interrupted snore that turned into a snort.

Sepharia paused until the woman resumed snoring.

At the side of the mat, Sepharia tugged on the tunic lightly to determine how difficult it would be to dislodge.

It barely moved, only a slight fold giving her slack. The majority of the tunic lay trapped under Astrela's mat.

Astrela's wide nostrils vibrated with each snore. Kneeling so close was like standing in a windstorm.

Sepharia kneeled for a long time trying to determine how to remove the tunic. She feared waking the woman, but had to get to the workshop.

She'd just about convinced herself to do the yank and run, but then fortune smiled and Astrela rolled onto her side, away from Sepharia.

The tunic came freely away and Sepharia tip-toed from the room without making another sound.

Changing into the tunic only took moments as she let her robe fall from her shoulders. The chilly night air kissed her body lightly, bringing goose bumps.

She bunched up her clothes and tucked them under her own mat and fixed her disguise before she went out.

Her hair had grown since she'd cut it Roman style a few weeks ago, but she had no shears to trim it. Sepharia decided the darkness would hide the flaws in her disguise if she was stopped.

Just in case she needed a pretense to be wandering the streets at night, she grabbed a small stoppered vial with a cleaning acid she used for jewelry and tucked it into a hidden pocket on her belt.

Sepharia straightened her tunic, squared her shoulders and went into the night.

The streets were quiet, dead almost.

A cold wind sliced right through her tunic. Sepharia shivered.

It'd been warmer in the house. The heat from the day had been stored in the stone.

She made her way toward the workshop, avoiding the Roman patrols easily. They carried lanterns that made them as obvious as the day.

At one point, creeping along a wall, the stench of burning hair assaulted her nose. She couldn't determine its source, it was faint and disappeared quickly.

Her mind was so wrapped around that smell, she didn't notice that she'd come upon an unlit Roman patrol until the deep voice rumbled from the darkness.

"Halt in the name of the Empire."

Sepharia had to hold up her arm to block the light as the lantern, previously hidden, flooded across her.

"Ave," she whispered, the words getting caught in her throat unprepared.

"You're not supposed to be wandering the night, boy," said the soldier.

Sepharia let the knot in her stomach loosen slightly at the calling of "boy."

"Apologies," she said, lowering her voice. "My mother was sick and I was getting medicine from the apothecary."

A second Roman soldier began laughing.   The knot tightened.

"Hear that, Gradicus?  Sounds like the boy's balls haven't dropped yet."

More laughter followed.

"Say something," came the command.

Sepharia squinted into the light.  "What should I say?"

The two soldiers began laughing harder.  "Bet they're still bald as a Thracian's arse."

Their laughing doubled and Sepharia waited silently, trying to make sense of their joking.

The first Roman soldier stepped into the light with his sword drawn, and put the tip of it against the bottom edge of her tunic.

"Shall we take a look, Gradicus?"

Fear seized her throat.  If they lifted her tunic they would see she wasn't a boy at all.

The other's laughing trailed into a chuckle.  "Nay," he said, bringing relief.  "I've seen enough bald balls to serve a lifetime, campaigning with the Gauls against Tolosa.  Damn Gauls sent a legion of hairless boys to fight along with us.  Only one in ten survived the assault on the walls."

The sword was sheathed, but the light stayed firmly on her.

"I would like to see this medicine," he said.

Sepharia nearly dropped it pulling it from her belt pouch. She tried to keep her hand from shaking as she handed the vial to the solider.

The soldier took the stopper out and sniffed at the opening.

"Smells like lime," he said.  "Not like medicine at all. Medicine always tastes bad."

The solider with the vial leaned toward her.  "What would happen if I drank from it?"

He held it up to his lips tentatively. If he touched the vial to his lip, she was prepared to run. Even the slightest contact with skin brought immediate blistering.

Sepharia cleared her throat. "It's for painful constipation. The medicine is supposed to liquefy my mum's bowels so she can shit again. Since yours, I assume, are in working order, you would shit through a sieve for a week." She did her best to hide the shaking in her words.

The soldier immediately pulled the vial away from his lips and stoppered it. "Well, that would be unfortunate."

He stared at her a moment longer, his brow hunching in thought. And then he handed the vial back to her.

"Let's not see you again tonight, shall we?" the soldier asked.

Sepharia nodded her head enthusiastically, no acting this time, and scampered into the darkness as soon as they gave her leave.

She was quite proud of herself for lying so skillfully to the guards. The bit about the liquification of the bowels was the perfect touch to keep the guard from being too curious.

When she was verbally sparring with Plutarch, there were no repercussions, other than the gentle ribbing she'd receive for it.

This time, she kept her guard up as she finished the journey to the workshop, watching out for soldiers lurking in the darkness with their lanterns hooded.

But her attentiveness wasn't enough to spy the two men hidden in the alleyway on the street before the workshop.

The thin moon, which had been hidden behind the bank of clouds entirely, slipped a stray beam through, illuminating the street.

She cringed as the light fell upon her white tunic, making her visible for all to see. She didn't want to come up on the workshop in such light, so she backed into the alleyway, peering into the street for signs of soldiers.

Sepharia kept her attention to the streets, thinking about the Roman soldiers.  Soldiers never lurked in alleyways.

The scuffed step was her only warning and there wasn't time enough to react as rough hands grabbed her by the shoulders, yanking her backwards, deeper into the alleyway.

She couldn't yell out, lest she draw the soldiers, but she thought she might have to, to save her life.  Murder on the streets wasn't uncommon in Alexandria.  Especially at night.

Sepharia struggled against the hands.  A knee shot forward and hit her squarely between the legs.  Sepharia tried to double over and feign injury, but there was no hiding her lack of male genitalia and she'd never thought to make a harness like Aunt Ada's.

A dim light flickered from a small handheld lantern.  The barest of flame was revealed, casting heat across her face.

"How interesting," said the voice in the darkness.

Sepharia knew it right away.

Lysimachus.

She'd walked right into his waiting arms.

More light was loosed from the lantern and she could see Lysimachus leering at her in the darkness.

Instead of his usual fashion flare, resplendent in vivid colors, he was dressed in an all black tunic.  His blond curls caught the lantern light, making them appear reddish, even blood tinged.

"Do you like?  Not my usual colors, but for this evening, I'll make an exception," said Lysimachus.

Sepharia kept her mouth shut, not wanting to give herself away.

Lysimachus strolled forward like an arrogant peacock. He reached his hands between her legs and cupped upwards.

Sepharia tried to keep her face still, but his touch made her want to recoil.

"How *very* interesting," he said.

Sepharia pulled herself away from the Alabarch.

"Oh, don't be coy. I know who you are," he whispered menacingly. "You're Heron's daughter, dressed up in boy's clothes."

She felt the grip on her shoulders change. Suddenly the man behind her was pressed against her backside. Horrid breath washed over her and she tried not to retch.

"Don't worry," said the Alabarch. "I want you all for myself."

Lysimachus drank her in with his penetrating gaze. He stared at her like he wanted to suck the marrow from her bones.

Sepharia wasn't sure which way to shrink from, so she tried to withdraw inward.

"I would claim my prize and take you home right now to begin your training, but I've set too much into motion and need to complete the evening's festivities. It won't be long now anyway," he said.

Then the Alabarch paused, tilting his head as he reviewed her face. "It just occurred to me how much you look like your father. Especially with the haircut. How uncannily like him." His eyes sparkled with deviousness. "Everything makes sense now. I thought I was losing my touch the night we hobbled him."

Lysimachus ran his hand across her cheek.

"Yes. Yes. This evening has gotten more interesting by the moment. I think I shall enjoy this even more," he said. "We shall have to make special care that your *father* is not harmed." His lips made special care when he said father.

Sepharia cringed. Not only had she given herself up,

she'd given up Aunt Ada as well. Even if she survived, she was ruined.

Lysimachus noticed the despair on Sepharia's face, and ran his hand through her hair possessively. "Don't worry. Soon this will all be over and you can begin your new life with me."

# 21

Lysimachus ran his fingers through the girl's short black hair, relishing its silky feel. He could feel himself rise with excitement. The girl was trembling in fear of him, but he knew in time, and after thorough training, she would come to accept his touch with relish.

He grinned to himself, pushing an errant curl from his vision. The night was going better than planned.

He'd planned on killing Heron and taking his...correction, *her* workshop as payment for the debt. And then sell the contents to Philo, who would pay grand sums to get his greedy hands on her papers.

That way he would receive much more than the meager cut he took of the taxes he collected.

But now, given his new information, a delicious twist as it was, he would take her into his house as a slave. Since she was a woman masquerading as a man, she wouldn't be able to raise a fuss or she'd be put on trial and hung at the first dawn.

Gragne cleared his throat. "They should be breaking

down the doors right soon."

Lysimachus let his gaze lazily drift over his henchman, who pawed at the girl as he held her.

Lysimachus frowned at Gragne. He was getting right too familiar with property that wasn't his. It was possible there would be additional casualties than just the ones in the workshop.

The Alabarch fingered the blade at his hip. When events were firmly in control, he would consider giving the man his final reward. Lysimachus couldn't much stand the man's odorous breath anyway.

The mercs that he'd hired to do the evening's job could be added to his retainer. He would be able to afford them after the sales to Philo. They would be more disciplined than the pair of thugs he'd rescued from the fighting pits.

The other one with the nasty cursed finger seemed to have disappeared anyway. Probably killed by a cheap whore when he got too friendly.

A heavy thump followed by a crash echoed from the end of the street.

"That would be the door," said Gragne.

"I know, you idiot," said Lysimachus. "I made the plans, if you don't recall."

Gragne opened his mouth and then after a surprising bit of thought, closed it again.

"And if you tell me they're breaking down the back gate now, too. I'll give you a limp in your other leg," Lysimachus spat. As his henchman shrunk beneath his gaze, the girl elbowed Gragne in the ribs and broke from his grip in a sudden burst.

The girl might have gotten away if Lysimachus hadn't been preparing to kick his henchman. So as his foot flew forward, he redirected it slightly to catch her heel, spinning her into the dirt.

Gragne recovered quickly and was on the girl like a cat on an injured mouse.

Then Gragne reared up, shouting, "Ow! She bit me." He smacked her hard across the face. "Miserable whore!"

Lysimachus kicked Gragne in the back. "Stop that. You'll wake the whole street."

Gragne had the girl's arms pinned against the ground and turned his head. "But she bit me," he said with a surprisingly pathetic voice.

"A just payment for letting your guard down," said Lysimachus. "If I hadn't been paying attention, she would have gotten away and I think you and I would be having a very different conversation right now."

Gagne looked momentarily confused as he processed the words, until his eyes widened slightly and then his head dipped like an oft-beaten dog.

Lysimachus sighed and whispered under his breath. "Idiot." Then he tilted his head and listened for sounds of battle in the workshop.

His many spies had reported the barbarian had taken to helping Heron and that they'd been devising defenses. Unfortunately, he'd lost his eyes inside the workshop when Heron had finally realized there was a spy in his shop and released his workers from his service, so he wasn't entirely privy to the final state of the defenses. Still, the numbers he'd sent in should make for easy work.

"Pick her up. We're going in," he said, kicking Gragne in the shin.

His henchman pulled the girl up by her hair, producing a pained moan from her. Lysimachus thought about reprimanding Gragne, but decided the girl needed to fear the thug, so she would be more amiable to his own advances.

Lysimachus checked for patrols before they went to the doorway. He wasn't worried about getting into trouble with the soldiers. As soon as they realized it was him, they would let him go.

But he wanted to keep the night's adventure quiet. The streets had been restless since the new taxes and Flaccus had warned him not to incite the Alexandrians any more than necessary.

As Lysimachus nudged Gragne to go through the door first, the high pitched scream of a man dying cut through the air. He couldn't be sure if it was one of his or one of theirs, so he pressed on. He'd sent twenty mercs, so he could assume they could take three men and one woman, and a gimp woman at that.

Then before he left the entryway and entered the workshop, Lysimachus noticed a heavy whine punctuated by a regularly spaced tapping. It almost sounded like a great beast growling in the dark, while occasionally gnashing its teeth.

Of course, he knew Heron's skills. The *Michanikos* had probably devised an automata to defend the workshop. But he'd also seen the miracles performed in the temples and nothing he'd ever seen inspired fear.

A few more shouts and heavy thuds let Lysimachus know that events were still unfolding. He thought about waiting, but knowing the truth about Heron had gotten him excited. He'd strip her down just to make sure he was right.

Lysimachus whispered to Gragne, "Let us see what the workshop brings. Give her to me and pull out your knife."

The Alabarch took control of Sepharia, inhaling the sweet scents of her hair as he held her tight.

He nudged Gragne to scout ahead, not expecting to find much more than his mercs cleaning up.

The scene confused him as he stepped into the workshop,

Gragne creeping ahead with his knife held out. The mercs had brought hooded lanterns with them to use once they had achieved surprise, but he saw no signs of them except for a broken one burning in the middle of the floor.

The lights flickered against the stacks of lumber nearby. Glints of bronze and other metals reflected like eyes in the darkness.

Lysimachus heard a few shouts from the back, the sound of swordplay and then a muffled thump.

He wondered if he'd entered the workshop too early. It sounded like his mercs hadn't taken control yet.

He didn't want to shout to find out if the mercs were still active in case the defenders had bows, but he had to know if he needed to leave.

Lysimachus pushed Sepharia in front of him as a shield. "Vartus? Have you secured the area?" he shouted.

As he waited for an answer, he decided to move from his current location in case arrows were being readied to fire.

Gragne crouched along the wall, eyes wildly searching the darkness.

"What in the Sha-Gu's name did you get us into, Alabarch?" shouted Vartus, his voice heavy with breathing.

Lysimachus scowled. "Five to one odds not good enough for you?"

At the twanging of strings, Lysimachus reflexively ducked. The girl tried to use the distraction to break away, but unlike Gragne, he had a proper hold on her tunic.

He kneed her in the back of the leg in payment for attempted escape.

Vartus' voice rang out of the darkness, shot through with worry. "It's not five to one. They have metal demons and the gods themselves at their command." The man sounded absolutely terrified.

Lysimachus closed his eyes, wishing he could cuff the man upside the head for his cowardice. "These are no demons. The *Michanikos* makes them. Like the statue in the Sun Square."

He had to do something quick to get his mercs from thinking they were beset by demons. He was regretting hiring the superstitious Gauls. His two thugs were at least too stupid to fear the gods.

"Heron! I've got someone here with me. Do you recognize the screams of your daughter?"

Lysimachus grabbed her by the back of the hair and pulled as hard as he could. Her rising scream made his ears hurt.

When he stopped pulling, he whispered in her ear. "Now tell them you want them to give themselves up."

Just to be sure, he placed the tip of his knife against her side.

Sepharia whimpered.

"That's right. Just say it," he said.

Then she shook her head, refusing him.

The bile rose instantly in his throat. Lysimachus pushed the knife into her side. She let off another ear piercing scream.

"Say it," he told her.

She shook her head again. Still refusing.

"I will cut her, bit by bit," he yelled.

The silence unnerved him. He couldn't imagine that Heron would let him torture her daughter very long.

Lysimachus considered his options. He knew more ways to make people do what he wanted, but he needed his hands free. He had to make sure she wouldn't get away.

"Vartus. Come to my side of the workshop," he shouted. "And bring your men with you."

The merc almost sounded embarrassed when he replied, "They're all dead. It's just me."

For a brief moment, like a flash of lightning, Lysimachus

felt fear. He briefly considered that he wasn't in control and that events had gotten wildly out of hand.

But as a man of his stature, he quickly dismissed it. He was the Alabarch, after all. Events would just require a bit more creativity.

He was glad there were two of them. Mother and daughter. That way he could kill one of them and have the other for his pet.

He just wasn't sure which one he would kill.

But the night was still young.

Lysimachus slowly brought the knife to Sepharia's throat, setting the edge against her soft skin.

"Don't move," he whispered through gritted teeth.

Then, he shouted into the darkness. "If you don't give yourselves up, I'll kill the girl."

Lysimachus waited confidently for an answer. When he was about to apply pressure to his knife, Heron yelled from somewhere nearby.

"How do I know that it's her?"

Lysimachus hesitated, trying to control the rage he felt before he spoke again. He didn't want Heron to get the satisfaction of goading him.

"If you'd like, I can cut her into pieces and you can examine them at your leisure." Lysimachus grinned, mentally applauding himself for keeping a level, venomous tone. Saying it in nearly the same way someone might offer a nice vintage glass of wine.

Heron might be the miracle maker, but he still ran the city.

With equal neutrality, Heron replied, "We sent Sepharia from the city weeks ago. I think you're bluffing."

Lysimachus had a moment of doubt. What had the girl been doing creeping around in the dark dressed like a boy?

No.  While it sounded plausible, he didn't believe it.  She'd been scouting for them and had gotten caught.  Simple as that.

"I guess I'll start cutting," he said casually.

Waiting for an answer, Lysimachus glanced to Gragne's position.  The henchman was gone.  He hoped he was still guarding his flank, but with Gragne, he never knew.

The best he could hope for was that Gragne had pinpointed Heron by the sound of her voice and was silently dispatching her.  A more likely scenario was that Gragne had left him.

The thought seemed quite likely now.  For all he knew, Vartus had fled too and he was alone with them in a workshop full of nasty traps.

And if he killed the girl, they would descend on him for certain.

The Alabarch dragged Sepharia backwards by the neck, keeping the knife pressed against it.  The girl struggled lightly against him.  Not quite escaping but pushing against his hands and whimpering.

He backed up until he thought he was at the archway that led to the entrance, but he found nothing but blank wall.  The broken, burning lamp didn't cast enough light for him to see if he'd lost his way going back.

Lysimachus shifted up and down the wall, but blank stone stared back at him.  He would have ran a hand along the wall, searching for an edge in case they'd blocked up the exit, but then he'd have to let go of Sepharia.

He cursed Gragne for leaving him.

Then the beastly growl with the tapping, that had been background noise, increased in volume.  Before he could pinpoint the location of the growl, a series of slams, like wood hitting wood, echoed throughout a region to his right, not but a few lengths away.

A dull drawn out scream followed.  It was a man dying and

it was close enough to give him chills. Vartus, he assumed.

Now he really wanted to leave the workshop.

Lysimachus held Sepharia tighter and whispered, "We're going to move now. If you flinch, I'll cut your throat and leave you to bleed to death on the floor."

At this point, Lysimachus was expecting a certain amount of limpness from the girl. Usually when he put the fear into them, they went all limp. Instead, her posture was tense and she seemed poised to run at any moment, despite his threats.

"By the Gods of the Nile, I will cut you," he growled.

Then, with equal menace back, Sepharia said, "Cut my throat, if you want. Once you do that, they'll be free to kill you."

Lysimachus had nothing to say. The truth hit so squarely in his gut, he just grimaced and dragged her along with him.

He didn't know where he was going, but he didn't have much choice. He didn't dare chance the wide aisle that led to the center of the workshop. Instead, he took the wall, following the way he thought Gragne had gone. Maybe they could meet up and find their way out.

The girl squirmed under his grip, so he kneed her in the back of the leg again.

"Stop doing that, you cursed pile of dung," she said.

Before he could restrain himself, he lifted his dagger and hit her upside the head with the hilt, knocking her to the ground.

As if she'd been expecting him to do that, she was up and running instantly. Lysimachus had no choice but to chase after her. If she got away, then he was dead for sure.

There was only one way forward and the girl ran ahead, just out of reach. Lysimachus was so focused on her that he did not notice the beastly noises increasing in volume.

Then, the moment before he was going to reach her, a great

black falcon head loomed out of the darkness and grabbed the girl with its beak.

Lysimachus fell to the ground, dodging the beak, and began scrambling backwards to get away. Behind him, the girl was making grisly screams as if the god Horus was eating her alive.

He scrambled under a table and crawled away, hoping Horus wouldn't follow him. Feeling safe for the moment, he pulled his legs to his chest and sat quietly.

The girl's screams had stopped. Lysimachus wasn't sure if that was a good sign or bad. His hands shook and he kept glancing around, expecting something else to loom out of the darkness at him.

Once his breathing had gotten under control, Lysimachus thought hard about what he'd seen. It had to have been a trap that Heron had laid for him. He'd been lucky that the girl had run into it for him, or he might be dead by now.

Lysimachus listened for the sounds of approaching feet, but he could only hear the beast noises carrying through the workshop.

Did they have some caged beast at their disposal, ready to loose on him?

Lysimachus shivered, imagining claws raking down his back.

He shook his head. He couldn't think like that.

After saying a quick prayer to the gods, Lysimachus began crawling along the floor with his knife in his mouth.

Then from ahead, footfalls made him look up. He was near enough to the broken lantern that he could see the creature running toward him. A metal demon with eyes of glass and a great bronze sword.

Fear consumed his thoughts, and Lysimachus leapt up, dropping the knife in his haste, and ran from the creature. He was aware after a moment that he was screaming.

His path was constrained by scaffolding on both sides, and without sight, since the lantern was directly behind him, so he ran headlong into the wagon.

Lysimachus coughed, trying to catch his wind again. Bent over, he realized he was leaning on the wagon with the secret compartment. The worker he'd bribed had explained all its secrets, including the latch on the inside.

The Alabarch crawled under the wagon to the hitch and pulled the lever. He heard the wagon bang open, and hoped it hadn't made enough noise that they knew what he was doing.

The compartment was tight, but he was able to crawl in, despite his pot belly. If he survived the night, he promised to eat a little less so if he were caught in a similar situation, the hiding space wouldn't be so miserable.

Lysimachus grabbed the handle on the door and pulled it closed. It clicked into place. He pressed on the door just to make sure it was tight.

Lysimachus took a deep breath, relieved that he had escaped death. They would think he'd snuck out and the next time they took the wagon out, or if he thought them properly unaware, he would sneak out.

He congratulated himself for quick thinking. He would celebrate his escape with a full scale assault on the workshop. Called in favors with Flaccus would give him access to Roman soldiers.

He would arrest them in the daylight so they couldn't defy the soldiers, put them on a sham trial, and then torture them in the main square near Pompey's Pillar. Lysimachus would make sure no one ever trifled with him again.

Lysimachus rotated around in the secret compartment. He wanted to be familiar with the escape latch so he could get out when he needed to.

His belly got in the way of spinning around, the space was made for a small girl and not a man of his girth around the middle.

The spy had told him the latch was on the back wall in the center. Lysimachus felt around with his palm, expecting to quickly hit a lever, but the wall was completely blank.

A deep foreboding feeling began to settle in his gut. Lysimachus instead used his fingertips and ran them across the surface, finding nothing again.

His hands began to shake.

Lysimachus rotated to the side wall and searched it too, in case the spy had made a mistake.

Then he searched the other.

Nothing.

His breathing, which had only just leveled out, started getting quicker and shallower.

Lysimachus spun around in the tight compartment, feeling each wall with his finger tips, scraping the wood for purchase.

The space, which had been a sanctuary from the horrors of the workshop, started closing in on him.

He was feeling the back wall with both hands, madly pawing at the wood, hoping to find a crack indicating the hidden lever.

He didn't even want to think about what the lack of one meant.

Just before he thought he might scream, his fingers found a rough edge.

Using both hands, he felt around the area.

It was an edge. And the shape was round.

But as he felt around the space, the awful truth began to dawn on him.

It was the lever.

But it'd been broken off and smoothed over.

The heavy thud of a person jumping onto the wagon startled him.

When he heard his name being spoken, he screamed.

# 22

Heron leaned on her poles and listened to the Alabarch screaming in the box. Plutarch was busy relighting the workshop, but the others watched her closely, waiting for the next command.

Only Agog was not watching her expectantly. His eyes drilled into her and when she caught his gaze, it was all she could do not to look away.

Sepharia, who had been freed from the Horus trap with minimal damage, ran to her side. "You're bleeding."

Her niece used a rag rescued from the floor to wipe the blood from her ear.

"It's nothing. I slammed my head on a scaffolding when one of the Gauls tried to take my head off with a sword," explained Heron. "Our barbarian friend returned the favor, but with better results."

Agog gave a slight bow. Heron noted how the big man barely had a scratch on him. He didn't even look winded.

Heron turned to the two additional members of their

defensive stand. The Egyptian couple wore simple clothing and no adornments of any value, even though they were of the merchant class.

"Mohani. Ossora. Your assistance this evening was invaluable. I desire to speak longer with you, but you have a difficult journey ahead."

The man, Mohani, glanced to his wife to let her know he was still too stricken to speak. He'd barely spoken five words since they'd met.

Ossora hesitated, speaking softly at first, but after glancing at the wagon, her voice raised. "Apologies that we should leave so soon. The gods will speak kindly on you that you should give us this precious gift. Once we reach our destination, we will care for it as it deserves. But we should leave the city before suspicions are aroused."

The woman glanced at the others and Heron read her intent. Heron motioned for the others to load the wagon. Mohani joined the others, while Ossora moved nearer.

"I understand not, why you have given us the Alabarch, rather than kill him yourself," Ossora asked. "You have as much claim to his life as we do."

"It's best the man does not die here in Alexandria. Rome does not look kindly on the killing of its tax collectors," explained Heron. "And because your needs far outweigh my own. He did not torture me in the square for all of Alexandria to see."

Ossora nodded with a thoughtful but pained expression. "Yes. Rome already bleeds us dry. Another reason to squeeze the stone will only make the governor happy."

"Yes," said Heron. "You see my point. And when you reach your destination, you will make the Alabarch copy the letter I gave you..."

The next part was difficult to say, even though Lysimachus

had brought misery to her workshop. She knew then what it was like for a king or queen to pass judgment on a subject. They did not swing the headsman's axe, but the words served the same purpose.

"...and once he has written the letter, he is yours. Just make sure the body never surfaces," she finished.

A terrible grin rose to Ossora's lips. With a crocodile's smile, her dead eyes bore right through Heron.

Heron looked away to see the wagon was nearly loaded.

Ossora grabbed Heron's arm and whispered into her ear. "And when we send the message, we shall send along the black stone. And when the Alabarch's time on this earth is done, it will be the red."

Heron nodded and pulled away from Ossora. The husband and wife were followers of Sobek, the crocodile god. Heron knew enough about their customs to almost pity Lysimachus. Almost.

When the wagon was hitched and loaded, the Egyptian couple left the workshop.

A knot formed in Heron's stomach. The supplies in the wagon should muffle noises from the hidden compartment, but until they'd left Alexandria, she wouldn't feel safe. It was a risk to give them the Alabarch alive. If he managed to escape, there would be no easy deaths for them.

Only the Northman's suggestions had saved the Alabarch from dying in her workshop. He would die eventually, but his disappearance would further tweak the Roman Governor.

"What now?" asked Plutarch.

Heron took a long look at the state of her workshop. The destruction from the battle pained her.

Arrows littered the floor, sticking out of wood planking and dead mercenaries. The huge Horus falcon head had an axe wound in the bronze skin. Blood trails from dying men were mixed into the dirt.

Her metal two-legged automata, which now hung limply by the ropes it ran along, hadn't killed any mercenaries', but when it sprinted out of the darkness, it shook the mercenaries will to fight. It wasn't until late in the battle that the mercs even fought back. Unfortunately, the hastily created automata hadn't held up to the battle. Parts had been torn off by frightened sword blows.

Along the wall on a platform, two cheirobalistras sat behind a wall of wood planking, watching over the entrance to the workshop. Gaul-made arrows with dark fletching covered the surface of the wood.

The cheirobalistras had done a fair amount of damage, but the real star of the battle had been her steam powered arrow launcher. The contraption fired wildly and without good aim, but it put out an ungodly amount of arrows so accuracy didn't matter.

Heron gave the workshop one long look. It would take many weeks and much coinage that she didn't have to repair the damage from the battle, but they were for the most part, unscathed.

Punt had a bloody bandage along his arm. Nothing too serious. Sepharia had bruising along her stomach from the Horus head. The falcon trap had been meant as a way to capture the Alabarch. Thankfully, she hadn't made it lethal or the mood of the workshop would be much different.

Heron straightened up, and though she was exhausted and absent the violet powder that she relied on, gave commands for the clean up.

"We can assume Roman guards will be here by morning," she said. "We have much to do before then."

Her friends looked ready to drop on their feet. She wanted them to have their rest, but they weren't safe yet.

"Agog. Please take the vinegar and dump it all along the entrance and whereever the Alabarch walked," she said. "Once the vinegar is poured, put a little chicken blood in the alley down the street."

The Northman nodded and immediately got to work.

"Punt and Plutarch. Disassemble the Horus trap and unhook the steam mechanic."

Once her foreman and blacksmith were busy, she found Sepharia waiting at her side with eyes downtrodden.

"I'm sorry..." she whispered. "I should have stayed at Punt's."

Heron took her into her arms, giving her a hug, trying not to let the tears well up in her eyes. She'd come so close to losing the only connection she had left with her twin.

Heron kissed Sepharia on the forehead. Holding her niece in her arms, she realized the girl was wearing a man's tunic.

"Sepharia. Go change out of those clothes. When the Romans get here, I don't want them to get the wrong idea, or make any unwanted connections," said Heron.

Her niece shuddered and shrunk away from her. Heron raised her eyebrows.

"Is something wrong?" Heron asked.

"The Alabarch will be dead soon, right?" whimpered Sepharia.

Heron tensed. "He didn't do anything to you, did he?"

Sepharia shook her head. "No."

"Oh, good." A relieved sigh slipped from her lips. "Yes. He'll be dead soon."

At first, Heron thought Sepharia was holding something back, but then she decided her niece was still shaken from the night's events and let the hesitation pass.

Sepharia gave her one last hug before scampering up to her room to change.

Heron was worried about her. She couldn't keep her locked in the workshop forever. She would have to find a way for her niece to grow without smothering her.

As the night progressed, Heron directed them in cleaning up the workshop. They left the arrows as proof of the battle, but stacked the bodies like wood in the courtyard.

As the skyline faintly betrayed the sun's arrival, a platoon of soldiers appeared at her gate, accompanied by a magistrate and a cavalry officer astride his horse.

When word had reached her ears that they were coming, she sent the barbarian away and Sepharia to bed. Heron greeted them alone while Punt and Plutarch continued cleaning the workshop.

She knew the Magistrate from the Library. His mental agility was not up to the task of his position, as he'd earned it through a political appointment, but his passions for learning made him at least a likable government figure.

The Roman soldiers were unknown to her and she didn't like the grim faced officer on the horse. He ignored her and led his horse around her courtyard suspiciously.

"Ave, Magistrate," said Heron, leaning heavily on her poles. Her knees and ankles were enflamed with pain from the long night, and she let that pain show on her face.

"*Michanikos*," said the Magistrate as a sign of respect, eyeing her leg harnesses warily. "By the gods, what manner of contraption do your wear on your lower half?"

Heron gestured upwards. "I had an accident weeks ago. I fell from a scaffolding while working my latest miracle. This device merely helps me with my mobility until I heal."

The cavalry officer had taken his horse to the pile of bodies stacked near the entrance of the warehouse.

"Do you have a habit of staging pitched battles in your workshop?" asked the officer.

Heron met his steely gaze. "Only when I am attacked by thugs out to rob me."

The officer made a dismissive noise. "These aren't mere thugs. These are Gaul mercenaries. While no match for a Roman soldier, they should make quick work of your workers."

"Officer Minatus," said the Magistrate. "Heron is a citizen of Alexandria with impeccable standing."

Minatus whipped his horse around to face the Magistrate. "And massive debts owed to the Empire. Need I remind you that our fair city's tax collector has gone missing as well?"

The Magistrate's face paled. "Troubling times. Troubling times."

"So how again did you kill a score of battle hardened mercs?" asked Minatus.

"Please follow and I can explain," said Heron.

Minatus dismounted and handed his reins to a soldier. The Magistrate followed right behind.

Heron cleared her throat as they entered. "We got word that the Gauls were planning on attacking the workshop, intent on stealing the cheirobalistras I had just made."

She indicated the two man-sized multi-firing crossbows on the platform. Punt and Plutarch, busy putting the workshop back to rights, paused to watch. Heron made get-to-work motions with her hand behind her back. She didn't want Minatus or the Magistrate to question either of them.

"They had intent to mount them on a wagon and take to banditry in the south past the boundaries of the Empire," she said. "Thankfully, we were able to put up a defense using the very weapons they intended to steal and making a little luck of our own to turn the battle."

Minatus climbed onto the platform to examine the cheirobalistras, running his hand along the bow portion.

"Yes, I could see how you could take down many foes with

just these two weapons," he said.

The Magistrate pointed to the metal two-legged statue hanging on a rope. "And what, by the gods, is that? A new miracle?"

Heron gave the man a knowing grin. "You have good eyes, Magistrate. You are correct. The injury to my legs proved fortuitous as I finally devised a locomotive method for my automata. Thus, I was working a prototype to show the temples."

She kept her story as close to the truth as possible. Her story had too many holes as it was.

"In the dark of the workshop, we sent the automata in on the ropes and the superstitious Gauls thought a metal demon attacked them," she said and then turning to Minatus. "No proper Roman would be fooled by such simple devices, but you know these Gauls."

Heron shrugged dismissively, indicating the pile of bodies at the entrance.

Heron could see the way Minatus coveted her cheirobalistras and made her next move while the fire was hot.

"Officer Minatus. I am concerned about this plot by the Gauls. What if another group of mercenaries decided to take the weapons? We were only fortunate that we were warned by a concerned citizen. I do not feel safe with them in my workshop," she said.

Minatus nodded along with her reasoning. "Yes. You're correct. These would be a devastating weapon for a group of bandits. No simple caravan could stand against them. What do you suggest?"

Heron sighed heavily, trying to convey her utmost concern. "Would the Roman guard of the city confiscate these two cheirobalistras? I was hoping to sell them to you anyway, but until such a deal could be struck, the guard could take them into custody."

She paused for a moment, before finishing. "For the safety of the Empire."

Minatus nodded agreeably with her proposal. "Yes. That would be the best course of action."

Once they had agreed to the deal, Officer Minatus spent his time removing the cheirobalistras from the workshop. Agog would be furious that she just gave away two of his war machines, but she had to allay suspicions before they began to fester.

With the Magistrate and the soldiers gone from her workshop, she finally retired to her room. The sun had come up and the Lighthouse of Pharos shimmered white in the morning rays.

Heron closed the dark curtains on her room, but even the faint light disturbed her sleep. So instead, she sat in the dark and considered how close she'd come to losing everything.

Then, she thought of her dead twin. The one whose name she'd taken.

"Oh, Sunny," she whispered. "This would be so much easier with the two of us."

# 23

The following weeks, the workshop bustled with activity. Heron had hired a select group of workers back, after Agog vetted them. She didn't know what contacts he had in the city, but she was prepared to trust him, given his defense of the workshop. He had to promise not to threaten or injure them first, since she was well acquainted with the information he extracted from Blackfinger.

Heron rented a house next to her workshop that the workers could live in. She told them it was a benefit of their employment, but really she didn't want them to wander far out of sight. She'd hired back only the workers without families. It pained her to exclude some, but she didn't want them to risk their family's lives.

The added labor still didn't meet their needs and after a suggestion from Punt, they started sending work to other workshops. They only sent components of the steam mechanics to the other workshops and assembled the final product at hers.

Nothing, however, was sent to Philo, and once she started selling her steam mechanics to the other workshops, she learned he was trying to buy up pieces to figure out how it worked.

The lesser workshops, careful not to anger the great Heron and his new miracle that turned steam into power, sold him nothing and told her about his schemes.

The other challenge had been making the steam mechanic in a way that it couldn't be copied. Their initial designs were transparent and Heron refused to let this design be lost to Philo and his thieving mentality.

The meager funds of the workshop had required it, as well. The interim tax collector had come by and given her a proper payment sheet. The pay schedule was steep but one she could live with after being blackmailed to give up her niece.

Agog, however, balked at the coinage, claiming that his well was drying up. Or at least, in his terms, "he couldn't bail as fast as the hole she'd punched in the boat."

So in a fit of nocturnal design, fueled by need and the violet powder, a crutch she desired to be rid of except that it deepened her voice to help her pass as a man and helped her survive the long sleepless nights, she redesigned the steam mechanic so its parts could not be seen.

The real feat of her engineering was hooking the power transference rods to the casing that hid the mechanic. Should anyone try to remove the covering, it would break the central pin and the parts would come loose.

After the first workshop tried to reverse engineer her steam mechanic and broke it taking it apart, she barred them from purchasing another.

She hated treating a fellow inventor so harshly, but the example ended any further investigations, because every workshop that had purchased one had seen a sudden increase in output, even if they owned slaves.

It wasn't that the mechanic allowed for work without a slave, it allowed for work that couldn't be done by slaves. Each time Heron made a visit to a workshop to sell another, the owner would show her the clever ways they were using the steam mechanic to perform new tasks like grinding metal surfaces flat or lifting heavy objects effortlessly with pulleys.

Heron brought those ideas back to her workshop, promising a discount on the next steam mechanic for sharing their ideas. What she gave up in coin, she made up in productivity, which earned her more coin.

She knew the design would eventually be copied. She just needed to make enough coin from it to erase her debt before it did.

Then one day, in the span of a few hours, Heron received two urgent letters. The first was from Governor Flaccus. The contents didn't surprise her, though the length of time it'd taken for it to happen did.

The second was a reminder from her secret benefactor, the one that wanted the truth about the Library fires. The tone was abrupt and somewhat rude, claiming she'd taken the coin for the investigation without making just efforts.

The arrival of the two letters in the same day bothered her, since they were linked by a common theme.

The truth was that she hadn't made any efforts into the Library fires since the assault on the workshop. Rebuilding the workshop and selling the steam mechanics had taken all her time.

And she was out of ideas on the fires. The darkness of her room, which often was the canvas to which she painted her ideas, had become a suffocating gloom.

So the day after she received the two letters, Heron sent a message to Agog to join her on an errand in the city.

She'd asked him along for three reasons. The first that she couldn't spare Plutarch or risk the production schedule, the second was she needed a keen mind to bounce her ideas off of, and the third was to have him along in case of another attack.

There was a fourth reason, buried down deep, but it'd been so long that she'd considered such things it didn't weigh in her decisions except in ways she didn't understand.

Heron was astride her own horse when Agog rode up on a brown warhorse. Punt had made her a new set of harnesses that could be used in the saddle.

"That poor horse," said Heron. "Did it lose at a game of straws with the other horses in the stable?"

Agog chuckled. "I guess the sun keeps the horse flesh from growing too large. In the cloud stricken north, we grow them to a proper size."

Heron walked her horse forward. "I think that one wishes it'd come from the north. Its knees look ready to buckle."

"Then let us keep to a slow meander," he said.

They rode for a while, keeping a leisurely pace and staying out of the thick of traffic. Though their city-bred horses were well inured to the noise and bustle, they skittered nervously along the side of the crowd. The frustration in the city seemed to be boiling over and even their horses sensed it.

Agog pulled next to Heron. "To what purpose do we ride? Taking the pulse of the city?"

Heron patted the horse, squinting in the bright sunlight. "The pulse is well known. Bitter at the crushing taxes and hunger from a lack of food. We ride for a different task today."

"I'll let you reveal your purpose in good time." Agog paused thoughtfully, and asked in a matter of fact tone. "Have the streets of Alexandria ever been this restless?"

Heron detected Agog's interest in the subject though he

tried to hide it.

"In the decade I have been in the city...no," said Heron. "Rome is hungry for new coin to feed its constant warring and presses Alexandria too harshly. Even the governor is concerned he sits on a tinder box."

Agog raised his eyebrow at her playfully. "Are you now privy to the mind of the governor?"

Heron pulled the note from inside her tunic and handed it to the northerner. She noted how quickly he read the document, like a scholar well versed in books.

She realized then that the Northman had a history and identity she knew almost nothing about. He made references that indicated he was a king of sorts, but anyone could claim such an honor. Or even be one, but of a pocket kingdom, lording over squirrels and deer.

She'd pressed the man for details in the past, but he'd expertly diverted her inquisitions. She vowed to find a way to get the man to talk.

"He's swinging at shadows if he believes your automata play about Caesar will cause an uprising," said Agog.

Heron nodded. "True. But his perception that it will is dangerous."

"Dangerous only for Hortio, should he continue to show the play to other like minds in the city. You're too busy to make another, anyway," he said.

"You speak our language fluently, yet you do not understand the politics of the Empire." Heron purposely needled the Northman to gauge a reaction. "Because I made the play in the first place, Flaccus will lay blame at my feet. Not because it is logical, but to leverage his power with me."

Agog narrowed his eyes at her. "I'm well acquainted with the politics of intrigue. It's no different from a battlefield and with no less at stake."

They rode a while longer in silence while Heron enjoyed the breezes from the sea. The streets led downward to the warehouse district and the docks. The Lighthouse stood proudly on the island of Pharos guiding white sails into the harbor.

"How are my war machines coming?" Agog asked.

Heron detected the aggravation in his voice. The man had been patient with her, and generous with his coin, to a point. But she could tell his patience and generosity were growing thin.

"I have two steam powered arrow launchers complete," she said, catching the hard look from the Northman.

"Two? My orders were for ten," he said, increasing their pace.

Heron tugged at the reins. "I have the structure complete, I'm short on steam mechanics."

Agog spurred his warhorse with his heel in anger and had to pull back on the reins to slow the horse when it had surged forward.

"That's because you keep selling them to the other workshops," he said, grimacing.

"If you were more free with your coin I might be able to hold off the new customs man while I made them, but you've turned as hard as a mule's rump. I must sell them to pay my debts."

She said it more harshly than she'd planned, but he'd been bothering her about the war machines constantly. He seemed restless and fidgety about the state of the work and it was driving her mad.

She assumed he had some war he needed them for in the north and was itching to get back. She was beginning to look forward to that day because they'd been getting on each other's nerves for the past week.

"What about the metal soldiers? Or have you forgotten about them?" he asked, frowning suspiciously.

Heron blew hot breath out her nose. "I have not forgotten, mind you. I've been working on the designs each night. I cannot make the steam mechanic small enough to fit in the soldier."

Agog opened his mouth, she assumed to make a quick retort. Heron decided she didn't want to hear it, and launched into a counter attack before he could get his words out.

"I thought being freed from the temples would be better than this. They were always asking for bigger and better miracles. Complaining that their followers were growing bored with the current ones," she said, with a bit of venom. "And now, I've traded those high priests and priestesses for a barbarian, claiming to be a king, and wanting machines to fight his wars for him."

She regretted the words instantly. Not the part about the temples and the wars, but about claiming to be a king. If he truly were, then he would be supremely offended by her tone.

When Agog's head snapped back and he began laughing earnestly, she felt her anger deflate.

"I was merely going to offer a suggestion," he said, with a twinkle in his eye.

"What?" she asked, sheepishly, expecting a pithy come-back.

"Make the soldiers bigger," he said and spurred his horse forward.

Heron had been ready to dispute whatever he was planning on saying, but the suggestion hit her like a thunderbolt.

It made sense, she thought.

Heron caught up to Agog, who slowed when he saw her.

"I'm not sure why I'm rushing ahead. I don't even know where we're going."

"To the warehouse district," she said. "And apologies for what I said."

Agog raised a curious eyebrow. "The quip about being a king? I'd think the same of an overgrown trained bear come tromping through the sands and demanding such things. My only saving grace is my shiny coins."

"It was still rude," she said.

He shrugged her comment away. "How would you truly know if I were a king? The kings in the north do not carry themselves like the Romans or Egyptians. We just happen to be the ones strong enough to keep the peace."

"Then why do you desire these war machines?" she asked, curious beyond just the point of business.

"I'm owed a debt and I mean to collect it," he said.

"What debt?"

Agog pulled up and gestured to the row of warehouses before them. "We've arrived at your destination."

He flashed an impish grin at her, indicating he had no intention of answering her question.

Heron turned her horse towards the bay and inhaled the salty air. The breeze fluttered Agog's hair behind him.

The sails of dozens of boats crossed the choppy waves of the harbor, while a hundred more waited at the docks. Dock workers carried crates and bags from the ships in droves.

Customs agents pored over documents, their papyri flapping in the gentle breeze. Any writings found were taken to the Library warehouses to be copied by a team of waiting scribes and returned before the ship left port. If the copying wasn't complete before the ship had to leave, they were compensated, though rarely for the full value of the book.

This was how Alexandria had grown her Library. The port sent grain from the delta throughout the known world. No reputable merchant fleet could ignore a port Alexandria's size and when they arrived to trade, the Library borrowed the books and papyri that were brought.

The huge stone warehouses, devoid of anything but a simple door at the base, were across from the docks so the copying could begin immediately. It also made the ship captains more agreeable to the confiscation that the books hadn't left the docks.

Heron explained this to Agog as they watched the stream of Library scribes running papyrus scrolls and the occasional book back and forth between the docks and the warehouse.

"You brought me to the docks to show me this? I'm aware of how Alexandria gets its books, even though I have not seen it myself," said Agog.

"No," she said, shaking her head. "I have another job I need help with."

"Another job? Did you bring me out here so you could delay my war machines yet again?" he said, leaning over and patting his horse.

She couldn't quite see his face to judge his reaction, the Suebian knot had flung his long hair in the way.

"Months ago, I was requested to investigate the source of the fires that burned the Library's precious books." Heron glanced around to make sure no Roman soldiers were within ear shot. It was a fine day for patrolling and a few patrols wandered leisurely across the docks, but none near enough to hear.

"The fires?" he asked, sitting up as if he'd been pinched. "Did they not happen one hundred years ago?"

Heron curiously noted the exact knowledge of the timeline. She found it rather surprising that he would know such a fact.

"Yes, and I've been asked, no...paid, to determine who did it," she said.

"Was it not Caesar when he escaped the Ptolemaic army?"

he asked, glancing out at the bay.

"You know a lot about Alexandrian history?" she asked.

Agog shook his mane of hair from his face where the breeze had blown it and he seemed preoccupied by the sudden interference.

"Ah...can't see a damned thing that way," he said, bringing his horse around to face the dock side so the wind kept hair out of his face.

"Yes, the winds are tricky here. Blowing across the Temple of Artemis on the long pier," she said, indicating the massive columned building at the far curve of the bay, opposite the Lighthouse.

"Do I have a budding historian in my midst or have you been keeping secrets?" she demanded.

Agog gave her a long look. "I'm a student of war. Only quick thinking saved Caesar when he lit the ships in the bay. I've studied it to learn the mistakes of others so I do not make them myself."

"And what was Caesar's mistake?" she asked.

"Throwing in with Cleopatra when her brother offered a stable alliance." He paused, his focus seeming to leave the moment. "But we men can be fools when it comes to women."

Heron stared at the whitecaps on the waves. The day was very similar to the day the Library burned. The tides and time of year were nearly exact.

"Right?" Agog asked. "You've been a fool for a woman before? Or are you inclined like Plutarch? Don't forget, you've admitted lies about your whoring ways."

Heron chuckled remembering the tales she spun at Hortio's party.

"I'm a fool for my work and that is the only woman I will know," she said. It was a question she'd been asked before so it came readily to her lips.

They paused as a pair of Roman soldiers wandered by. Heron nodded her head at them. They eyed Agog suspiciously which made Heron smile after they had left.

"So what did you come here to learn? Did you figure out who started the fires?" he asked.

Heron glanced up at the warehouses and then back to the ship-filled bay.

"No. But I know who did not do it, at least based on the stories that have been told and read," she said.

The Northman had turned his horse slightly, so the wind was blowing his hair partially across his face. Heron waited until she could study his reaction before she spoke again.

"There's no way it could have been Caesar."

Heron swore she saw a moment of disappointment, but then the wind switched slightly and threw hair in his face again.

"Damn wind," he said. "And why do you say that?"

"The damn wind," she replied. "Today marks the ninety-fifth anniversary of the fires. The tides and seasons match the day perfectly. And at that combination of conditions, the wind blows south-west across the Temple of Artemis, which means the wind could not have blown the fires into the warehouses."

Heron extended her hand to the pier on the south side of the harbor. "Instead, it would have pushed the burning ships along the coast, but not into the city."

Agog laughed. "Is not the weather a plaything of the gods? How can you not know if Apollo or one of the others threw their weight with Caesar?"

Heron felt that Agog was mocking her. "You know my feelings for the gods. I did not think you such a fool."

"I jest," said Agog. "But, by the gods, you've made quite a boast that you can know the weather from a century before, just by the similar nature of the day?"

Heron nodded, understanding him. "Yes, I would be a fool. But I consulted the weather charts of the day, Alexandria is studious about its collecting of information, and the winds were blowing south-west that day."

"Then why did we come out here?" he asked.

"To get out of the warehouse and stretch my legs, as it were." She motioned to her harnesses and shrugged. "And to see it with my own eyes. Because one cannot always trust what was written in books."

"A fair statement," he replied. "So now that you've determined Caesar isn't the culprit, do you know who is?"

"No," she replied, turning her horse to head back to the workshop and holding her hand up to block the piercing sun. "But I have another place to check in a few days, if you'd care to join me."

Agog shrugged, too casually by her accounting, and said, "I could, I seem to have a little free time coming up."

"Good," she said, speeding her horse ahead. "I'll have a new invention ready to show you then. Come on foot, you won't need your horse." Heron paused, letting a smile rise to her face. "He wouldn't be able to carry you that far anyway."

Heron left Agog there on the docks and rode back to the workshop alone, wondering the whole time if she'd uncovered a new secret about the Northman or was just imagining things.

# 24

Sepharia slipped past the line of chained slaves, her eyes wide, barely containing a grin. Even their unwashed bodies didn't bother her.

She'd seen slaves from the window of her room at the workshop before, but walking the streets amid them made her feel alive. A thought which came with some trepidation because she pitied the slaves. Her aunt had taught her as much, but given her lifelong sequester in the workshop, being on the streets during the day dressed as herself seemed like being freed from slavery.

A shoulder slammed into her. Sepharia spun around to catch a hateful look from a richly dressed man.

She tried to rein in her giddy enthusiasm. Heron had given her a special errand. She'd waited fourteen years to walk the streets of Alexandria during the day, she didn't want to ruin it and get locked up again.

There was a book Heron wanted from a particular merchant. Sepharia touched the coin purse under her robe, chastising herself as she did it. Plutarch had warned her even thinking about one's coin purse would give thieves its exact location.

She glanced around to see if anyone looked like a thief, but realized it was foolish. She wouldn't be able to tell.

Guilty feelings faded fast as she passed a kabob vendor. The scents of spiced meat made her mouth water.

Sepharia passed it and then in a fit of impulse, ran back to the vendor.

The blue-eyed vendor, wrapped in layered desert gear, squinted as she came up to his booth. She could feel his eyes paw at her. Sepharia regretted stopping but deciding leaving without food would be worse.

"How much?" she asked, trying to sound casual.

"Three ha'pennies," he said.

His toothless smile gave her shivers.

Sepharia pulled her purse out and handed him the coins. She knew she was supposed to haggle with him, but she didn't feel like it.

When he handed over the stick of meat, he rubbed a finger across her hand.

Sepharia skittered away, glad that she had purchased her meal in the daylight. She wrapped her light turquoise robe around her and continued her journey.

The way to the book seller passed by the Library. The ornate columns outside the main entrance enticed her to stop. Three men in togas stood outside on the steps, engaged in a fierce argument.

It seemed to Sepharia that the chubby scholar with bright pink cheeks was winning the argument. She could only tell by his body language, confidant and punctuated with deft thrusts of his outstretched hand. As if he was skewering his opponents with his verbal barrage.

Sepharia snuck closer, feigning her admiration of the architecture. Her ruse wasn't so outlandish as others stood in the shadows of the Great Library, pointing and gesturing toward the building.

She wondered if the men argued on the steps so they could demonstrate their intellect to the gathering crowds.

Sepharia kept moving closer and closer, careful not to reach the steps, which were forbidden to women, until she could hear their debates.

"...but Man fits amid the Earthly clockworks as was intended by the Heavenly masters," said pink cheeks. "We are but perfect tools of creation."

A hawk-faced scholar with an all too serious grimace scowled the words out of his mouth. "Man is but a locust by a different name. We must lay waste before we can build, thus creating our own order, without reason to Earthly matters. Therefore, the Heavens intend for us to be lords of the Earth, crushing that which does not amend itself to our ways."

The third scholar, a man with pale skin the color of chalk, squeaked out his argument. "Ahhh...and that is where you are both wrong. Man must tread carefully through a den of sleeping lions, lest they awake and rip the heart from our chests."

The three scholars constantly glanced at the audience assembled before them. Sepharia detected a rising of their voices whenever the crowd moved away, as if to lure them back in.

"Basking in the glow of the Library's wisdom?" asked a man in a toga standing on her right.

He was barely taller than she, though she was tall for her age, and he had a distinct Roman nose.

"I'm afraid someone left old fruit out to rot on the steps of the Library," she said, hoping the man would wander off.

He raised an eyebrow. "Is someone an amateur philosopher?"

Sepharia regretted her choice of words. She wasn't supposed to be learned at all. Only queens like Cleopatra had ever dared spar with the scholars of the Library.

"They sound like actors rehearsing their lines," she said, covering. "And they preen like peacocks at the Royal Palace."

"And you have been to the Palace?" the man asked, his eyebrows nearly at his hairline.

Sepharia shifted from foot to foot. "Um...no. I heard it once. I'm not even sure what a peacock is," she said, then scrunched up her face.

The scholar seemed to accept her excuse and reached out his hand in greeting, beaming a wide smile.

"I'm Gnaeus Genucius Gurges," he said.

"Seph..." she mumbled.

"Pleasant acquaintances, Sef," he said.

She nodded, deciding if leaving would be rude. She couldn't make up her mind so she stayed and feigned continued interest in the debating scholars. Gnaeus stayed as well.

After a span of time in which she heard three logical fallacies and one *reductio ad absurdum,* Gnaeus spoke.

"So which side of the argument do you come down on? The Naturalists, the Man as Tyrant, or the Lion Walkers?" he asked.

Sepharia glanced around, wondering if Gnaeus was trapping her into admitting her knowledge. But his face seemed amiable enough. Almost encouraging.

The rhetorical villainy espoused by the three scholars had been gnawing on her thoughts and finally, at Gnaeus' urging, the words burst from her mouth.

"All. None. Pieces of others they've failed to mention. Arguing Man's place in the world is about as possible as counting the sides of a crystal tumbling from the top of the Pharos. Man is Man by doing, not observing."

When her words tumbled to a stop, she put her hand to her mouth and looked around to see if anyone else had been listening.

Gnaeus laughed. "Pay no mind. I do not subscribe to the idiocy of women. My mother had a deadly wit and whipped my feeble mind into the slightly less feeble shape it is today."

Sepharia let out a relived sigh.

"And I appreciate your viewpoint," he said. "A practical view of Man makes for thoughts that improve the daily lives of ordinary men."

Gnaeus put a hand to his mouth as if he were telling an important secret.

"And these three fools are merely espousing ideas they read in forgotten books, hoping to generate a bit of fame and snare a patron," he said under his breath. "Sophists by a different name, I say."

"And what kind of view of Man do you have?" she asked.

"An historical one," he said quickly. "I study the acts of man, so I can better understand how he will act in the future. Specifically, those rough men from the distant north beyond the reach of the Empire."

She opened her mouth, the coincidence was unbearable. She wanted to ask a question about Agog.

Gnaeus looked to her expectantly.

She shook her head. "I have to go. I'm late for an errand."

Gnaeus bowed. "May we meet again, so that we might once more cross verbal swords," he called out as she scurried off, holding her robe above the dirt.

Sepharia gave a returning nod as she checked the sun for position. Being late wouldn't earn her any more chances to explore the city. She would just tell Heron that she had to avoid a tipped wagon.

The book dealer had a diminutive shop between a temple and a snake meat seller. Two priests in red robes milled around the front of the temple, calling to anyone within earshot to step inside. Sepharia had never heard of their god, but new ones popped up and disappeared faster than seagulls' shit on statues.

Before she ducked through the doorway, she felt the hair on the back of her neck rise up, as if someone was watching her.

Sepharia spun around. A quick scan of the people passing by the shop revealed no one suspicious.

She watched for a minute longer until she was comfortable that no one had followed her. Why she'd suddenly become spooked bothered her. Heron wouldn't have sent her out by herself if there was danger.

Sepharia ducked inside and blinked her eyes, waiting for the spots to clear so she could see. The momentary lapse of vision made her want to step back outside.

As her vision returned, the details of the little shop came into focus. At first, she thought the book dealer kept a messy shop. Scrolls, papers, and books were scattered over the tables.

But then she realized the shop had been ransacked. The books had deep gashes. Snatches of papyrus were littered around the room.

The instinct to flee was strong. She could practically hear Heron telling her to leave the shop and return instantly, but she knew the book she'd been sent to get was important. She wanted to show her aunt she could help.

Sepharia picked up a scroll at her feet. The papyrus had deep slashes and a strong smell.

The opposite end was wet. She sniffed the wet area and

her face screwed into a knot when she realized it was urine.

Sepharia dropped the scroll and took one step forward, holding her robe up so it didn't touch the floor.

Surveying the room, she realized that every book or scroll in this part had been ripped apart. The book she wanted was not going to be in this section of the store.

A dark curtain led to the back.

Sepharia took another step forward and put her hand to the curtain. After a deep breath, she whipped aside the fabric.

The book dealer lay on his stomach in the middle of the back room, clearly dead with blood pooling around his corpse. The books in back had been treated the same as the ones in front. His hand lay on a book yanked from a shelf.

No other exit could be seen and since the back room wasn't even as big as the first, the examination only took as much time as it took to turn her head left and then right.

Seeing the body didn't bother her after the battle in the workshop. In fact, it seemed almost anti-climatic to find the book seller dead.

The only thing that kept her from searching the back room was the chance someone could enter the shop and think she'd killed the man. Without turning around, Sepharia took one big step backwards. Putting her back to the body wasn't an option at the moment.

Heron would want to know everything she'd seen, so she memorized the state of the room. Maybe the others would come back with her and search the store for the book, but by then, the magistrate might be investigating the crime.

Sepharia was focused on the room, noting details that Heron might quiz her on later. As she prepared to take another step backwards, she became faintly aware that someone was standing behind her.

Then a hand firmly clamped over her mouth.

# 25

Heron hobbled upright around the steam wagon while Punt and Plutarch looked on. The ratio of length between the casings and the back axle seemed wrong.

"The drive mechanism is bunched. The pistons will bind up," she said.

She could feel Plutarch cringing from across the wagon.

"The measurements on the drawing were off a smidge," he explained. "I had to make necessary adjustments."

"The measurements were not," the last part she said in his high lilting voice, "*off a smidge.*"

Heron leaned against the wagon to take the weight from her back. She'd been hunched over using her poles so long, her back had forgotten how to hold her up since she'd gotten rid of them.

"To leverage the proper force into the axle from the steam mechanic, the placement has to be exact. With your meddling, the steam wagon might rip apart from the bound forces and kill everyone on it."

The devastation on Plutarch's face made her wish she could take it back.

Her foreman looked dead on his feet. Black rings circled his eyes. She'd been pushing them hard for months without respite.

Even Punt appeared exhausted. He'd been sleeping at the foundry so he could trade his travel time across the city for working the forge.

The wagon wasn't as bad as she'd said. It might break apart when pushed to its limits, but she doubted it. She'd mostly been angry that Plutarch had tampered with her design, not an uncommon occurrence within the workshop and one which normally didn't bother her.

"Apologies, Plutarch," she said. "I over spoke out of pettiness. The adjustment will be fine."

Plutarch gave her a full bow. "The fault is all mine. I should have checked with you first before making such a crucial change."

"I'll have none of that," she said. "You've been working yourselves to death for me. Plutarch, you're looking like a collection of bones wrapped in loose skin. And Punt, you haven't seen your wife in a month."

Plutarch raised an eyebrow playfully. "I get starved while Punt gets rewarded?"

The joke snapped the tension between them. Heron hobbled over and clasped hands with them both.

"I'm giving you both the next three days off with pay," she paused. "Make that with double pay. Triple."

Their eyes went wide. "Master Heron," they said in unison.

Plutarch continued. "There's so much to do right now. We cannot afford to stop."

The stoic Punt nodded along with Plutarch.

Heron put her hand upon Punt's shoulder. "I cannot

afford to have my most important friends fall dead on their feet. And the workers are merely assembling more steam mechanics. A job they can perform in their sleep now."

Plutarch opened his mouth, but Heron cut him off with a palm forward hand gesture. "I'll be gone the next ten days on an errand with the Northman, testing the steam wagon and investigating a lead."

Plutarch and Punt shared glances. "A lead?"

She shook her head, remembering they knew nothing about her investigation into the fires. "For our next project."

"But who will take care of the workshop?" asked Plutarch.

"Sepharia, whenever she returns from the book dealer," said Heron.

Heron was suddenly reminded how late in the day it had gotten. Sepharia should have been back already.

Heron checked the entrance hopefully and to her surprise, a shadow passed across the lantern, indicating a person about to enter the workshop.

Her heart sunk when she saw Agog.

Agog stopped. "Am I not wanted here? Even when I bring a gift?"

He had a mischievous grin on his face.

"I was expecting Sepharia," she said.

Agog laughed. "My gift has been spoiled. I brought her with me."

Sepharia slipped past the Northman and seeing the worried look on Heron's face, ran to her.

Heron embraced Sepharia, noting how much her niece had grown in recent months. She wouldn't be able to pass as a boy any more without binding her chest.

"I was worried when the hour grew late," said Heron.

"And worried you should be," said Agog, suddenly grim. "We found the book dealer dead."

Sepharia nodded. "We couldn't find the book you wanted either. Though his hand lay on this one. I thought it might be important."

Heron took the book, glancing at the title written in golden ink: *Sumerian Myths*. She threw it on her desk. All her dealings with the temples had made her an expert on religion, so she doubted she would need to read it.

Heron gave Agog a sideways glance. "I didn't realize I'd sent you along on the errand, too."

Agog shrugged away her comment. "I was headed here and saw Sepharia, so I followed her a bit to make sure she was safe. When she went into the book dealer, I decided I would surprise her, only to find the place ransacked. After that, I guarded the door while she searched for your book."

Sepharia had a shy smile on her face and out of the corner of her eye, she caught Agog's longing glance at her niece. Heron suspected Agog wasn't following her out of concern. Men of the north had their reputations. Another complication she wasn't ready to deal with.

"Who killed the book dealer?" she asked absently, still thinking about her niece.

"We don't know," said Agog. "But he'd been killed the day before, but not any longer than that."

"Are you an expert on the state of the dead?" she asked.

"I've made my fair share of them on the battlefield. When the dead are left to rot a few days, they get bloated and stink. His blood had dried, but no bloating," said Agog.

"Was there anything else that you learned?" said Heron sarcastically.

A flicker of amusement trickled across his lips. "Yes. The killers used curved blades and wear obsidian necklaces."

Heron laughed. "Are you a seer now as well as a warlord and a scholar of the dead?"

Agog threw an object to Heron. She caught it. It was a necklace with a simple obsidian crescent on it.

"Sepharia found it," he said.

Sepharia nodded proudly. "The merchant had it in his hand. He must have ripped it off during the struggle when they killed him."

"And the curved blades?" she asked soberly. "Did they leave one as well?"

"Battlefield knowledge," said Agog. "The cuts were from curved blades. They chopped up so many books and scrolls it was easy to know the shape."

Heron paced around on her modified leg harnesses. A job more laborious than it was worth, but she couldn't quite stand still.

She'd tracked down a book about the Carthaginians that had survived the destruction of their city from Rome. Supposedly, they'd formed a secret society bent on revenge through any means necessary. A scholar at the Library that she'd shared letters with had suggested it.

Lost in her thoughts, she didn't realize they were all staring at her until she looked up.

"Master Heron," said Plutarch. "Whatever this is, it seems very important to you. If you would like, we can help you in whatever way we are capable of."

Punt and Sepharia nodded along with Plutarch. Agog stood to the side, watching the exchange carefully.

Her first instinct was to not tell them. She'd caused them enough pain with her debts to Lysimachus.

But she realized that they were involved already. If the book dealer had been killed because of her investigation into the fires, it put all of them at risk. She had to tell them.

Heron motioned to follow to her desk. Once there, she explained everything, including how she had received the job.

The only part she hid from them was the size of the payment. Not out of greed, but of concern they would think it a scam.

Except for the regular payments of coin, she might as well thought it a scam, but she'd made enough from the deal to help stem the tide of debt. It'd been a profitable venture, even if she never could determine the source of the fires.

As she explained what she knew, she realized it was more than the payment driving her. The fires had been a great blow to civilization. The greatest of all blows.

Her inventions had been built on the shoulders of giants before her. Aristotle. Archimedes. Geminus. Eratosthenes. Aristarchus. Pythagoras.

She couldn't even imagine what she might have discovered by now had the Library not been partially destroyed.

Finding out who caused the fires in the Great Library in Alexandria had become more than a job. She wanted to find out because if it'd been done by human hands, justice should be brought to them.

After she finished, they stood around in silence, each to their own thoughts.

Plutarch spoke first, "Does the murder implicate the Carthaginian secret society?"

Heron shrugged. "Maybe. Without seeing the book, I cannot know for certain."

"What about the necklace I found?" asked Sepharia. "What does it mean? Is it a temple's sign?"

Plutarch shook his head. "There are probably two dozen temples that use the moon as their symbol. And even that does not help us. The killer might be associated with a temple without being from it."

The Northman had been listening quietly, but when he spoke up, Heron could detect more than just curiosity.

"Are there any suspects you've ruled out?"

Heron thought for a while before speaking. "The Ptolemies. And Caesar, maybe." And after another pause. "That's it. I have ruled out almost nothing."

The enormity of the task weighed on her. How could she dare solve a mystery a century old? It seemed foolish to try. Yet she knew she could not give up on it.

"What clues lie outside the city?" asked Plutarch.

Heron considered confiding her reasons for visiting Siwa. But she dared not explain this one, lest they believe her a fool.

"This one I'll keep to myself, for now," she said.

They seemed to accept her answer, all but Agog, who studied her.

"While you're gone, I can find out from the Magistrate what they learned of the book dealer's death," said Plutarch.

"I thought I told you to rest? You look terrible," she said.

A naughty grin rose to his face, transforming Plutarch from the stern foreman to someone else entirely.

"I plan on visiting an old friend," he said. "He has the ear of the Magistrate."

"Hortio?" she asked.

Plutarch nodded playfully.

"Fine. But don't overextend yourself," she said.

Plutarch rolled his eyes.

She noticed Punt straining to speak. "Yes, Punt?"

"I will check with the temples of the city to find which has a crescent obsidian symbol," he said.

She shook her head again and was prepared to forbid him, until she saw the look on his face. She sighed, exasperated.

"Are you just going to walk up and ask them?" she asked, then switched into her best imitation of his deep voice. "Have any of your followers lost this necklace when they were murdering an innocent book dealer?"

"No, Master Heron," he said. "I still have lamps to sell. I

will make inquires with my eyes only."

"Clever, Punt," she said, nodding appreciatively. Then to the others, "Never underestimate the gruff exterior of our master blacksmith. His intellect is as keen as the blades he fashions."

"And me? What can I do?" asked Sepharia.

"You're in charge of the workshop while we're all gone," said Heron.

The pride welling up in her niece's eyes was worth all the nervousness she would feel while headed to Siwa. But she didn't dare let Sepharia know.

Besides, she didn't have much choice.

"Now that I've dragged you into my schemes, are we clear on what to do next?" she asked.

They nodded.

"Good. Start loading the steam wagon and harness the horses. We'll have to make it look like a regular wagon until we get out into the desert. Then we can see how it works."

The others got to work immediately while Heron slumped onto her desk, desperate to take a quick nap before she and Agog left.

But sleep eluded her. So she spent her time thinking about all the reasons she shouldn't be going to Siwa.

# 26

The wagon rumbled across the desert, pulled by a pair of mottled gray horses. Agog had volunteered to drive the wagon until morning. Heron had crawled in back, stuffed amongst the boxes that hid the steam mechanical.

Mercifully, she'd gotten a fair amount of sleep. More than she had in years at the workshop. Maybe travel was a remedy for her sleeplessness.

Heron crawled back onto the seat to munch on hard bread while the sun anointed the horizon with color.

Agog had chosen desert clothing and a head wrap for the journey. Only his green eyes peeked out from the garment. Except for his size, he could pass for a desert nomad.

"Care to get a rest?" she asked, refreshed and awake after sampling her ornate box.

Agog shook his head. "I don't sleep when I travel. I'm too often reminded of the hard ride to battle."

Sensing the Northman in a pensive mood, Heron decided to press his history. She knew so little about him otherwise.

"Have you fought that many battles?" she asked. "I myself am city born and bred. I only know of war through the occasional machines I make."

"I have fought in a few," he said. "Won some. Lost others."

Heron rubbed hands together to warm herself. The chilly desert air was made colder by the passing of their wagon.

"I find it hard to believe that you've lost even one battle," she said, blowing warm air through cupped hands.

Heron pulled a woolen blanket from the wagon and wrapped it around her midsection.

"When the Romans came, our side was crushed by their superior weapons, armor and tactics," he said after a time.

"Were you leading it?"

He shook his head. "The first time, I was but a lieutenant in another king's army. We'd raided too far south into Gaul and angered the Romans. Afterwards, those of us that survived, tucked tail and scurried back to our homelands."

"The first time?" she asked.

"I had a hard head in my youth and the lessons of the first battle did not quite sink in," he explained. "The thoroughness of their thrashing led me to study their tactics so that I might turn the tide should we meet again."

"So you did not agree with the way your side was led?"

Agog chuckled lightly and snapped the reins, guiding the horses around a dune that had blown onto the old road.

"There are a thousand opinions in any army but the only one of worth is the one yelled the loudest."

Even though she couldn't see his mouth, she sensed there was a smile.

"So the key to being a good battlefield leader is having a loud voice?" she asked.

His quick glance was followed by silence. They rode a while longer. The wind teased at their wagon, throwing enough sand in her face that Heron pulled the blanket around her head.

"The second time I faced the Romans," he said eventually, "we were skirmishing with a nasty Germanic tribe that'd been raiding our villages."

"Were you a lieutenant again?" she asked.

He shook his head. "This was years later, after I had traveled and learned and fought other wars and found a wife."

Heron had never heard him mention a wife before. Had never even considered that he'd had one.

"I could not dare attack the tribes without leaving guard, but I needed every soldier. So we packed up the villages and brought them along," he said.

Heron could hear a different timbre in his voice. It was hard as steel, as were his eyes, staring forward without blinking.

"My strategy was perfect and my troops were flawless in execution. We moved from valley to valley surprising them at every turn. They must have thought we were three armies hitting their lands." The hint of smile that had been creeping upon his lips was squelched as heavy thoughts overtook.

"But we didn't expect the Romans up from the south. When the southern tribes realized they would lose, they offered fealty to the Romans for their support."

Heron could hear his disgust plainly.

"Tired from the constant march and battle, we were routed again, despite a superior strategy. For fear of losing my people, I lost them anyway. The Romans did not give quarter."

Heron's heart clenched. "Was your wife there?"

The piercing glance was all she needed.

"Has there been a third time?" she asked softly.

After a long pause, "Not yet," he said, laced with venom.

It wasn't until the sun shown down on their backs that either spoke again. Heron, for fear of disturbing the Northman and Agog, clearly lost in the events of the past.

When Agog spoke again, after many hours of travel, Heron was surprised.

"Aurinia was a seer as well as my wife. I'd claimed her from the forest and though she was younger than the other priestesses, they feared her. When she spoke, even they made warding signs," he said with a secret smile.

He'd thrown his face covering over his shoulder once the wind had settled.

"Before the battle, we brought prisoners to the priestesses, who were bare-footed and girt with girdles of bronze. Aurinia was raven-haired while the others were grey," he said.

The look on his face made it seem he was witnessing the action as he spoke.

"They crowned the prisoners with wreaths and led them to the wicker wagons. We had captured one of their kings and Aurinia claimed him for her prophecy."

His face grew wistful and forlorn.

"After his entrails spilled upon the grass, she leapt to them, feet splashing in the pools of blood around his body..."

The description was gruesome, but the manner in which he spoke made it seem that it was a normal practice for his people.

When it seemed he wouldn't speak again, she asked, "What was the prophecy?"

He shook his head, shaking off a bad dream.

"What?" he said, gazing down with dream soaked eyes and the reins held loosely in his hands.

The wind and the removing of his covering had loosened his knot, so the hair formed a wispy halo around his head. Heron had never seen him so lost before, but then as quickly as it'd happened, it was gone.

"The prophecy," she said. "What did she say?"

Agog sighed, his eyes steel again. "That I would defeat the tribes so soundly that I would not have to return my people north." He paused. "Or at least that's what I thought it meant."

"Did you defeat them?" she asked timidly.

"Soundly," he replied. "The tribes sold themselves to the Romans too late. I crushed them so thoroughly we would have had peace for generations."

The 'but' could clearly be heard in his words.

"Joyous that the prophecy foretold my victory, I had given orders to my people to decamp and ready themselves for a long stay. They had traveled hard and bled often and I wanted them to enjoy the victory," he said.

"When the Romans came, too soon after the last of the southern tribes were defeated, we couldn't flee north. They slaughtered us whole since they themselves were too far away to conveniently take prisoners."

Agog gripped the reins tightly with one fist. Veins popped on his arms and his forehead. He straightened his knot with the other hand until the hair was pulled from his face.

"How did you survive?" she asked carefully.

"My closest lieutenants and I fought our way out of the Roman's trap. We tried to make it to the seers, but they'd already been killed by the time we got to them. Aurinia's throat had been slit like the prisoners' she'd killed only days before."

His rage was so unbridled that when he glanced over, she thought he might strangle her.

"My sorrow was only worsened by thought that had she not given me her prophecy, she still would yet live," he said through gritted teeth.

"What do you mean?" she dared to ask.

"Normally, we traveled light, ready at wagon to move to the next camp or battle. It's how we had confused and beaten the southern tribes. But at her words, I thought the war over and had them plan for a longer stay. If I hadn't given the command, we could have slipped the Romans and fled north."

His words stitched tightly in her gut. Not only for his loss, but for her destination and what she prepared to do.

They continued their journey mostly in silence, taking turns at the steerage, taking breaks only when the horses required it.

The winds swept south by southwest, blowing across their backs and making the journey quicker. As they grew closer, Heron found herself growing more anxious.

She kept going back to the Northman's story about prophecy. While there were other more tangible, more logical reasons for coming to Siwa for her investigation, the one that bothered her most was the one she could not escape, nor talk herself out of doing, despite the story.

She was going to speak to the Oracle of Ammon.

# 27

"We are being followed," he said, matter-of-factly.

Heron nodded. She'd seen them since the road had turned more eastward.

"One man to the north, running parallel," she said proudly.

When Agog clicked his tongue, she knew she had missed something.

"Another behind on a camel," he said.

Heron resisted the urge to turn and look. "How can you be certain? You've been facing forward the whole afternoon?"

Agog pointed to his nose. "The wind blows at our backs and camels smell like shit."

"Raiders? Shall we fire up the steam mechanic? Siwa can't be far," she said playfully.

"Since the horses will have to be loosed to use the mechanic, I'd rather stay on the wagon," he said with a gentle nod. "Unless you were planning on riding the horses in and letting me steer the wagon."

"Well, then I guess we'd better hope they aren't raiders,"

she said.

Agog gave another exploratory sniff. "I detect the faint scents of incense. I believe our camel rider is from the temple."

Heron laughed lightly.

It had been a long time since she'd been in the presence of a man for so long. Her life was dedicated to the workshop and except for the rare occasions to raise funds or sell her inventions, she never left its walls.

Not that Heron couldn't admire the men of her workshop. Punt was a broad-chested Egyptian man with bronze skin and a pleasant face, but he was married. Plutarch was tall and slender and handsome, but not inclined to women.

They'd been working for her so long that she thought of them more as brothers than men. Not that it mattered. She couldn't dare expose the illusion, lest the workshop be taken from her and Sepharia sold into slavery.

Distant anguish tugged at her heart. She missed her twin. As much for his comforting presence as the cover he would have provided. If he were alive, she could have stayed Ada and worked in the workshop, while he stayed the face.

Then she could even consider a man like Agog. Heron tested the winds for the airs of the camel, but all she could smell was Agog's salty man scent.

She wondered if he suspected. Their conversations during the second leg of the journey had been flirty. But she didn't dare.

Deep down she didn't trust the northerner. He'd been keeping things from her, so there was no reason to involve him in her secrets. Even if she did ache to feel a man's touch again, just for a night.

Hours later, cresting a sand swept hill, they both gasped upon seeing the Oasis of Siwa stretch out before them. Palm trees fluttered in the wind over the hidden valley.

In the middle of the valley of palms, a white temple thrust out from the greenery. Even in the fading light of dusk, the temple shown like a clear jewel against the sky.

The road to the temple was clear as a white snake slithering through the palms, beset with columns at intervals. Heron steered the wagon toward it.

When Agog shifted, visibly tensing, she knew visitors approached.

As they reached the palms, a man in sheer white desert robes stepped from a column. It had appeared the man had slipped out of the stone, but Heron knew better than to believe an illusion she'd performed herself in the temples.

"Salutations, Heron of Alexandria," said the man.

Heron found herself not surprised in hearing her name, though she noticed Agog had flinched.

Upon closer approach, Heron could see the man's crystal blue eyes studying her with amusement.

"Greetings," she said. "Might we know your name, since you know ours?"

The man bowed deeply. "Ahhh, but in your heart I think you know my name, your waking mind just hasn't discovered it yet. But I will humor you, because you are our guest. I am Salhaed, priest of Ammon."

"Greetings, Salhaed," she said.

When she sensed Agog wanting to speak, she placed a hand on his arm. Agog gave her a sideways glance but she shook her head.

After Salhaed straightened, he spoke again, "I do not know the name of your companion."

"He is my bodyguard. His name is Garn." The deception came easily to her lips though she hadn't planned on it. Because they'd known who she was upon arrival, she thought it best not to give them more information.

"Salutations, Garn," said Salhaed.

Agog nodded his head reverently and kept silent. She let out a tiny breath, glad that the northerner had agreed to her lie, even though she wasn't quite sure why she had said it.

As Heron brought the wagon next to Salhaed, the priest began studying the boxes and diverse shapes contained within.

"I've never seen a wagon so strangely loaded for a trip to our humble oasis," said Salhaed.

"We sought to confuse those who might be watching as we left Alexandria, but it seems we could not deceive the priests of Ammon," she said as flatteringly as possible.

Salhaed grinned and gave her a slight bow of appreciation. "Yes. Our sight goes beyond the mortal realms. Mere oddly shaped boxes cannot confound us."

"Shall we give you a ride to the temple proper or will you walk the whole way?" she asked.

Salhaed winked at her and then put two fingers to his lips and whistled. A white stallion appeared from the trees and the priest expertly grabbed onto the horse and slung himself upon it as it ran by.

Even Agog clicked his tongue in appreciation at the display of horsemanship. Heron found herself slightly annoyed that she could interpret Agog's subtle clicks of the tongue.

"There. Now I may continue our conversation without slowing your journey," he said, riding next to them.

"We were not slowed," said Heron. "The horses could use a break from their hard journey across the desert."

"Well, then. We are not but a moment longer and then we shall unbridle your horses and wash the dust from your faces. The Temple of Ammon has long been looking forward to your visit," said Salhaed.

"Your hospitality in the harsh desert is unmatched," she said.

As they neared, Heron realized that the temple was perched atop a small hill in the center of the valley. The temple building had appeared above the palms because it rested on the peak.

The steep slope would be challenging for her to climb with her leg harnesses, no matter how improved they were.

The waters of the oasis came into view as they made the final turn. A sizable village sat beneath the temple. Torch light flickered across the water surface as the day darkened.

From the number of houses, at least two hundred lived at the oasis. Children could be seen running from house to house, playing games. Women in colorful robes with baskets teetering on their heads walked back from the water's edge.

Heron didn't see any men, but she sensed they were being watched from a distance. She assumed that if Agog made threatening movements, guards would appear and surround them.

Salhaed lead them to stable that was nothing more than a thatched roof with no walls and a few posts to tie horses. A withered man scurried from a nearby hut and unhooked the horses from the wagon.

Heron supervised for a moment until she realized the man would gently care for their horses by the way he cooed and rubbed their long noses lovingly. As she hobbled after Salhaed, she noted that he did not mention her leg harnesses.

A stone cut doorway opened into the cliff. Heron thought they would enter the passage, until she saw a table set amid a grove of palms and surrounded by torches.

Salhaed led them to the table, motioning for them to take a seat. As soon as they did, women appeared and poured them water in golden goblets.

Their host had not spoken, so Heron kept quiet. Agog's eyes clearly studied their surroundings. She was glad she'd said he was her bodyguard, otherwise his tense movements could have been interpreted suspiciously.

Heron wondered about the three seats at the table. Normally a bodyguard would not be seated with his charge. But maybe they had not really known who he was upon approach and she liked that reason better than that they knew his real identity but were letting her think she was deceiving them.

"It is quite an honor to have the *Michanikos* visit our humble shrine," said Salhaed.

"Humble shrine? No. The honor is mine," she said, raising a goblet in salute. "The Oracle of Siwa's role in Alexandria's rise is well known."

Salhaed waved his hand at her dismissively. "We have no role. We are but speakers for the gods."

"But without the Oracle's assertion that Alexander was descendant from Ammon, the city, along with its Great Library, would have been killed as a stillborn by the Egyptian elites," she said.

Salhaed made a face that Heron detected as a flicker of anger or regret. But it passed so quickly, she couldn't be sure she'd seen it. It might have just been a trick of the torch light.

Salhaed expertly steered the conversation to more mundane topics as roast bird and seasoned dates were brought for their meal. The priest asked questions about the current happenings in Alexandria, though Heron got the impression that he knew them already by the nature of his questions.

As they plucked the meat from the bones and sipped from their cups, Heron presented a question, "When will I get to speak to the Oracle?"

The priest gave no adverse reaction to her request. He seemed to be expecting it, in fact, as a faint smile rose to his lips.

"One does not speak to the Oracle," said Salhaed, his

crystalline blue eyes coldly regarding her. "The Oracle speaks only to you."

"Then how do I give my question?" she asked.

"In truth, the Oracle already knows your question, but most visitors wish to speak the question just to be sure," he said.

Heron tilted her head and threw a bone back onto her plate. "If I must speak my question, but not to the Oracle, how will she hear it?"

Salhaed inclined his head. "Your humble servant, Salhaed, will bring the message to her this evening. Then the following night as the crescent moon reaches the peak of its journey, high above the temple, you shall hear the answer from the Oracle."

Agog shifted in his seat and she heard the tell-tale click of his tongue.

"When shall I give my question?" she asked.

Salhaed offered his hands in a receiving manner. "Whenever you feel it is necessary. Even now, if you'd like. And then I will begin my journey to the peak."

Heron nodded and pushed herself away from the table. Not because she was full, but to see both their faces as she asked the question.

Agog was trying hard not to appear interested, but she could see the tenseness in his shoulders. The man was bristling.

She was glad that Salhaed was focused on her, otherwise he would clearly see the bodyguard's discomfort, throwing her deception into question. Before Salhaed might notice, or she lost her nerve, Heron asked the question and found herself not surprised by either man's reaction.

"Who started the fires that burned the Great Library in Alexandria?"

# 28

"Have your wits flown your mortal cage?" Agog breathed as they were led to their sleeping quarters.

Heron shushed him, knowing the slaves attending them would report their conversations back to Salhaed.

Then she realized Agog was walking at her side. She snapped her finger and pointed discreetly to a spot a pace behind.

Agog practically growled at her with his eyes, but fell into step behind her.

They were led to a grove of trees with a stone hut in the middle. It had wide, curtained windows and an arched door. Colorfully striped cloth ribbons hung in the entrance, shifting slightly in the breezes that were deflected from the cliff.

The woman slave with a gentle flourish of her hand indicated Heron should enter. Heron looked back to Agog. The hut looked barely big enough for one.

"Where will my bodyguard be sleeping?" she asked.

The slave repeated the gesture indicating Agog would

sleep in the hut.

Heron felt great discomfort when dealing with slaves. She disliked giving them orders, but she didn't want to share a small hut with Agog.

"That hut looks too small for the both of us," she said, mimicking the tone of command she'd heard too often on the streets of Alexandria. "I desire separate sleeping quarters for my bodyguard."

The slave blinked twice and glanced toward the temple. Then she made the slightest of grimaces and indicated the hut a third time.

Heron sighed. She had hoped to have privacy to clean and adjust the molded genitalia she used as her gender disguise. It allowed her to urinate standing as a man, but it had gained an aroma from the constant use.

"Fine," said Heron. "Then lead my man to the water so he may fetch us more to drink. I am parched."

The slave pointed to herself and shook her head, indicating that Agog would not be allowed.

Glancing back to the Northman, she noticed he was staring into the trees. She subtly followed his gaze to see glints of steel in the darkness. They were being watched by armed guards.

"Let us retire," she said, defeated.

The stone hut was even smaller inside than she first thought and Agog had to hunch down or hit his head on the ceiling. There was a cot along one wall and a blanket along another with only space between for another person. A candle attached to the wall spread its meager light in the small space.

Agog slipped into a crouch on his blanket, scowling. He clicked his tongue in annoyance.

Heron glanced out the window, careful not to disturb the cloth covering.

"They keep us prisoner here," he said, hunched over and brooding.

Heron shook her head. "Yes and no. The temple does not wish to harm us, but they keep us together for a reason."

"And what reason is that?" he asked.

As her vision adjusted to the dim light of the hut, she was struck by how much a beast of a man the northerner was. The candlelight cast menacing shadows on his form. She felt like she was waiting in a cave with a great bear.

A contrast to the eloquent and learned man he portrayed himself to be in the workshop. Of course, she'd seen him fight twice: once in the streets of Alexandria and the other in the darkness of her workshop.

In the workshop, she'd only seen flashes of him slipping through the shadows and then a scream. She had almost pitied the mercenaries.

Heron shrugged. "Besides annoying me with your presence?"

She gave him a half-grin, which he ignored and continued his sulking.

"What's gotten into you?" she demanded.

"I was wondering the same of you," he said. "Why travel here to ask a foolish question? I thought we embarked on a real errand. At least if we would have tested the wagon, we might have learned a valuable truth."

Heron peeked from the opposite side window. She hated the way the trees and walls kept her blind. A person could be sitting outside their window and they wouldn't know it.

"I have my reasons," she said, not wanting to admit them out loud. She could barely even admit them to herself. Might she be chasing at shadows?

"By what reasons could your investigations lead you here?" he asked.

Heron waited until the Northman was looking up at her, so she could indicate her true meaning with her eyes.

"Enough talk from you," she said, invoking the haughty tone of a slave master. "My servant should not be questioning me so vehemently, even a hired one as yourself that I have given much liberty."

She hoped that if the temple was truly spying on her that her words would give reason enough not to distrust their ruse.

As Agog's eyes narrowed, she indicated the outside with a nod of her head and cupped a hand around her ear.

Agog nodded, understanding.

"Apologies, Master Heron," he said. "My brain is much addled from the long journey across the desert and a lack of sleep."

Heron marveled at how quickly the Northman changed from brooding beast to delicate conspirator. His pose seemed noble and thoughtful now, rather than beastly.

"I am not tired yet, though I feel myself growing in that direction," she said. "So I would hazard a tale that would help soothe us both on our way to sleep."

One eyebrow rose questioningly. Heron smiled in response.

"Have you heard the story of Alexander's visit to this very Oracle?" she asked.

Clearly as a student of history he had, but he played along and said, "No, Master Heron, I have not."

"I will be brief then, as I am growing tired already," she said. "The story is told in the book *Life of Alexander* from Plutarch, not mine, but a scholar from the Library."

Heron sat on the cot, content that it wouldn't matter if the temple overheard her tale.

"As a military venture, Alexander conquered Egypt easily. But running your troops through a country as proud and historied as Egypt and convincing its leaders to pledge fealty wouldn't actually hold the country and Alexander needed Egypt for its gold and food and slaves," she said, skipping the details and only hitting the highpoints of the story.

"Alexander was wise beyond his years, a benefit of having Aristotle as his teacher, I presume, and he knew that Egypt would only follow a divinely inspired leader. A pharaoh. So Alexander came to the Oracle and asked two questions. The first, he inquired if any of his father's murderers had escaped. The answer was that he shouldn't ask such questions because his father was more than a man."

Heron paused and held out her hand in a stopping motion. She realized she'd plowed into the story too quickly.

"First, I think I should point out that when Alexander came to the Oracle, he came with his army. Secondly, he was the only one to go into the Oracle. His entourage waited outside."

Agog clicked his tongue and Heron took that as a signal to continue.

"Alexander then asked a second question, directly to the Oracle and received his answer. He asked whether he was fated to conquer all of mankind. The Oracle granted this to him and then he proceeded to reward the temple with gifts," she said.

"And with the belief that he was fated to victory, his troops followed him across the whole world in his conquest. And the people of Egypt, believing him descendant from the god Ammon, the very god that speaks through this shrine, fell in behind him and supported the great city of Alexandria as its new capital."

The Northman appeared deep in thought at the conclusion of her lecture.

"Well, that story did the trick for me," she said with a smirk, lying onto the cot. "Sleep well, loyal bodyguard, I hope this story has proved instructive."

Agog didn't acknowledge her, so she turned and went to sleep. Surprisingly, she slept well, though awoke well before the dawn. The candle had been snuffed, but light from the moon filtered past the curtains, revealing hazy shapes in the darkness.

Heron found herself staring at the sleeping form of the Northman. She watched the slow heave of his chest as he slept comfortably on his back.

In the dim light of morning, Heron imagined running her hands across his chest. It had been so long since she'd been with a man that it seemed like another life.

Lost in her fantasies, Heron didn't notice that Agog had awoken and stared back at her. Embarrassed by the unfiltered eye contact, Heron rolled onto her back.

Heron was saved by the entrance of a slave, the same girl from the night before. She motioned them to follow.

They were led to the table in the clearing. Only two chairs remained. They were given wet cloth to wash their faces and then they ate a breakfast of bread and sticky green fruit.

Heron avoided Agog's gaze, though he studied her closely. She spent her time looking at the hill she would have to climb, her knees already aching from the thought.

No one attended them after eating, so they wandered into the village. The villagers moved through their daily routines like an automata play. Heron walked up to a woman threading a rip in a tunic, sitting in the shade of her doorway. The woman would not make eye contact or respond to Heron's questions.

Heron repeated the exercise until she grew certain that the villagers were forbidden to speak to them. Even the slave girl attending them remained silent.

Along the way, Agog occasionally nodded toward distant locations around the oasis. Heron found men in steel and white desert robes spying on them.

Heron went back to check on the wagon to find the boxes hiding the steam mechanic disturbed.  She checked the important connections, finding that they hadn't been adjusted.  Not that she thought the temple priests could interpret the gears and levers enough to damage it.

They spent the rest of the day by the water's edge.  Agog tried to strip down and swim in the oasis, but men appeared and shouted at him until he started putting his clothes back on.

Once the men left, Agog shot her a sly glance and put his feet into the water.  They chatted quietly while they waited for nightfall.  Agog told tales of his village life when he was a young man.  He had questions about hers, but she shrugged them off.

In all, Agog's anger from the previous night seemed to have dissipated, either from the tale about Alexander or an acceptance that she was going through with speaking to the Oracle.

During quiet moments, Heron caught Agog staring at her in a way that made her feel uncomfortable.  Did he see past her disguise?  Was he just considering their task?

Heron almost wished it was the first.  Besides her niece, no one else knew about her deception.  It weighed on the heart to keep a secret for so long.  She'd always been able to confide in her twin, knowing he would always keep her secrets safe.

And in another time and place, she would be interested in the Northman.  Maybe before he returned to the North, she could reveal herself for one night of revelry.  Maybe.

But she knew that would never happen.  It would risk too much.  He would probably leave once the war machines were complete.

Before the sun set, the slave girl led them back to the

grove. They ate a flaky white fish caught at the oasis, and a bowl full of nuts and berries.

When the appointed time finally came, Heron felt restless and alert. Salhaed appeared in a white temple robe, adorned with gold inlay. His bronze skin shown against the white, making him glow in the moonlight.

"Greetings, Heron of Alexandria. I hope our hospitality has held you well received," he said.

"Gratitude, Salhaed," she replied. "Your hospitality has been well received."

Salhaed led them to the bottom of the hill. Next to the upwards leading path was a gold goblet on a single white pedestal.

"Before you ascend, you should partake of this cup of honeyed wine to aid you on your journey to the Oracle," he said, indicating the goblet.

Heron lifted the goblet and downed it in one long draw. She assumed it was drugged, but knew she wouldn't be able to refuse. It was safer to let them believe she didn't know.

"The Oracle awaits," said Salhaed and he began walking up the path to the peak.

When Agog started to follow, Salhaed motioned for him to stop.

"The answer is for Heron alone, since he was the questioner," said Salhaed.

Agog hesitated, glancing to Heron.

"I'm certain I am safe within the temple's capable hands," she said. "Though I would have preferred your shoulder for the climb."

Salhaed tut-tutted softly. "One must make the climb on his own power or not be worthy of the Oracle's wisdom."

Salhaed took to the path in long confidant strides. He would reach the peak long before her.

"Plato have pity," she muttered.

Not far into the climb, Heron wondered if she would make it to the top. Her leg harnesses were not made for climbing, only walking across flat surfaces. The joints dug into her leg. She stopped frequently to rub the life back into her legs and adjust the harnesses.

At a quarter of the way up, the drug from the cup took hold. The simple stony path up the mountainside became a treacherous landscape of unreality.

The periodic torches that marked her way began to sway like serpents. Despite her internal certainty that they were still torches, Heron avoided them, scraping along the walls to keep her distance.

The shadows between the islands of light became yawning pits. Her logical mind knew there was stone beneath her feet, but she crawled across the shadows, fearful she would fall to her death.

Glancing to the moon, she frequently became enthralled by its crescent shape. Doubts that she would be safely received at the top crept in.

The crescent moon matched the shape of the necklace from the assassins. She wondered what Punt and Plutarch had learned in her absence. She wondered if they were even alive. All these thoughts careened around in her head like water spiders.

Fears that whatever sinister forces arrayed against them had risen up and slain her friends and her niece while she was gone took hold and could not be dislodged. Even Agog had probably been set upon by a host too numerous to stop and he lay in the dust with blood pooling around his throat.

Heron crawled up the mountainside, tears dripping from her face, harnesses loose and partially dragging behind.

As she neared the top, her waking mind began to assert

control over the drug induced one. Shadows stopped being pits and torches became torches. Even the thoughts of her friends being dead had ceased.

A new thought replaced the others, one that made her chuckle lightly as she fixed the harnesses around her bloody knees.

Salhaed had given her the drug at the bottom, expecting her to be in its throes when she reached the peak. The difficulty of her climb had delayed her progress enough that the drug, while still in her body, now only served to mute the agony within her legs.

Heron finally stood and continued her journey with an awkward gait as she hadn't been able to fully repair the harnesses.

The path gave way to an arched gate. The haze of smoke filled the courtyard beyond. Heron stepped through to find Salhaed greeting her.

The priest's face was cast in a welcoming light, though Heron could see by his tense shoulders that he was perturbed by her lateness. Heron kept her eyes decidedly vacant.

Other priests in lesser robes bowed as she passed. She caught many a glance toward her bloody, ruined knees. She was certain blood still ran down her calves but feared breaking the illusion by tending to them.

The white stone temple on the far side of the courtyard waited without adornment except columns carved into the stonework. She was disappointed by the plainness. She had hoped to find clues amid the frescoes and paintings normally found on temple walls.

Heron crossed the distance until she stood at the doorway.

An old priest with a gray, grizzled beard stood before her. His face was lined in wrinkles and his robe was simple white. Crystal blue eyes like Salhaed's watched her approach.

The old priest moved to the side and motioned for her to enter. Heron heard noises of protest from behind.

"What is the meaning of this?" asked Salhaed. His voice seemed both distant and near.

The old priest held his hand up to silence Salhaed. "The Oracle wishes to give her answer directly."

Salhaed bristled beneath the command of the older priest. Their hierarchy was apparent by the exchange. Heron assumed Salhaed the high priest due to his gilded robes, but the old one asserted power. Maybe given from the Oracle's command.

The old priest motioned again for her to proceed. Heron entered before Salhaed could stop her.

The adytum, the interior of the temple, erased her concerns about finding clues. The walls were lavishly decorated. Heron proceeded slowly and drank in the details.

On the right wall, King Amasis, in whose reign the temple was built as she read from the cartouche beneath his carving, stood with his arm outstretched to the east. Slaves offered wine vases to the eight gods that followed: Amenre, Mut, Khonsu, Dedun-Amun, the goddess Tefnut, Haraphis, Nut, and Thoth.

On the left wall waited Ammon, whose name and voice had been given to the temple. Ammon's lower body was wrapped in white cloth and he held a resurrection staff.

Behind Ammon and fed by more slaves, eight more gods looked on: Haraphis, Sutekh-irdes, Hebenu of the Two Lands, Nehem'awa, Amenre, Mut, Khonsu, and Thoth.

Heron couldn't be sure of the meaning of the same gods on both walls. She made her way through the hallway, trying to memorize every detail. Had she not been going so slow, she might not have noticed the procession painted into the background.

In the distant mountains, far beyond the gods and

goddesses painted to be standing in the room as she, a line of men danced before a tiny altar.

The portion of the painting was up high, so she had to stand on her toes to study it, a feat of balance, given the harnesses and drug.

Then she saw it, hiding behind the altar. A darkened crescent moon, almost black except for hints of shimmer across its surface.

Aware that she'd been taking a long time to walk through the hallway, Heron continued, content that she'd found at least one clue. She couldn't be certain that the dark crescent matched the one from the assassin, but it was more than they had before.

Heron went through the second hall, under an archway depicted with the head of a ram, Ammon's symbol. Other adornments of the god were painted upon the walls. After an inspection, Heron moved to the inner sanctuary.

A woman was seated on a dais covered in crimson silken pillows. She wore a simple shift across her bosom. Heron knew her as the sibyl of the Oracle when she realized the woman's eyes were sewn shut. The thick thread looked old and bonded to her eyes.

She'd been blinded by the temple for her prophecies. Heron wondered if it were as much to keep her from escaping.

The woman would have been a beauty in the streets of Alexandria. Heron felt sorrow for her, trapped in a secluded temple to speak mysteries. She was a slave worse than chained.

The haze of incense drifting through the room made her cough lightly.

"Heron of Alexandria," said the Oracle with a clear, high voice.

"It is I," Heron replied.

The Oracle tilted her head and a secret smile of amusement flickered across her lips. The Oracle patted the pillows beside her. Heron was almost glad the Oracle was blind so she would not see the pity on her face.

Heron glanced around, certain she was being watched. She assumed that once she climbed upon the pillows, guards and priests would rush in and drag her away.

Heron made her way tentatively, the drug having worn off enough that her knees began to ache.

The Oracle took her hand and whispered, "I will tell you the answer to your question, but first I must know."

Before Heron could react, the Oracle leaned forward and unerringly, placed her lips against hers. Surprised, Heron had no time to flinch and once the Oracle's lips were against hers, she dared not pull away.

The Oracle pushed her lips insistently against hers. She had soft, plush lips like the petal of a flower. Heron felt a tingle at the base of her spine.

Then, as quickly as it had begun, the Oracle was upright and away.

"I will give my answers now," said the Oracle, motioning for Heron to return to the spot before the dais.

Heron noted the mention of answers in the plural rather than singular. Will she receive answers for questions she did not ask?

Before she had much time to weigh her thoughts, the Oracle spoke again in fluent Greek.

*"One question begets three and no man may be their master. As all things have a past, a present, and a future, so too does your question.*

*The future speaks first, in a city made of time, the error will be understood and set alight a new conquest.*

*For the present, wrapped in a knot of the mind, is owed a*

*divine debt that shall be repaid in full.*

*And last—the past, the truth fractured into meanings upon meanings, was set alight by the Empire's favored hand."*

The words burned themselves into Heron's mind, though the meaning of them was kept far from understanding. Only the last verse, pertaining to the past, was clear.

The Oracle had laid blame of the fiery destruction of the Great Library upon the Empire's favored son—Gaius Julius Caesar.

# 29

Heron hardly remembered the journey back down the mountain. Once she had received her answer, she left straight away, wanting to reach the bottom before the drug wore off.

Agog practically caught her as she stumbled down the last slope and carried her to the wagon. He'd had it readied during the climb.

The pain from her bloody, ragged knees grew to white hot intensity by the time the wagon left the oasis. She sat in back, and using water and a rag, tried to clean the mess that was her knees.

Pebbles and rocks had become imbedded in the flesh. Using a sharp knife, she picked the worst of the stones loose. A particularly nasty shard had dug deep and she had to cut away skin to remove it, only to pass out when it pulled free.

When she awoke, Agog had stopped the wagon and was wrapping bandages around her legs. Heron chided him for stopping the wagon and told him she could do it herself.

Heron did not sleep. The pain and the aftereffects of the

drug made sure of that. And the Oracle's words had so firmly lodged themselves in her mind, deeper than the rocks she'd pulled from her knees, she thought of nothing else in her half-asleep, half-awake state.

She didn't know why the Oracle had given her three answers when she'd only asked one question. What information was the woman trying to pass on to her?

After a time, which was no time and all time together because she was lost in her own mind, she began to come out of her dream-like haze.

Her tongue was stuck to the roof of her mouth and her bladder ached. The wagon sped through the desert passing over a tall hill that was losing a battle with a nearby dune.

A water pouch sat against her leg. She drew from it again and again, feeling like her thirst would never be quenched. When the pouch was empty, she threw it back down, partially sated.

Agog stared ahead, lightly flicking the reins. He was wrapped in his desert nomad gear. The sun neared the horizon and painted the earth in bright colors.

"Stop the wagon, Northman. I have to make water upon the sand," she said.

Agog tilted his head toward her. "Piss off the back. We're being followed and I dare not stop."

"The temple?"

He shook his head. "Bandits." He nodded south and pointed discretely with his elbow.

Heron followed the direction he indicated. It took a minute, but eventually, she caught sight of four men on horses shadowing them.

"Why haven't they attacked already?" she asked.

Agog clicked his tongue, which passed as a thoughtful shrug. "Freya's frigid tits, why would I know?" he said. "If it were me, I'd have already made my move."

Heron patted the boxes covering the steam mechanic. "Maybe they're afraid we've got a mini-ballista under here."

He chuckled and shouted his response back, "Or they're waiting to join up with others. Bandits hate to attack unless they've got overwhelming odds."

The wagon bounced and Heron grimaced, tightly grabbing her thigh. She shut her eyes until the pain dissipated to a low throb.

"Must you hit every bump and rock?" she said when she could speak again.

Agog pointed to the right. "If you prefer, I can steer that way. It's smoother near the bandits."

She could hear the grin in his words and shouted back her reply as she crawled to the back of the wagon. "Try to find a flat patch while I water the sand. Otherwise, you'll have to circle back around and pick me up when I fall out."

He laughed at her grim humor, to which Heron found herself doing the same, as she painfully crawled to the back.

Climbing to a half-kneeling position, she lifted her tunic and urinated through the molded genitalia. Complete, she made her way back and took the spot on the bench next to Agog.

"Want to get some sleep?" she asked, nodding to the wagon.

He shook his head. "I can't sleep before a battle and we won't outpace them unless your steam mechanic can drive this wagon faster than a horse," he said.

She pulled out a hunk of dried meat from a bag between them. "By my calculations, it should, but let's not try that right now."

"Why not?" he asked.

"We have to cut the horses loose to use it and we wouldn't

make it back to Alexandria. We're still too far away, unless I slept a second day."

Agog shook his head. "Only one day out, but I've been driving the horses hard."

Heron made a few more calculations. "If they haven't attacked by morning, we should be close enough to fire up the steamer."

"Morning? Ha!" he said. "We'll be lucky if our horses don't fall dead by then."

Heron shrugged. "Unless you'd like to stop and just get the fight over with, we'll have to wait until morning."

Agog gave an exaggerated scowl. "I should have procured a weapon before our trip. I can probably take the four of them bare-handed, but I can't vouch for your safety."

Heron glanced south. "Make that six, two more have joined them."

"I could take a weapon from the first?" he playfully asked himself.

"We're in a race for our lives and you're joking around," she said, raising an eyebrow.

"Humor is my secret weapon in battle," he said, smiling. "It's always the overly serious ones that die first."

"Can we talk about something else? We've got a long way until morning and I'd rather not dwell on it," she said.

Agog nodded.

The landscape veered smoothly away from the bandits, letting them put more distance between them. But the bandits didn't seem deterred by the change, they rode along patiently.

"Can you tell me of your words with the Oracle?" he asked. "Or will that violate the sacred mysteries and void your precious prophecy?"

Heron detected a hard edge to his question, despite his grin. She hesitated, deciding if she should reveal what she learned.

"We might die on this errand of yours," he said, nodding toward the bandits. "It would be common decency to let me know the worth of the journey."

It was Heron's turn to scowl.

"Caesar did it," she said without fanfare.

He raised a questioning eyebrow. "Caesar? I thought you'd ruled him out."

"I did," she said. "But that's not what the Temple of Ammon wants me to believe."

"Believe?" he asked, and then quieted, clearly in thought. "You didn't expect the real answer, did you?"

His green eyes bored into her.

"Took you long enough to figure it out," she said.

Agog shook his head. "I should have realized it from your story about Alexander." He paused and then asked. "Why did you go, then?"

"A couple of reasons," she said. "The night we were attacked, the man who you killed last called me a 'heretic' before he died."

"You never mentioned that," he said.

"I didn't think it important at the time," she said. "My failures in the temples were well known, as was my curse. I thought it nothing more than petty spite from a dying man."

"Tell me we didn't come all the way out here based on one dying lunatic?" he asked.

"When I was taking Sepharia to Punt's house in the secret wagon, I was accosted by an old hag who told me that the 'fires can only be found within the hidden waters of Ammon.'"

Agog nodded and let a sly grin rise to his face. "Prophetic words from an unlooked for source."

"Yes. The words seemed gibberish to me that day. I was too busy thinking about getting Sepharia safely through the streets," she said. "Later on, reflecting on everything I knew about the fires, I recalled the hag's words. I might not have thought much of them, except for my own experiences making miracles for the temples."

Heron glanced south. The bandits were keeping a safe distance. The contented nature of their following unnerved her. The sun would pass the horizon soon and they'd be traveling by moonlight alone.

"And?" Agog prompted her.

"I have made minor oracles before," she said. "Some give bird song to indicate a positive or negative answer, or others point to a prophetic item. The answer is given randomly, unless the temple in question pays an additional fee to add a secret lever that can direct the oracle's answer."

Agog let loose a short guttural laugh. "So my story about Aurinia was falling upon sympathetic ears after all."

"Was that story not true?" she asked.

He nodded grimly. "Sadly, yes."

Heron continued before he could grow maudlin again. "Besides confirming that the Oracle intended to mislead us, I also spied an important clue in the paintings before the Inner Sanctum."

She described the procession and the darkened moon. Agog immediately made the connection to the necklace as she had.

"So these hidden forces behind the temples started the fires?" he asked.

She shrugged. "They have not been ruled out, but I can find no proof of their involvement."

The Northman slapped his leg. "They've shown motive enough with their deception."

"They profit from the deception," she explained. "But that does not mean they are guilty."

Agog leaned back, considering her words with a hand to his chin. "I see your reasoning." And then a second conclusion appeared on his face. "What then of the temple's motive?"

Heron blew air out her lips in exasperation. "First, I don't even know which temple. A conspiracy among many or just a handful? They can't all be in on it, secrets are harder to keep the more who know about it." She paused. "But for motive, I can only guess. The city is a tinderbox, waiting to be lit, like my steam mechanic. Proof, for the masses anyway, that Caesar started the fires, might lend itself to a revolution."

She caught the way the Northman gripped the reins, rubbing the leather with relish. It did not confirm her thoughts but his actions lent themselves to her tentative conclusions.

Agog turned and with an almost deliberate calm, asked, "Will your secret benefactor take Caesar's name as an answer?"

Heron decided to test her theory. "I don't know. Will he?"

Without blinking, Agog answered right away. "Depends on the kind of man he is. Does he want the truth? Or just a convenient answer?"

His answer could be read both ways. Heron tried a different tactic. "I guess it depends on what he wanted the information for. To shore up the annals of history? To settle a grudge? And if the temples wanted this information out, will his needs outweigh the hidden agenda of theirs?"

Agog shrugged with a casual dismissal. "We're not even sure what they want. So how can you even compare two different hidden agendas?"

The Northman picked up the reins, steering the wagon around a clump of rocks. Heron found she had no answer for his question.

The night rattled by on the seat of the wagon. The pain and her long rest kept her awake. She wasn't sure how the Northman was managing.

Heron found herself worried about Agog's motives. She knew so little about him, even after hearing stories of his youth and conquests and the loss of his great love. She had no idea why he wanted the war machines, or why he was interested in the fires, if it were truly he behind the coinage.

For all she knew, he could be planning a conquest near Alexandria, either east or south. His troops could be moving into position while he waited for her to finish. It would explain his impatience with her progress.

Rome's displeasure at disruptions in the smooth workings of the Empire would be great. Heron shuddered to think what would happen if they traced the weaponry she was making back to her.

By rights, the Empire did not like her making war machines for anyone but them. But Philo had cornered the market with judicious bribes. She'd practically been forced into doing business with the Northman.

Heron casually glanced at Agog. He wasn't what she'd expected of a barbarian. His keen wit, erudite knowledge, and brutal strength made her wonder how Rome kept the hordes from traveling south.

While she liked the man, both professionally, and deep down, she could admit, a little privately, that he was an unknown that she was about to arm with weapons the world had never seen before.

Heron vowed to learn more about the Northman before she released the war machines to him. Especially since he knew what she'd learned at the Oracle.

Throughout the night, Heron dozed, briefly at best. Catching snatches as they made their way over dunes and long stretches of hard packed dust. The Northman piloted the wagon like a statue, barely moving and with a grim visage on his face, their previous humors lost to the night.

When the morning came, like a fire at dawn, Agog elbowed her deeply in the ribs.

"Four more have joined the six. Ready the engine," he said.

She climbed into the back, knees flaring with agony. The boxes in back made it look like they were hiding a camel. Heron removed them, keeping an eye on the horizon where the bandits rode.

The steam would take longest to rise, so Heron started the fire with a portable flint. Plutarch had packed a mixture of wood dust, oil, and wood in a steel bin. They'd lined the bottom with clay bricks so it wouldn't burn through the wagon, but they hadn't tested it yet.

They hadn't tested any of it, actually. Heron remembered Plutarch's adjustment to her design. Burning a hole through the wagon would be the least of their worries.

"They're coming," said Agog.

Heron didn't bother to check on the bandits. It would only slow her down and she was focused on the steam mechanic.

The flame was tickling the bottom of the water chamber. It would take time to boil and even longer for the mechanic to produce enough force to move the wagon.

"Should I release the horses?" he asked over his shoulder.

"Drive away from them," she said. "We need more time."

Heron blew on the fire, willing the water to turn to steam.

"I'm not going to have time to stop and release the horses if we don't do so soon," he shouted into the wind.

Heron glanced up. The bandits were bearing down on them, dust kicking up in plumes. She had an idea how they could keep going and activate the mechanic, but it would be dangerous. Less dangerous than ten bandits, though.

"The water isn't boiling yet. Can you release the horses while we move?" she asked.

Agog looked to the two horses, foam frothing at their lips as they thundered across the desert sands. He sighed. "Yes, I can climb onto the yoke and cut the harness if you can steer."

She nodded. "I'll have to steer from here. Throw me the reins."

The whooping of the bandits could be heard above the winds and the rattling of the wagon.

Heron knocked on the boiler with her knuckle. "For the love of Archimedes, get steaming, will you?"

As if on command, the first puffs of steam slipped from the joints and the piston began to move. The mechanic wasn't engaged to the wagon axle yet, but she would have to do that on the move. They would have no time to get up to speed slowly.

She just hoped Punt had forged strong gears that would withstand the hard coupling.

Heron pointed to the harness. "Cut them!"

Agog put the knife between his teeth and began crawling along the yoke. It seemed the bandits were right in their dust plume, waving curved swords and screaming.

Heron blew on the fire, stoking it more as Agog crawled across beam. She wasn't sure how the heavy timber held the big man.

Using one hand to steer with the reins, she kept the other on the lever that would engage the piston to the axle.

When Agog pulled the knife from his teeth, she readied the lever. The bandits would overtake them soon and she would be in reach of their swords.

Agog raised his knife and cut the first harness. The horse kept going even though it wasn't attached, though with only one pulling, the wagon slowed and the freed horse slowly surged ahead.

When he cut the second, it veered left. Heron nearly forgot

she was holding onto the reins and got yanked to her rear. Her knees exploded in pain. The bandits were astride the wagon as it was already slowing.

She barely dodged a sword blow, digging into the wagon side as she rolled to the back. As her fingertips touched the lever, she hoped that Agog was holding on tight, and slammed it into place.

As the gear caught, the wagon jumped a foot into the air and lurched forward, suddenly accelerating. Agog hung from the yoke with his feet barely caught onto the wagon edge.

The steam mechanic was chugging mightily and the wagon pulled away from the bandits. She could see their eyes widen with horror and surprise as the wagon drove away without horses.

Using a two lever system she'd designed, Heron steered the wagon across the uneven desert. The wagon was still gaining speed as Agog finally hauled himself onto the seat.

He had a maniacal grin, as his hair flew into his face, unbound from the knot on his head. "Your steam wagon works!" he shouted above the wailing winds.

Heron put her hand up to block the feeling of needles on her face. Sand kicked up from the harness hanging from the yoke.

The steam mechanic was whining with stress. She could hear the tension in the piston as she suspected, but there was nothing she could do, she had no way to stop the wagon. And she wanted to reach the city without the bandits catching them.

Checking behind, she saw the bandits had stopped. Either they'd realized they couldn't keep up or they were frightened by the lack of horses.

As the fire burned down to coals, the line of the city of Alexandria came through the distant haze. Heron sighed, thankful her calculations were correct.

Even from their distance, she was amazed by the growth of the city. The camps on the south side practically doubled the size. Permanent structures were being erected faster than the Romans could order them to be torn down. Huge tents of a style she'd never seen before hovered on the southern tip.

The wagon was slowing, but she knew they had too much speed, so she drove the wagon back and forth to shed momentum.

As they neared the outskirts, horses rode from the out-city to intercept them. Heron hoped it wasn't Roman soldiers and was relieved when a band of threadbare Egyptian mercenaries rode up. Heron threw water on the fire so they would roll to a stop.

The men rode up with wild eyes, staring at the empty harnesses.

"What manner of beast do you ride upon without horses?" asked the lead man, bare-chested and tattooed, dark skin soaking up the sun.

Before she could speak, Agog jumped from the wagon and declared. "It's Heron of Alexandria's miracle wagon. He rides the breath of the gods across the desert sands."

Recognition appeared on their faces. She was well known, especially to Egyptian Alexandrians, who took her as their own.

"And where do you ride from?" the man asked.

"The Oasis of Ammon," said Agog. "The gods favor Heron."

Before she knew it, Agog had convinced them to haul the wagon back to the workshop. Other curious men from the out-city followed the mercenaries, so the story of the miracle wagon was well entrenched by the time they passed under the city gates.

Heron knew that by nightfall, the story of her horseless wagon would be on every Alexandrian's lips. Which meant the governor would know soon, too.

And behind that, they would wonder what she had learned at the Oracle of Ammon.

Heron cursed Agog's loose tongue and wondered what he was getting at. She decided she could no longer trust him.

# 30

The heavy stare of the afternoon sun descended on Agog, bringing a coating of sweat as he rode through the crowded streets. His furs had been replaced by cloth, but worn in the style of his lands, over the shoulder and loose around the legs.

The oppressive heat reminded him that Egypt was not his home. He missed the cool embrace of the northern weather. Snow seemed a myth he'd once heard of.

Agog thought about Heron and found himself smiling. The old man he'd chanced upon when he first came to Alexandria had been right about the miracle worker. Heron had no equal.

The war machines were nearing completion. The first batches had been shipped.

Agog could scarcely believe what Heron could convince simple iron, water, and wood to do. If he didn't know better, he would have thought it magic or divine power.

The populous of Alexandria, however, didn't know better and had transformed the cursed miracle worker into a scion of the gods. The rumors had altered themselves until Agog barely recognized them himself and he'd started half of them.

He'd heard only yesterday that Heron could make metal statues come to life just by breathing into their mouths. Another rumor had Heron matching wits with a pair of powerful djinns and defeating them, forcing them to pull his golden chariot for eternity.

Agog laughed, thinking about the battered steam wagon being called a golden chariot. The poor hunk of wood had barely made it back to the workshop before falling apart. Plutarch flushed with embarrassment when he saw how close the engine had come to explosion.

The newer designs resembled chariots, though his coin had all but dried up in purchasing the war machines. He would find his way to new funds in short order.

Agog rode around a fight between two men, a Gaul and a Thracian. A crowd gathered quickly. From his high position, Agog could see no Roman guards in sight.

The Gaul made unbalanced lunges while the Thracian waited patiently for counterpunches. Agog moved on, content he knew the victor.

His thoughts fell upon the black stone that had arrived at the workshop only days before. Word had reached his ears that Governor Flaccus had taken his troops from the city. He would be gone at least another fortnight. As expected, the letter from Lysimachus had angered the man.

The remaining Roman soldiers could not handle a city that had been estimated at near a million souls and Agog doubted that estimate included the make-shift city surrounding the walled one.

After avoiding an overturned cart and a man beating his slave senseless, Agog finally made it to the Museum. He tipped the stable boy a pair of ha'pennies and strolled through the entrance, passing a trio of blowhard scholars that only parroted the words they read in scrolls, trying to convince a rich, foolish noble to patronage them.

Agog moved through the rooms easily now. Knowledge of the layout and less obvious clothing facilitated his ease. Though more than one scholar mistook him for a slave and commanded him to carry a heavy chest full of scrolls.

He passed through the Hall of Foreign Curiosities, spying a headdress he recognized from a Vandal village near his home. But that item was the only one he knew. The other strange and wondrous objects that populated the Hall were of materials and shapes he'd never considered.

A basket of carved demon masks sat near the exit. Supposedly they'd been sent back during Alexander the Great's conquest of the Far East. The masks had been painted in vibrant colors, but now were faded and chipped.

The Conservatory was packed for a lecture about the power of condensing one's thoughts with mental exercises about counting lines on a woven octahedron. The exercises were claimed to increase mental potential.

The lecturing scholar, a tall fellow who said his words in a distracting breathless manner, offered sale of the octahedrons for only a talent.

Agog could hear Heron scold the man, "Astounding feats of the mind wither there, unless put into practice."

He appreciated Heron's style. Agog kept the same counsel about his affairs in the north. Speaking about things did not make them so, only putting effort to action made them real.

Agog recalled that Heron never lectured his daughter. Only gave her tasks which unerringly taught her valuable lessons.

The way to his destination brought him through the Hall of Catalogs and around the Peripatos Garden. And though he'd passed through there numerous times, Agog marveled at the wealth of papyrus scrolls stacked in shelf upon shelf.

Agog finally found himself in the Histories section and wound through the shelves and tables until he found Gnaeus in a side room seated by three scribblers.

"Agog! My barbarian friend," said Gnaeus, holding his hands out in greeting. "I expected you some time ago."

Agog ignored the chiding. "Delays. The streets are growing overfull."

Gnaeus' eyes alighted with secrets as he motioned for Agog to join him in a nearby room.

"I acquired the scribes to copy your document," he said.

Agog frowned. "I thought there would be five."

"No worries," Gnaeus said. "I hired the best. These three can do the work of five."

"But do they know all the languages I requested?" Agog asked.

Gnaeus' face screwed up like he'd smelled a fart. "The *charakitai* do not care what language they copy. They're trained to scribe the exact copy of the original. Knowing what they were writing might invite editorial copying."

Agog hadn't known that. He nodded, agreeing with the wisdom of the Library.

"Do you really mean to go through with it? To make—"

"Silence, scholar," said Agog, slicing the air with a hand gesture. "I'd prefer to keep my council private."

Gnaeus rolled his eyes. "Then scheming with Hortio was the wrong way to go about it. The man has a looser tongue than Caligula."

"Speaking of him," Agog said. "How fare his efforts among the people?"

"You mean Heron's automata plays? A smashing success. The other workshops duplicated it quite thoroughly. Alexander has been killing Caesar nightly in the Juden Quarter, the Old

Egyptian noble houses, and in the lesser places of the Rhakotis District."

Agog rubbed his hand across his chin. He almost felt bad for having the automata play remade in another workshop. Heron would be quite cross with him, he was sure, but then again, Heron probably wouldn't approve of the plan either.

"And my letters?" he asked absently while still deep in thought. "Have you received replies yet?"

Gnaeus pulled a roll of papyrus from his toga and handed it over with a curious eyebrow raised.

"They left Tyre as soon as your message reached them. They wait for you as directed," he said.

Agog unrolled the papyrus and laughed when he saw the crude drawing on its inside.

"Is it a secret signal of some kind?" Gnaeus asked.

Agog was still laughing as he patted the scholar on the back. "Grimm made a drawing of me fucking a goat. Or at least that's what I think it's supposed to be. He's not so great an artist."

"Why would he do a thing as this? Are you not his king?" asked Gnaeus in horror.

Agog stooped down to Gnaeus' level and stared deeply into the scholar's eyes. "In my lands, we don't powder our noses before we shove them up someone's ass. And kings aren't fragile vases to be kept on a shelf." Agog paused. "In fact, it's probably a reminder from Grimm that I'd better not forget where I'm from."

The Northman straightened, keeping his hand resting on Gnaeus' shoulder. Agog realized then when Gnaeus actually met his kinsmen, assuming the plan went well, their actual behavior compared to what he'd read in his scrolls was going to break his little mind.

"So this Grimm, then," Gnaeus asked tentatively. "He can

read and write?"

Agog bellowed a laugh. "Freya's frigid tits, no. He's as illiterate as a stump. My horse can read and write better than he can. Smells better, too."

"What about the rest?" he asked. "Can they?"

"Most of the men cannot read or write but a few simple words. The women are a different story all together." Agog paused, considering. "And I suppose we'll probably pay for that little imbalance one day."

"So how did they read your message then?" Gnaeus asked.

"Quadi can read. He's my scholar of the North," explained Agog, thinking about the man and his affection for the color purple.

"Enough of them. Your scribblers need to get to work."

He handed Gnaeus a papyrus of his own. The scholar unrolled it and read the words quickly.

"Your Latin is quite lovely for a barbarian," Gnaeus mused.

Agog decided he would have to help Gnaeus learn new terms for his people. Agnar, of all of them, could be quite prideful and he didn't want to upset his allies.

Gnaeus rolled the papyrus up and slapped it against his hand. "I'll get them working on it right away."

Agog patted Gnaeus on the shoulder again. "Do not release them until you've been given the signal."

He left the scholar giving directions to his scribblers. The way back through the Museum did not distract him as it had on the way in. His mind only wheeled upon his plans, picking apart each decision, and wondering if it had been the right move.

As he walked down the steps of the Great Library, Agog tried to shake off his doubts, even though he knew there was no time for second guessing. His actions would place his head firmly into the Empire's mouth.

Agog wondered if his hesitance came from Aurinia and the desire to claim her weregild. But he knew that wasn't it. Aurinia would have admired his boldness. Even though that same boldness had gotten her killed.

Then, he thought back to Heron's workshop. He hadn't properly said goodbye. Maybe it was a guilty conscience for what was to come for them.

He felt a fondness for them as if they were his own people. Although he'd thrown them into battle without a second thought, he wasn't sure why his thoughts lingered on Heron and his friends. They were essentially hired help.

But Agog knew it was more than that. His people knew what they were getting into when they followed him. Heron knew nothing of the sort.

In fact, Heron was probably patting himself on the back for finally climbing out from beneath his debt, without a clue that those efforts would be for nothing. The world, and of more immediate concern, the streets of Alexandria, were going to change forever.

And for Heron, things were going to get a lot worse before they got better.

# 31

Sepharia sat on a barrel, sipping a cup of wine, watching her Aunt Ada break a smile across her face that spoke of long relief.

She was supposed to only think of her as Heron, but Sepharia found it hard to do. Heron was her father, though he was a man she barely knew.

Sepharia recalled the laughing smile that sprung easily to his face as he spun her around when she was scarcely taller than his knees. It was the smile on Ada's face that brought those memories back to her. Ada rarely smiled. Her lips were normally bleached white with purpose.

With the last of the war machines shipped out the day before and her debts with the new Alabarch covered, her aunt had much to celebrate.

Sepharia felt a bit guilty about keeping her father's name separate in her head from the new Heron, her aunt. It'd been her father's poor business sense that had created the debt. The feelings for her father were more like a mirage in the desert, distant and hazy and when she reached them, they faded to disappointment.

Ada deserved the name more than her father had.  The name had little meaning when he'd owned it.  A fledgling workshop among many and without weight to the name.

Despite his problems, her aunt had whispered stories of his genius to her at night, under the blankets.  She even claimed that when she was stuck on a particularly thorny problem, she'd think about how her twin would approach it and sometimes the answer would appear, as if he'd sent it to her from the beyond.

Sepharia liked to think of it that way, and maybe it was even true.  That her father, feeling guilty about the way he left them, had brokered a deal with Annubis to let him pass along his knowledge to his sister.  She just hoped he hadn't given away too much.

Her aunt hobbled over using a cane to keep her steady and leaned against a barrel next to hers.  She removed the harnesses a few days before and still seemed unsteady just using her cane.

"A raven steal your thoughts?" asked Ada.

Sepharia shrugged non-committal.  "Just thinking about..."

Ada nodded and patted her on the arm.  "Been thinking about him, too.  Never stop, actually."

The party seemed to be winding down, though it wasn't much of one in the first place.  Only Plutarch had dressed for it in a light blue toga that matched the desert sky.  The others had worn their typical workshop gear.  Punt, much to everyone's surprise, had worn a shirt.

The workers had left earlier.  Heron had given them each a skin of wine, a few days off, and a nice bonus.  Plutarch had carped after they'd left, that he'd given them too much, but

Heron had waved off any argument.

Punt came by on his way out, looking sheepish. "Apologies for the interruption, Master Heron."

"Please, Punt, I'm too tired for the formalities." She gave him a soft smile and a brief nod of the head.

"My apologies for ever doubting you," said Punt while staring at his feet.

Ada's head rose and her face screwed into curiosity. "Doubting?  When of all people have you ever doubted me, Punt? You've been my stalwart. A rock amid the stream."

Punt's hands took on a life of their own, opening and closing, until Punt shoved them into his armpits. "It's Astrela. A while back, the bones said..." he let his voice trail off with implication and glanced up cautiously.

A smile transformed Ada's face into the spitting image of her father. "Dispel the thoughts from your concerns. It takes more than a few bones to bring me down."

Punt shrugged hesitantly.  "I didn't believe her at first, but then after the accident, I began to wonder if the rest would come true."

"Prophecies can be dangerously self-fulfilling if we let them taint our thoughts," said Ada.

Punt shifted from foot to foot. Sepharia wanted to hear what Astrela had said. Like her aunt, she didn't believe in them, but she was curious.

Her desires were answered when Ada asked, "I'll bite. What was the prophecy?"

Punt wiped a hand across his bald head, knocking loose a few beads of sweat.  "There was something about crows and staffs and then she said there would be a great accident and afterwards, the pillars of Rome would shake."

Ada's eyebrow went up in mock amusement.  "And you believed the explosion with the first steam mechanic was our great accident?"

Punt met Ada's eyes and his posture grew less confident. "Well..."

"How many other accidents did we have last year? Last spring, didn't you blow up a crucible, throwing you across the foundry and nearly killing Plutarch?" she asked.

Punt scratched his head. "I'd forgotten about that."

"And what about the miracle we made for that little temple with the goat-legged god? Didn't a rotten timber nearly kill Plutarch when it snapped in half, sending the whole structure after him?"

"And that one, too. I guess," mumbled Punt.

"For that matter, didn't I have a reputation of bad luck from previous accidents?" she said, the amusement spreading quickly.

"Apologies, Master Heron," said Punt.

"No need, my friend," said Ada. "We have accidents because I'm constantly pushing the workshop to newer and untested designs. That's what's been causing the ill luck. It hasn't been luck at all, but just my stubbornness to keep pushing the edges, rather than capitalize on past success."

Sepharia had never thought of it that way, but it made sense. She'd also wondered in the past if they were cursed. The realization that Ada was right dawned on Punt, too.

"As for Rome shaking. They're worse than my workshop. The great Roman Empire strains itself regularly," she explained.

"Then I will push questioning thoughts from my mind."

Punt accepted Ada's offering of a clasped hand. "Questioning thoughts are always welcome in the House of Heron." Ada paused. "Just base them on your own eyes and ears rather than the tilting of bones."

Punt laughed and then a remembered thought appeared on his face. "Master Heron, I nearly forgot something."

Heron indicated he should continue.

"Our investigations, while you were at the Oracle. Plutarch learned nothing useful from the Magistrate and my wanderings only proved that nearly every temple in the city has some crescent shaped moon on their walls."

She nodded and Punt left with a sack of self-trimming lamps over his shoulder.

Ada turned to Sepharia once the blacksmith had left. "It's just us girls," she whispered. Plutarch had left while they were speaking with Punt.

"What now?" Sepharia asked.

Ada took her hand in her own. Her eyes sparkled with excitement. "Without that awful debt weighing us down and the wonder of the steam mechanic at our fingertips, we can do anything we please."

"Can you be Ada?" Sepharia whispered, and regretted it when her aunt's shoulders slumped slightly.

Ada shook her head. "Not here. The world is not ready for that."

"What about in the North? Agog told me that in his lands, women aren't only legally a hair above slaves. They have as much power as men," said Sepharia.

"Maybe, when we've accomplished our goals here, we can travel up to the North and visit. Then maybe I can be someone else." She paused in thought. "Though I'm not sure if I remember who that is."

"You like him," Sepharia said. "I've seen the way you look at him."

Ada shook her head. "I'm fascinated by him, but no. Not him. His heart is spoken for."

Sepharia could see the longing in her aunt's eyes. The resignation of her station and role in life.

Sepharia wondered if Ada believed the sacrifice was worth

it, so that she could create her inventions. But she dared not ask.

"He's gone anyway. Didn't have the courtesy to even say goodbye. Just took his machines and left," said Ada with a hint of anger. "And as Heron of Alexandria, I have much to do."

"He's gone for sure?" she asked.

Ada nodded. "He'd been restless to move on for weeks. Especially after the black stone arrived."

Ada jumped like she just remembered something important. She glanced to her desk and then back to Sepharia.

"What do you think he's going to do with those war machines?" Sepharia asked eventually.

"Hopefully take them far from Alexandria. If the Romans find out I've equipped a warlord with new technologies far superior to their own, they will come knocking on my door," said Ada.

A distant bell began to ring.

"That's odd. No bells are to ring at night," said Ada.

Sepharia agreed and then, as suddenly as the bell began to ring, it stopped.

"We should see what that is," said Ada.

A faint orange glow could be seen from the courtyard. Sepharia indicated it with an outstretched arm.

"Fire," Ada whispered.

"Let me go to the courtyard to look," said Sepharia.

Ada limped toward their living quarters. "I'll check from the upper floor. I hope it's not..." Her words trailed off, the concern obvious in Ada's eyes.

Sepharia ran to the courtyard. The orange glow was definitely a fire in the city. It was hard to tell exactly where it came from. The buildings blocked her view. At best,Y she gathered it centered in the Juden District.

Then she thought she heard a rumbling sound, like the sound of a heavy rain on a stone roof.

Up the street would be a better place to see the fire. She went to the gate, but paused when she heard distant shouting, like the sustained chatter of a gladiator arena waiting for the fight.

Her palms grew clammy. She hesitated.

Judging by the direction of the glow, her aunt wouldn't be able to see what was happening.

Sepharia unlocked the gate and went through.

She didn't make it five steps when men appeared out of the dark. A bag was slammed over her head.

"Who'd we get?" asked a rough voice.

Sepharia struggled against the hands, but they were too strong.

"His daughter," said a smooth voice full of silk. It had a strange accent she didn't recognize.

"Shall we go in and get the miracle worker?" the rough voice asked.

"I think not," said the silky one. "I'm not partial to going in that cursed place. Let him come to us. Plus, the streets aren't going to be a safe place much longer."

The silky one snickered and then Sepharia felt herself being picked up and thrown over a shoulder. She tried to throw the man's balance off by squirming, but he was much too strong.

As Sepharia was being carried away from the workshop, she shouted for help.

The man carrying her punched her in the head, silencing her as she reeled in pain.

Tears formed in Sepharia's eyes.

The only solace to her abduction was that when she'd shouted for help, she'd yelled "Heron" while thinking of Ada.

# 32

Heron's heart was relieved when she saw that the fire did not come from the Library. It seemed to originate in the Juden Quarter past the lake harbor, but she couldn't lean out the window further.

Still, fire in the city was dangerous and could eventually spread to the Library if not contained. She hoped the harbor and canal would help keep the fire in the Juden Quarter. She had little to fear for her workshop, being on the south side of the Library. If her workshop was in danger, then the city would be a cinder by morning.

What worried her were the other sounds of the night. The winds had ceased their usual bluster and from her perch she could hear metal ringing against metal, reflected from the stone buildings.

For a brief moment, she considered the Northman was involved, but that was ludicrous. Even with her war machines and the governor's depleted garrison, he couldn't field enough troops to take on a city the size of Alexandria.

Even if his armies hadn't been wiped out by the Romans, he couldn't get them south without alerting someone. Heron chuckled, amused by her own wild imagination.

Realizing she wasn't going to learn anything new from her window, Heron went to the courtyard. Sepharia might have a different idea of what was happening.

The open gate didn't immediately bring fear into her heart. At first, she assumed Sepharia had gone into the street for a better view of the fires and just wished she would have waited so they could speculate together.

Then, when she saw the shadow of a man standing in the open gate staring into her workshop, her heart seized with worry. Especially when a hint of purple fabric flashed across the opening as the man disappeared.

Limping toward the gate, her eye caught a locking nail lying on a timber. It was the closest thing to a weapon she could find on the way out, so she grabbed it and tucked it under her belt. The thin shaft of metal had a piece of string attached for temporarily pinning the nail into place and she used that to make sure it wouldn't slip from her belt.

Halfway across the courtyard, she heard Sepharia yell her name.

Heron hobbled faster.

She reached the gate in time to see a group of four men carrying a struggling form around the corner.

Heron followed.

Before the last man slipped around the corner, she thought she saw purple again.

And he'd glanced back toward her, as if the man wanted her to follow.

She had no choice but to do so.

At the corner, she hesitated, remembering she'd left the gate open. She had no worries about her neighbors, they knew enough to stay out from the incident with the Gaul mercs.

But the streets were beginning to fill with curious onlookers, wondering what the distant shouting and orangish-red glow was.

On the next street, Heron found she was falling behind Sepharia's abductors. They were two blocks ahead.

Only the moon from the cloudless night made it possible to see that far.

Moving east, she wished she still had her harnesses. The cane wasn't enough support for her to run and her knees were still weak.

Passing Pompey Avenue, she caught her first glimpses of fighting.

The avenue straddled the line between the Rhakotis District and the temples, going north to south. At the southern end, near the inner wall, flashes of steel and flame and a strange hulking shape drew her eye as she crossed.

Fearful to even pause or look away, lest she lose sight of Sepharia's abductors, Heron only caught brief imagines.

But as she ran she wondered if the hulking shape she saw looked like a huge metal lion.

She might have thought it was one of her steam chariots, except she'd never made one to look like a lion. She'd kept the designs simple so she could produce Agog's ambitious orders.

Her knees ached.

Heron switched hands with the cane. The handle had begun to rub a blister into her palm.

The group of four men turned down a distant street.

Heron was thankful Alexander had devised a logical city with long, straight avenues and streets. In any other city of tortured stone buildings built around the whims of the growing populous, she would have already lost them.

Heron pushed forward.

The streets were awakening. Torch light popped up at random intervals.

She had to get to the cross street the men had turned down soon. If they turned again, she'd lose Sepharia.

Heron was knocked over by a shape running out from an alleyway. Her cane was kicked away in the impact.

The man got up and ran before she could even figure out what had happened.

She crawled to the cane, disoriented. Along with her cane, she found a piece of papyrus in the dirt. She climbed to her feet, still clutching the papyrus.

Vertigo overtook her for a moment. Heron used the Lighthouse to orient herself to the chase. As she continued hobbling down the avenue, she mentally remarked how red and ominous the glow from the Lighthouse had been.

She made it to the street she thought they'd gone down. Glimpses of a man disappearing down another street caught her notice, but she didn't know if it was them.

The street they'd gone down was too close for it to have been the men. They had a bigger lead on her, especially with her being knocked down.

Her only hint was a flash of purple.

Yet, the only way she could have caught up was if they'd waited for her.

It dawned on her then that it was likely they were luring her onward using her niece as bait.

Heron considered going for help, but Punt's house was the other way and by the time she got back with him, Sepharia would be gone.

When she got to the next street, she made her way cautiously around the corner. It was empty.

The orangish-red glow of the fires had grown stronger during her chase.

The sounds of battle carrying over the city were clearer now.  A squad of Roman soldiers ran the other way behind her.

She'd been rushing through the streets so headlong, she'd barely paid attention to her location, but slowing to a walk, she knew where she was.

Temples lined the street going in both directions.  Places of worship could be found anywhere in the city, but the largest grouping was where she was standing.  It wasn't an official district, but it was called the Temple District by habit.

Heron had been in and out of almost all of them.   In creating miracles, or scouting the competition.

That the abductors had run to this region worried her. She'd been so focused into the chase, she hadn't considered why Sepharia might have been taken.

Walking through the temple district, she realized it had to do with her investigation into the fires.

The temples kept their fronts well lit, even during the night.

Heron remembered the parchment clutched in her hand. She held it up to the torch light.

It read: *"Caesar started the fires, Flaccus desires to finish the job, rise up and throw out the Romans."*

The message was written in Greek, Latin and Egyptian.

Heron thought to Hortio and his nobles.  Could they be bold enough to overthrow the Romans?  Didn't they know, even if successful, Rome would crush them mercilessly?

She shook her head.  It seemed improbable, but it explained the fires and the battle.  Looking down the street she saw other parchments lying in the dust.

Whoever had started it, had spread the pamphlets throughout the city.  Though most were illiterate.  In a city of scholars, there was always someone near enough to read.

Despite the importance of the mystery, Heron pushed its

consideration from her mind, she had a niece to find.

The marching of feet alerted Heron to the troop of Roman soldiers entering her street.

She was between lights, so she scurried to an alcove along a lesser temple. She fit herself beside a statue of a minor god with a face like a frog and a whip in one hand.

As she waited for the soldiers to pass, she realized another person was on the other side of the alcove.

"Apologies," she whispered in Egyptian. "I did not know anyone else was hiding here."

"No matter," came the reply in rough Egyptian. "Enough room for two to hide from them thieving Romans."

"What's going on?" she asked.

"We're throwing them out," he said. "Even the gods are on our side."

"The gods?" she asked.

The man made a grunt of firm commitment. "I saw one myself kill a whole squad of Roman soldiers. The beast growled and then they all fell dead one by one."

"Growled?" she asked, as what was probably the truth of his words dawning on her.

"Like the mythical manticore spewing its deadly spikes. I saw it with my own eyes," he said.

"Just the gods are fighting this war?" she asked, fearful of the answer.

"The nobles too and their allies. Big beastly men. I saw one myself. Just about pissed myself." The man paused. "They say even the *Michanikos* has thrown in with the revolution. That's a good sign."

That's a bad sign, Heron thought.

Whatever the result, she was now an enemy of the Roman Empire. She knew who the nobles' beastly allies were as well.

Agog was behind the war. She knew it by the man's

words. But how he thought he could take Alexandria from Rome was beyond her.

The soldiers had passed, so Heron ventured a question, "Friend, did you happen to see a group of men carrying a girl just a short time ago."

"Yes, I did," he said quickly. "They were a rightly strange group. They turned onto Hepta street. The one in purple robes kept checking backwards as if he were seeing if anyone was following. Except if they were, they'd surely find him, waiting like that."

Getting knocked down in the street and hiding from the soldiers had delayed her long enough that the man in purple robes, a priest likely, had probably thought she'd gotten lost.

That was a good sign. If they knew she was coming, she was at a disadvantage. If they thought she'd gone a different way or had been delayed, they wouldn't be expecting her. She had to hope.

"Thank you for your assistance," she said. "But I must be going."

He mumbled a common farewell.

Heron stopped before she got too far from the statue.

"Friend. If you'd like to earn a talent for your troubles. Go to Heron's workshop and wait there until someone arrives. When they do, let them know that Heron's daughter has been abducted and tell them to come to the temple district."

The man mumbled a response.

Heron took to the street, hobbling to Hepta street.

As soon as she was about to turn the corner, she knew exactly who had taken Sepharia.

Instead of turning down Hepta street, she went past. It would take longer, but she could circle around through the back alleys and approach the temple from the rear. Then she could surprise High Priest Ghet and rescue Sepharia from the

Temple of Nekhbet.

Heron raced up the street, as fast as she could manage, pushing herself though the pain as it shot up her thighs, making each step agony.

Then, before heading up the alley, Heron paused and looked down to her wooden cane and swollen knees.

She shook her head, deciding that she was a fool to think she could rescue Sepharia alone. But if she went to get Punt or the others, they would possibly move her.

The only way to save Sepharia was to go then, while they thought she wasn't coming and wouldn't be there yet with reinforcements.

The city was no safe place, either. There was no guarantee she could even get back to the workshop. The battle lines could move across her path and she'd be cut off. If Sepharia was going to have a chance, she had to go now.

Heron sighed heavily, imagining the sight of her assaulting the temple with only a wooden cane. She knew Agog would laugh.

But she was Sepharia's only chance.

# 33

The layout for the Temple of Nekhbet was a huge cathedral, surrounded by a labyrinth of lesser rooms and apartments for the priests, acolytes and slaves. The lower level, beneath the main worship chambers, held the sacred mysteries.

While the temple had fallen on hard times, it was still one of the oldest and grandest in the city. Newer temples were bigger, but they lacked the ornamentation and detail of the Nekhbet.

But the esthetic value of the building meant less to attracting followers than it had in the past. Heron had been a part of that change. Minor miracles and curiosities had always been a part of the temple retinue, but Heron had brought it to a higher level.

As Heron stood in the shadows of a nearby temple, scouting a way to enter, she considered the irony that her success as a miracle worker had created the conditions that had brought the Temple of Nekhbet low and she wondered if that factored into their abduction of Sepharia.

It'd been half a year since the disaster in the temple, but wooden scaffolding still clung to the front where the statue had fallen into it. The structural damage had been severe. The repairs appeared to be nearing completion.

During the setup, she'd been allowed in the side rooms and the upper chambers, but passages to the basement had been watched by temple guards.

She knew of three entrances. The first went through the main doors that only opened when a fire was lit in the brazier. There was no way she could open that door without alerting every temple on the street, even if she could find the wood.

The second was the secret door by the alcove. They had used that to enter and exit on a regular basis. But Heron knew they would be expecting her to enter that way.

Through the courtyard in back was the third entrance. The pulleys to lift the statue had ended at the well. There was no way to sneak up to that door and she assumed it was well guarded.

Heron wracked her brain trying to remember another way into the temple. She couldn't just stroll in and ask for her niece back. She had to find a way in.

Heron studied the north wall for windows on the upper floors that she could climb to, but none could be seen and she doubted her ability to scale the wall.

She thought about everything she knew about the temple layout. She was about to give up when she thought of a fourth way.

To make the main doors open, the brazier had to be lit, pushing air down a pipe and into a large vessel of water. If the diameter of the pipe wasn't too small, she might be able to fit.

The scaffolding was conveniently blocking the view of the brazier from the upper windows. Heron made her way through the shadows to the platform next to the stairs that held the brazier.

The burning bowl was as wide as she was tall. Ashes covered the bottom.

She put her shoulder into the bowl, pushing as much as her knees could take, but it didn't budge.

Frustrated, she slumped behind it and examined the skyline. A fiery glow blanketed the northeastern section of the city.

As she imagined the bucket brigades dousing the spreading fire, the wind shifted, bringing a chorus of steel from one street over. The smell of burnt stone assaulted her nose.

The new direction of the wind would make putting out the fires more difficult, especially while the battle was still raging.

Heron put aside thoughts of the fire. There was nothing she could do about it and Sepharia needed her.

She wanted to go to Agog's soldiers and solicit their help. With a squad of his Northmen, they could assault the temple and rescue Sepharia.

But she knew better than to rush off into a war expecting rationality. Archimedes, the inventor that had most influenced her, had been killed during the Siege of Syracuse by a Roman soldier, despite orders that he should not be harmed.

So she dismissed the idea of running for help and sighed heavily.

Heron tapped her fingers on the bronze brazier. Even though she hadn't made this particular miracle, she'd been the one to design it. She'd been hoping the constant fires had weakened the moorings on the brazier making it easy to knock loose.

She thought a while on the other weak points of the structure. She might be able to wrap a rope around it and use the scaffolding to leverage the bowl from its perch. But she didn't have a rope and she couldn't climb, anyway.

The hole at the bottom of the bowl would be an easy way through except she had devised a clever alternating iron vent that would allow air to pass through without getting clogged with ash.

A simple grate would have worked, except she'd been concerned slaves would fall through once the metal had been weakened from the constant flame.

The thought gave her an idea. She crawled around the base until she found the maker's mark. Stamped into the backside of the bowl was Philo's crescent moon paired with a hammer.

She climbed into the ankle deep ash and felt around with her cane. Then she cleared away a section, making a little depression in the ash. Satisfied, Heron took a deep breath and stomped down hard onto the grate.

The jarring pain nearly made her black out and she had to grab the edge to remain standing. After another deep breath and a second stomp, the grating snapped open. The ash drained around her ankles, disappearing into the hole at the center.

Philo had no concern for the lives of slaves, so when he'd copied her design, he'd use a cheap grate instead of her more expensive and complicated venting. For once, Heron was glad she'd lost a job to Philo the Maker.

Heron sat in the remaining ash with her feet in the hole. She wasn't so sure about the next part. The chamber beneath had to be able to collect pressure to push the water into a bucket. If she couldn't get out of the chamber then she'd likely drown or be stuck for days and possibly die down there.

She eyed the pile of timbers lying near the scaffolding. After a few minutes of hauling, she dropped two timbers into the hole. Each one made a splash and a *thunk*.

Heron lowered herself into the hole. The sides squeezed

her shoulders, but she was a slender build. She squirmed her way down the pipe, smearing ash along her body, until her lower half hung free.

After taking a deep breath, she pushed with her elbows. She hit the timbers with her ankles, cartwheeling her into the wall head first.

Her mouth opened, sending brackish water down her throat. Heron coughed and sputtered, half-climbing onto the timbers in a desperate attempt to stay above water. It had a thick, greasy feel from the constant ash and her eyes burned.

She tried to use a corner of her tunic to wipe her eyes, but not enough light from the moon slipped down the long tube. She coughed and gagged until she almost threw up.

Once her stomach settled and she spit enough times to get the large chunks from her mouth, she tried exploring the water chamber.

It was round and made of bronze. She felt around with her fingertips for an opening, standing on her tip-toes to keep her head above water. She cheered silently when she found the edge of the seal.

Heron repositioned the first timber to lay against the molded bronze. She climbed on the wood, which was a tricky feat since the ash had slimed the surface.

Then she pulled the second timber up and jammed it perpendicular against the wood. Carefully lying on her back, she pushed her feet against the upright timber, feeling the door bend beneath her back. The two timbers served as a pair of tongs, prying the door loose.

With a crack, she broke the seal open. Using the second timber to make a ramp, and after she'd rescued her cane from the murky depths, she climbed up and out of the chamber.

The platform beneath the opening made for a more graceful exit. The slaves needed it high enough to dump more water in.

She still couldn't see, but she remembered the layout from her previous time in the temple. Water dripped nearby and the strong smell of dampness made her steps careful. She tried not to imagine rats scurrying in the darkness.

With outstretched hands, she found the stairway and made her way to the top.

No one guarded the stairway, so Heron gained the main level without alarm. She reviewed herself in the dim candlelight flickering at the top of the stair. The previously white tunic was now dingy gray with streaks of black.

She squeezed her tunic until it was merely damp. She didn't want to leave a trail of drips as she searched.

The hallway split from her location as she tried to ignore the heady scent of burnt cinnamon. The temple must burn buckets of the incense daily.

The left passage led to the labyrinth of rooms housing the faithful. Far on the other side was a stairwell to the lower areas. Intuition told Heron that Sepharia would be kept below.

But she didn't want to creep through the rooms. There was no way she would make it through without being found. So she went right, in the direction of the main cathedral.

She knew a hidden passage lay in the center of the floor, so the priests could appear suddenly during a distraction and amaze the flock. They'd used the passage during her miracle, though the idiot priest had gotten overzealous and nearly brought down the building.

Heron was surprised to find the statue of Nekhbet standing in the center of the huge room amid a lattice of scaffolding. The vulture-headed god had been damaged from when it had heaved into the wall and it appeared progress on the repairs had recently stopped at the beak.

The structure looked surprisingly flimsy. She wondered

how none of the stone workers had been injured.

She was about to move in when a flicker of light alerted her to the approaching priests. Heron ducked into an alcove, clutching her cane defensively.

Either her stained tunic blended into the stone easily or the two young priests were too busy discussing the best ways to request a tithe to notice her. They passed a couple of steps from her hiding location.

Heron relaxed after they were gone and limped as quickly as she could to the hidden stairwell. Kneeling around on the floor behind the statue, she found the latch which opened the trapdoor. Heron dropped into the hole, grimacing from the short drop onto a stone platform.

The temple used an inelegant way of getting their priest into the cathedral quickly. Three acolytes would crouch where she was standing, holding up a wooden pillar while the priest balanced on top.

At the appointed moment, the priest would slide open the passage and they would thrust him upward. The pillar matched the flooring, completing the illusion that the priest had appeared from nothing.

Heron regretted her time working with the temple charlatans. She silently promised to atone her abetment of the temples by creating a city that didn't need them.

The lower chambers were a mystery to Heron. She'd never been beyond the top of the stairs.

She crept through the stone hewn passages, restraining the urge to use her cane, fearful of making a sound. Torch light was sparse, so she spent half the time creeping through the darkness.

The rooms were mostly storage for the sacraments and costumes of the priesthood. Heron thought about putting on a vulture-headed mask, but decided that would only make her more obvious and make it harder to escape, should she be spotted.

The hallways were painted with scenes of the temple's history, but the light was so dim, Heron couldn't make out the details.

Once she came upon a lighted passageway, past a room filled with dried incense, including the offending burnt cinnamon, and with paintings that immediately made her heart clench.

She'd found a duplicate scene on the walls at the Oracle of Ammon in which the line of robed men danced around an altar beneath a darkened moon. This painting had more detail and she was able to see a bloody sacrifice on the altar.

The sacrifice was a woman, carrying a scroll in one hand and a leafy branch in the other. The men around the altar wielded curved knives.

Seeing the duplicate painting connected many previously remote facts in a web that stretched wider than she first thought. Even the book dealer's death meant more now in retrospect than it had then.

The flicker of an approaching torch distracted her from further examination of the painting. Heron fled as fast as she could, each step a tiny grimace of pain.

She never saw the torch-bearer, but couldn't find her way back to the painting. A scene to the right, hidden by shadow, had promised more insight into the temple.

But investigating the fires wasn't why she'd come to the temple. She'd come to find Sepharia, and in her surprise, upon turning a corner, she found her.

Stretched across an altar, much like the one in the painting, lay Sepharia. Her chest appeared to be moving up and down, so Heron assumed she was alive.

Heron barely noticed the rest of the room, despite

alternating between horrible strangeness and unusual familiarity, as she hurried to Sepharia's side. Her niece was strapped to the altar with stained ropes.

Heron had one strap partially loosened when she heard footsteps from the hallway. She had barely scrambled behind the altar before torch light flooded the room.

When she heard the man's voice, one she knew very well, her surprise was immediate, but then as the other facts of the investigation slipped into place, it all made logical sense.

# 34

"Come out, Heron. Your entrance to the temple was not unnoticed. Our priests see beyond this mortal realm and cannot be fooled by mere trickery."

Heron froze, hoping for a second his call was a bluff, but in the instant after, she knew it wasn't by the surety of his voice.

She turned, using the time to examine the room closer. It was larger than she first thought. A dyed screen hid familiar shapes. The altar was made into the shape of a ziggurat.

The walls had been painted into a dramatic vista. They were surrounded by mountains under a night sky.

Five crimson pillars ringed the altar. Fantastic creatures were carved into the stone. Heron could see the shape of a shedu—a winged bull man. Examination of the others was lost as she turned to face her antagonists.

"Greetings, Philo," she said. "I should have known you were going to be lurking in the bowels of this temple."

"Greetings, Heron. You look to be the one rooting around

in bowels."

Philo stood beside the High Priest Ghet. Her rival wore an azure toga with black silk edges. He looked ready to welcome guests into a party.

Ghet drummed his obscenely long fingernails against his robe, studying her with near erotic focus.

"I told you, he would come if we took his daughter," said Ghet.

Heron glanced at Sepharia, unconscious on the altar. If she couldn't wake her, there would be no way to carry her out, even if she could overcome the two men.

"I didn't realize the temples trafficked in simple kidnapping," she said. "I thought you were into more widespread destruction, like the burning of the Great Library."

Ghet laughed playfully. "Have we finally made your list of suspects?"

"More than suspect, Ghet. The temple's fingerprints have been all over the fires and my investigation. You might have been better off had you not tried to interfere," she explained.

Ghet sneered. "Even by your words, I can tell you have not fully comprehended the depth of your problems."

"Then elaborate," she said.

The two men blocked the only entrance from the chamber. The high priest had a curved dagger in his belt. Philo appeared unarmed.

"You are our guest. You first," he indicated her with outstretched fingernails.

Philo watched with casual amusement.

She needed more time, so she took his indulgence. "Fine." Then she stopped, glancing upward. "First, your priests did not *see beyond the mortal realm* in my coming here. When I dropped into the water chamber, I displaced enough water to open the doors."

She regretted not seeing that problem before, but she'd nearly drowned herself and all-encompassing thought had gone out the window. There was nothing to do about it now.

Philo chuckled and clapped his hands once, as if she were a child telling a first joke. "You see, Ghet. I told you he was of quick wit. It'll be a shame really."

His sideways glance was hate filled. She paced in front of the altar, using her cane to steady.

"The fires were started by one of your acolytes, posing as a scribbler or other such minor functionary in the Library. It might have been more than one, but the word was given to start the fires during the heat of battle. It was only luck that Caesar started his own fire, masking the one set by your people," she said.

"You say that as if I were alive then," said Ghet, tapping his fingernails against his chest. "Unless you think me a powerful necromancer extending my life through a pact with the dead."

"You or your temples. It's all the same. Whether it happened one hundred years ago or that you plot it again matters not," she said.

"Ah, yes," he said wistfully. "It would be great fun to wipe out another swath of the Library. Shame the fire protections are more stringent now, or that we didn't know of this battle before it started. We can't let the people see us tip our hand."

Heron breathed a silent sigh of relief. She'd been concerned about another fire in the Library during the battle, but his confession quelled her concerns.

"So you admit it," she said.

Sepharia seemed to be thrashing lightly as if waking from a bad dream. Philo stood where he began with his hands clasped behind him. Ghet had moved closer, hand on hilt.

"What does it matter if I admit it," he said. "You won't survive the night and even if you did, you have no proof of your accusation. No Magistrate would ever consider it." He paused. "But I am curious how you knew it was our acolytes in the Library."

Heron nodded. "When I was performing your miracle in the temple, I recalled seeing an acolyte with ink stained fingers like the scribblers. It was an odd sight."

Ghet played with the dagger in his belt, narrowing his eyes. "Yes, I suppose it is."

"And in the Library, I have passed scribblers that reeked of burnt cinnamon," she explained.

Ghet laughed. "That particular incense is rather strong."

"The rest is so obvious and heavy handed it's laughable," she said, hoping for a reaction. When none came, she continued, "The prophecy from the Oracle at Ammon was clearly a plant as were the hag's words that sent me in that direction. Did you think me that blind?"

She spun around, pointing the cane at them. "How long have you been guiding the wheels of history using your Oracles? Are they all yours?"

Ghet tried to act nonchalant about her accusations but she could see in his tensed shoulders that she hit squarely on the mark. Philo wasn't a much better actor and practically choked on her last comment.

"You had your thugs attack me in the streets, your assassins kill the book dealer trying to throw me onto the scent of the Carthaginian cult," she said. "Everything you did practically led me to you."

"But yet you know nothing about us," said Ghet in a practiced flippance that Heron saw right through.

"I know everything about you," she said, keeping the point of the cane firmly trained on Ghet. "You are not the Temple of Nekhbet. You are the Cult of Ur from ancient Sumer."

Before, Ghet seemed to accept her accusations cheerfully,

as if he expected them and he was a cat, merely playing with her, the mouse.

At the word *Ur* he stiffened and his fingers that had been teasing the hilt of his dagger, grabbed it angrily. Philo looked equally shocked though less dangerous.

Ghet glared at her with murderous intent. "How long have you known?"

Heron let her cane drop to the floor. "Truthfully, only this evening. It wasn't until I saw the mountain altar painting on your catacomb walls, the same scene I witnessed in the Oracle, that my mind first whirled around the idea. Add this altar, clearly shaped into the Ziggurat of Ur, and I could see nothing else."

Philo nodded appreciatively, as if he were a fellow scholar listening to an enlightening lecture. Ghet's eyes bounced around the room, clearly wondering what other secrets Heron could uncover.

"You see, under my long tenure as chief miracle maker of the temples of Alexandria, I have, unfortunately, become an expert on the religions of our time," she explained.

Sepharia made a soft moan. Heron turned, faking a moment of deep thought, when actually she scoured the room for a more formidable weapon than her wooden cane. With nothing in sight, she decided to make a play for the object behind the screen, though making use of it would require clever maneuvering.

"Interestingly enough," she continued. "The book dealer tried to clue me into your attack by pulling out a book from his shelves while he died called *Sumerian Myths*. I've read the book before, recalling mention of an ancient cult from Ur that sought to gain power through hidden means."

Ghet cleared his throat. "Our intentions are not to gain power, but to protect the sight of Man from the illusions of knowledge."

Heron leaned on her cane. "Yet you use knowledge in the form of illusions to hold onto your power? Your words are a dry scroll to the flame of my logic."

Ghet puffed himself up. "If you stare directly into the sun, your eyes will become burned out. Only by seeing the reflected light by the moon can we safely view the knowledge given by the gods."

"So knowledge is only safe through the filter of the temples?" she said, practically spitting the words out and then turned to Philo. "How can you be a part of that, Philo? While you're a snake and a cheat and lack an original bone in your body, you are still an inventor and a scholar."

Philo appeared not affected by her insults. "But I bow to the wisdom of the temples. They are right in their prudence. Look at the numerous accidents you've had pushing the boundaries of this knowledge. My path is the safer path."

"Lies," she said. "You might as well tie the yoke around your head and bend thine arse to them."

Philo's lip curled in anger. She didn't want either of them thinking logically if she were to escape. But she hoped she hadn't pushed them too far.

Heron wandered over to the screen, checking back with her antagonists to make sure they hadn't moved closer. Philo had a sanctimonious smile on his face.

"I see you've found your work," said Philo, mocking her as he moved the screen for her to see.

One of her steam mechanics had been hooked to a torture device—the rack. She'd seen Lysimachus use a rack in Pompey's square before. The victims' arms and legs were pulled in opposite directions until the joints separated from the body. The screams of the victims were haunting.

Heron glanced back toward the passage. The way out of

the room was clear, but there was no way she could outpace the two men with her ruined knees, nor carry the tethered Sepharia.

Philo leaned over and sparked a flint which caught the oil pot on fire beneath the water chamber. "It was quite troublesome to come upon another one of these once you blocked my purchases."

"And with good reason," she said. "My steam mechanic is meant to free man from the tyranny of slavery, not torture him for the gods' amusement."

"You mistake my purpose," said Philo as he whipped a sheet from a nearby table, revealing a host of knives and other jagged implements. "I seek knowledge of a different sort. While you are my teacher in the arts of the mechanical," he bowed, "your knowledge of the inner workings of Man pales beneath my sun."

"So you whore yourself to the temples in exchange for bodies to experiment upon?"

"Live ones," he said, raising his eyebrows at her. "For I seek to understand how the body works much in the same way I dissect your miracles once you have thrown them away."

Philo turned to her with outstretched arms. "Soon I will be presenting the Great Library with a series of tomes titled *Man, An Exploration*."

He moved closer to Heron, smiling wickedly. "No longer will Heron of Alexandria's name be spoken on the lips of her citizens. Instead, they will speak of Philo of Alexandria, the greatest scholar of the body physiks."

Ghet tilted his head, listening to distant noises. "I must go up and check on the state of the war for Alexandria. That pesky Northman of yours has created quite a stir."

Heron thought she was to be left with the unarmed Philo, when Ghet snapped his fingers and two temple guards appeared and restrained her.

The cane was stripped from her and in short order, she was strapped to the contraption, her arms and legs splayed out and constrained by manacles.

The steam mechanic had roared up to speed, requiring Philo to shout above its noise. "I can't wait to peer into your magnificent brain."

The tides had turned so quickly, Heron barely had time to catch her breath. One moment she was planning escape using her greatest invention to foil her captors, the next she was strapped to an ancient iron torture device waiting for the cruel attentions of her captor.

Heron looked up.

Philo held a short bladed paring knife over her.

# 35

Heron tried not to imagine the knife cutting into her flesh, but her mind saw the possibilities of his work too keenly. She closed her eyes, but that didn't help, either.

Then, she turned her head away from Philo, who had changed his mind about his knife and had gone back to rearranging his implements.

Sepharia had woken and stared wide-eyed back at her. If it wasn't bad enough that Philo would cut her apart while she still lived, her niece would be forced to watch, too.

Heron clenched her eyes shut, indicating to Sepharia to do the same. Once she had, she cleared her throat, which was harder than she thought, stretched across the metal rack.

"Philo," she said as calmly as she could. "What are your plans for my daughter?"

Philo looked up from his table and glanced over his shoulder at Sepharia on the altar. He'd been opening a leather bound book to a blank page.

"Don't worry. She's the temple's property. It'll be a quick

death," he said as if he were offering a favor.

Heron quieted. At least she would be spared the pain and agony Heron was about to experience.

"There," he said, settling comfortably on his stool. "Now where shall we start? Maybe a bit of more knowledge of the knee. I'm curious how the damage appears to the eye."

When the knife bit into her flesh, it was like a hot flame had been set to it. She wished she could have stayed quiet, to spare Sepharia the horror, but she found her voice betraying her in high screams.

Heron blacked out for a moment and came to, with Philo dabbing away blood from the bloody flower that was now her knee.

"Let's see how that looks when we apply pressure," he said, detached.

Philo activated a lever on the steam mechanic, initiating a gear that connected to the manacle on her leg. The chain pulled her leg taut until it felt like her knee would dislocate.

Heron blacked out at least twice more during the investigation of her knee. When she came to the third time, he was sewing up her knee and the chain had been loosened.

Philo gave her a sip of water from a cup that she drank from greedily. Her throat was dry from screaming.

Heron was relieved when Philo hunched over his book and began scribbling notes and sketches. An absurd thought crossed her mind, wondering what Philo would make of her gender once the truth was exposed. At least the insult that he'd been bested by a woman would be worth it.

"Is there anything I could offer that would get you to free my daughter?" she asked, gritting her teeth through the pain.

Philo made an amused grunt. "I told you, she's not mine to give. She's to be sacrificed in a few days."

Heron glanced at Sepharia to see her working on the

binding that she'd loosened. They'd used ropes on her, so there was a chance of escape. Heron was glad that Philo's back was to the altar.

"What if I offered a new design that was going to revolutionize the world?" she said. "A design so amazing it makes my steam mechanic a mere toy."

Philo's raised eyebrow betrayed his interest. "Go on."

Heron didn't actually have a new design in mind. She just had to hold his interest.

She wracked her brain for an idea she could confide. A design she read about in the Library sparked an idea. "It's...a machine...that can count."

Philo immediately laughed. "Why, that's absurd. You have no such device in mind. You're just stalling."

"No," she said, more confidently this time, the idea gathering speed like a stone rolling down a hill. "You are familiar with the Heavens Mechanism used by the Rhodes Astronomical Society for calculating the positions of the heavens?"

"Of course, don't count me a fool."

"Then, you would know a similar design could, with a series of inputs, relay calculations powered by the steam mechanic in iterations beyond man's capability, allowing us to even greater works," she said, hoping to pique his curiosity.

She wasn't entirely sure how such a device would work, but she knew enough that she could probably work it out given time. She hoped Philo would give that time to her.

"In addition," she said. "I will be as a cooperative a patient as possible. For the enumeration of knowledge."

The last part seemed to seal the deal and Philo clapped his hands together, eyes twinkling with import.

He stood, surveying his meager table and book. "With that design, they would name me the greatest of all inventors."

He rubbed his chin. "How large is such a device?"

Heron kept her eyes from glancing at his book. "A meter on two sides and twice as tall."

"Yes," he said. "I would imagine that a device like that would be rather large, dwarfing even the Heavens Mechanism."

He took a few steps away. "Well, I shall have to put our current investigation on hold while I have the acolytes bring down a larger table with the appropriate sketching implements."

Philo smoothed his pristine toga. "The wonders of this day never cease. I'll be back in a bit," he paused with a grin on his face. "Don't go anywhere."

As soon as Philo left the chamber, Sepharia began struggling on the altar. Heron tried to get loose herself but the manacles were inescapable.

It seemed to take forever, but eventually Sepharia got one arm free. Once she had that, she was able to work the other arm free and then the legs.

Sepharia grasped at the iron manacles frustrated. Tears immediately formed in her eyes.

"I can't get you free," she said.

"Don't worry, daughter," Heron offered, feeling closer to Sepharia than she ever had. "I can get loose and then we'll escape together."

"But how?" Sepharia said, wiping a tear with a forearm.

"Go to the rooms up the passage and find a length of rope at least one meter long," said Heron.

Sepharia left immediately. The silence after her niece left, even with the steam mechanic chugging along, was unbearable. She kept expecting Philo to return with a handful of guards and Sepharia held captive. Their deal would be off the table then and he would likely torture the design out of her. He might be planning that anyway, for all she knew.

Sepharia returned eventually with a long coil of rope.

"Cut a one meter length, tie the one end to my wrist manacle and the other to the pulling mechanism for my leg," she explained. "And they have to be tight."

While her niece was busy, Heron wondered if she was going to rip her arm and leg off in trying to escape. She had no other choice but to try.

With the rope cutting across her chest, pulling the wrist manacle toward her leg, she said, "Now engage the leg, slowly and be ready to switch it off once the manacle breaks."

She hoped the thin pin holding the iron around her wrist would break before the rope. The rope appeared to be sturdy.

Sepharia engaged the leg puller, which yanked on her wrist manacle. It wasn't budging.

Heron glanced toward the door, worried Philo would return any moment.

"More power," she said.

Sepharia engaged the lever another notch. The rope and manacle were both straining. She willed the pin to break.

"More," she shouted, setting herself for when one or the other broke. If the rope broke, it would yank her leg from its socket. If the manacle broke and Sepharia didn't switch the lever in time, it would pull her arm down and probably break it. As the mechanic wailed with worry, the manacle finally broke and Sepharia slammed the lever.

"Now the other arm. Use a second rope to make sure the ropes win," she said.

Sepharia tied the two ropes and they broke the manacles in order with minimal damage to Heron's body. Her wrists and ankles were bloody from when the manacle snapped, but it was a wound well worth the cost.

Before they left the room, they each grabbed knives from the table. Heron grabbed Philo's book after a moment of hesitation.

Then Heron realized they would have a difficult time escaping the temple. They couldn't really shimmy back up the hole in the brazier and all the other entrances were guarded.

Heron looked at the steam mechanic and then the rope and had an idea. She tied the end of the original rope, which was at least a couple hundred feet long, around the pulling mechanism. She also added more oil to the flame, worried it was losing power.

Then she gave the rope to Sepharia and they wound their way to the secret entrance into the cathedral. They still had plenty of slack by the time they reached it.

Heron hoisted Sepharia up through the hole, grimacing from the pain in her flayed knee. Once above, Sepharia tied the rope around the base of the statue, interweaving it with the scaffolding.

"Tie it around the mid-section," she whispered as loud as she dared. "Get off as soon as it's done. I'm throwing the lever."

Sepharia nodded and began climbing the scaffolding. Heron left the secret entrance to return to the sacrificial chamber. Limping back into the room using her cane, Heron found Philo standing near the steam mechanic with a knife in his hand ready to cut the rope.

She reacted immediately lunging toward him, but she would reach him too late. Her knee buckled from the strain, tearing the wound open.

Falling to her knee, she threw the cane at him. It spun through the air and struck him in the face. He dropped the knife and Heron scrambled toward him.

She dove onto him as he grabbed his knife, knocking him to the stone and pinning his arm under her leg. Blood ran out her knee over the both of them as they struggled. Neither were real fighters and their efforts were clumsy.

Even though Heron was on top, Philo was the stronger and she had multiple injuries. He eventually maneuvered on top, though she managed to keep his knife away using her hand and a leg.

But as he gained leverage, his hand broke free of hers and he thrust the knife up between her legs, victory apparent on his face. When the knife blade hit her wooden genitalia instead of soft flesh, his face turned sour. Heron used the moment of confusion to wrestle her other arm free.

She plunged her knife into his belly.

That she was a woman slowly dawned on his face as he died beneath the blade.

Heron clambered to her feet and engaged the lever. The rope pulled out the slack and began straining. The mechanic had been pinned to the floor. The steel whined under the pressure.

Sepharia better be clear of the statue, she thought. Heron grabbed the book and her cane with bloody fingers and stumbled back to the hidden passage.

Suddenly, the rope jerked forward and she heard a horrible crash, shaking the walls and knocking Heron from her feet. She hoped the statue had knocked a hole big enough for them to escape.

After throwing the book and cane up the hole, she climbed the rope. Her hands were slick with blood so she wiped them on her stained tunic before pulling herself up. With Sepharia's help she was able to make it out of the hole.

The statue had broken through the wall and a faint orangish glow peeked through. The walls looked fragile enough so the whole structure might fall soon.

Sepharia ran ahead. Heron reached down to pick up the book which lay next to the knife Sepharia had dropped. Heron had left hers in Philo's belly.

306   Thomas K. Carpenter

She was about to limp after Sepharia when she was tackled. Ghet had plunged a knife into the book as she'd turned. Heron yelled to get Sepharia's attention but the noise of falling stone covered her shouts. The knife impaled book lay a length away.

Heron kneed him between the legs, doubling him over. He grabbed her with his long fingernails, cutting her arm.

Ghet slammed his forearm across her face. Heron tried to fend off his blows but her arms were weak from blood loss. She glanced around for the knife, but it was out of reach.

Ghet's leg pressed against her knee, sending shoots of pain through her head. Heron flailed around for a weapon.

Then she remembered the pinning nail in her belt. She kicked him again between the legs, and used the moment to pull the nail free.

Heron looped the string from the nail around Ghet's belt while he punched wildly. Then she drove the nail through the taut rope. After another kick to the groin, she wriggled free and dove for the knife. Ghet grabbed the other knife and started moving to his knees, not realizing what Heron had done.

In one quick motion, Heron sliced the rope, which had been straining between the statue and the steam mechanic.

The rope snapped, and since Ghet was connected to the rope via the pinning nail, it yanked the high priest of Ur from his feet toward the hole. Stretched out on his back, Ghet couldn't fit into the hole and the belt squeezed his middle.

Heron turned away from his screams, grabbing the book and her cane and limped across the cathedral. Halfway there, a sickening crunch and gurgle ended the screams.

Heron and Sepharia scrambled through the stones together, dust blinding them until they made it to the stairs only to hear the tell-tale sound of Roman crossbows clicking into place.

# 36

Heron wiped the dust from her face, leaning heavily on Sepharia and the cane. Blood ran down her leg in rivulets. Ash stained her tunic and skin. Her joints felt like mashed roots and any moment, the temple behind her would come crashing down.

"I'd be careful," she said to the soldiers. "All who touch me come to ruin."

The dust and blood half-blinded her, so she used a corner of Sepharia's toga to wipe her eyes. Her ears still rang with the sounds of falling stone.

The heavy guffaws began from a deep voice far to her right and caught quickly with the rest, until the whole group of soldiers was laughing.

With her eyes clear, Heron began to see that they were not Roman soldiers, though they carried their crossbows.

"Using that curse to your advantage?" said Agog.

Agog leaned against the controls of his steam chariot, arms crossed, face tinted with soot and split wide with laughter.

The chariot he rode on had been fashioned into a mythical manticore, with her rapid arrow launcher as the spiked tail. A stocky bald Egyptian manned the tail.

The Northmen lowered their crossbows.    Agog was attended by three steam chariots and a squad of twenty well-armed men. A horse pulled wagon with supplies waited behind the chariots ready to resupply fuel for her steam mechanics.

Heron could see by the Northmen's eyes they'd been fighting all night. Most had small wounds and their weapons were bloodied, but they appeared in good spirits.

"Looks like your Master Heron didn't need us after all," Agog said to his gunner.

Heron recognized Punt.

"What are you doing there?" she asked.

Punt shrunk, glancing sheepishly downward.

"Don't be shy, Punt," said Agog. "It was you that led us here."

Heron remembered the man in the shadows. She didn't think he'd actually try to find her.

"Did you pay him a talent?" she asked.

"Yes, Master Heron," said Punt, still staring at his feet.

"Don't be that way, Punt. You've saved me a long walk across the city," she said, grinning.

Punt glanced up, a hint of a smile on his face.

"Speaking of the city," she said. "How goes your war, Agog?"

A different Northman spoke to Agog. He had an angled nose that had been broken in the past and a leather bag hanging around his neck.

Agog glanced to Heron and laughed.

"What did he say?" she asked.

"Jarngard says he thought you'd be much larger," chuckled Agog.

Heron and Sepharia climbed down the steps. Chunks of stone were still falling. Heron caught the glances her niece garnered from the soldiers.

"We're just rooting out pockets of Roman soldiers," said Agog, answering her earlier question. "The city is ours."

Agog helped her up to the steam wagon. There was enough room for her and Sepharia to ride behind Agog.

"It was just that easy?" she asked.

"No," said Agog grimly. "We'll still have to deal with Flaccus' troops when he returns in two days' time, but our superior technology will ensure a crushing victory."

Agog engaged a lever and the chariot moved forward. Sepharia made a concerned noise and knelt down to attend Heron's knee. She ripped cloth from her toga and began binding it to stop the blood loss.

"Don't you have other pressing duties than playing caravan to a tired and bloody engineer?" she asked.

Agog glanced back with an eyebrow raised. "Without you, this conquest would have been laughable. You have not seen your steam chariots in action. The revered Roman soldiers broke and ran like fodder when we first charged them, spewing arrows from our tails like rain."

As they exited the street, a great clamor erupted behind them. They all turned to see the Temple of Nekhbet fall in upon itself, sending a plume of dust from the wreckage.

Agog motioned for them to continue. The soldiers jogged easily next to the chariots as they moved through the city.

"So I feel it a great honor to carry the architect of this war back to his workshop," he said. "And making sure he gets there in one piece. There are still bands of Roman soldiers causing havoc."

"But how did you come upon Punt?" she asked.

"It was my intention to send a band of soldiers to guard your workshop, but when the winds shifted last night and carried the fire past our breaks, we had to protect the buildings."

"Last night?" she asked, bewildered.

"Yes, it's morning," he said and with an outstretched arm indicated the orangish glow on the horizon.

"Plato have pity, I thought that was the fires still," she said, then after a pause, "so those fires were yours?"

Agog nodded. "We set them in the Juden Quarter to draw the soldiers out. Mostly they were for show, but the swirling winds created problems once the fighting broke out. The last thing we need is to be blamed for another fire at the Great Library."

Despite her exhaustion, Heron felt a great anger well up. It didn't help that Ghet had told her of the cult's intention to use the distraction to burn the Library again.

"Are you a complete imbecile? Risking the entire treasure of knowledge stored within the Great Library for your petty war? If the fire had gotten lose, we could have lost everything! You're just like Caesar!" she shouted.

Heron might have gotten up and pointed in his face, except that Sepharia was still tending her knee.

She could tell Agog wasn't used to being called an imbecile or being compared to Caesar. His eyes burned with fury for a moment and then he narrowed his gaze at her.

"The fires were small and mostly for show and that's why we started them in the Juden Quarter, so if they got loose, the harbor and canal would protect the rest of the city. Your precious Library was safe," he said.

They rode the rest of the way to the workshop in silence. Heron felt bad for yelling at him, but she was angry at his foolishness.

The Library was the only thing that helped keep the people like Ghet at bay. It was the only hope man had for the future.

The knowledge contained within the Library was everything.

Agog left her at the workshop with a dozen Northmen and Jarngard, who he regarded as one of his lieutenants.

The first thing the broken-nosed northerner did when he reached her workshop was open the pouch around his neck and dump a few dice into the dirt and laugh at the results, glancing around the workshop with a maniacal grin.

Heron limped into the workshop without her cane which had been forgotten on the steam chariot. Plutarch welcomed her and immediately moved her to a comfortable location so he could tend her wounds.

Once her knee had been resewn and the events of the evening retold, Heron had Sepharia draw up a hot bath. While she waited, she ate breads and cheese shoved into her hands by her foreman, claiming she might die from malnutrition.

Finally she sunk into her bath, with Sepharia guarding the door, since they now had Northmen patrolling around her workshop.

The dust and the blood from the night's events washed from her skin, but she knew their imprint never would.

# 37

Agog defeated Flaccus' troops upon the plains outside the city easily. The Governor fled north toward Rome. Agog let him go because he wanted the Empire to know fully the method of their defeat.

Heron knew this through her discussions with Jarngard while she was sequestered at her workshop. Agog's lieutenant knew only a smattering of Latin and what he did know was mostly crude sayings and anatomical ways to fornicate with a horse.

Jarngard was always laughing. He began every statement with an uptilted laugh. He learned more Latin while she waited to be called on by the new Satrap at the Royal Palace.

Agog knew enough not to call himself King of Alexandria. The people would never stand for it. They were excited about being freed from the Roman yoke, especially through the inventions of her favored son, Heron.

It was enough for them to accept Agog, for now. Though she found Jarngard did not call him Agog. That seemed to be a name he'd taken during his time in Alexandria.

Jarngard called him Wodanaz. She knew enough of his language to know his references made Agog, or Wodanaz, the King of Kings in his lands.

When Heron pressed Jarngard on the subject of his King, he just laughed at her and pulled out his dice.

Heron found his dice as strange as his constant laughter. He threw them constantly, taking some guidance from the numbers shown.

Heron was able to communicate with Jarngard on one important item. Though, it took half a day to figure out enough words to understand. Heron had wanted to know the reason why Agog had taken the city of Alexandria, when it was far from his home.

When Jarngard had finally understood her question, he nodded grimly. She reasoned from his gestures and smattering of Latin words, that he had taken Alexandria as a weregild. The Romans believed in equal justice, based on the Babylonian codes of old.

The Northerners were different. They placed a monetary value on their crimes. Heron had heard of a weregild before. She thought its elegance made the Northerners more civilized than most thought. The blood feuds of the deserts could carry on for generations, while a weregild was paid and done.

Agog had claimed Alexandria from the Romans as his weregild for the killing of his wife and people. It was a steep price for a whole people and she would have thought him mad if he'd ever told her his plans. Heron had thanked Jarngard once she'd finally understood.

The anointing of the Satrap would occur in a few days time and Heron chafed at the waiting. She was forbidden to leave the workshop, though Plutarch and the others were allowed. Jarngard indicated that Roman assassins still lurked in the city and until they'd been rooted out, she had to stay in the workshop.

Heron didn't believe the reason. But she couldn't convince Jarngard, no matter how she tried. Even Plutarch and Punt seemed to be on Jarngard's side, arguing for her to stay safe.

Her wounds were healing, though she suspected she'd be permanently wedded to her cane. She had a few made for her while she waited, though none of them felt right. She liked the one she'd left under the rubble at the Temple of Nekhbet.

Of the Cult of Ur, there was no further mention. For all she knew, Philo and Ghet were the only ones privy to her knowledge of them. Still, she knew that was improbable. The cult had been around for millennia and was patient beyond the ages of time.

If she was able to exert any influence once the coronation was complete, she would have the Library vet its acolytes and sages more carefully. They would have to double their protections of the valuable information, maybe even copying the Library to hide in another location. That would be her first request to Agog once she got the chance to talk to him.

While she waited, the workshop had been busy making new steam chariots and arrow launchers, but Heron barely paid attention, letting Plutarch manage the daily work.

Since the battle, Heron hadn't put ink to paper, lacking the urge to create for the first time in her life. She hadn't even touched the lotus powder, despite having a full box.

When the coronation came, Heron wore a simple tunic. Her hair had been cut short as it had grown suspiciously long. Despite her friendship with Agog, she dared not let down the illusion of her gender.

Her twin's token lay against her chest, under the fabric of her tunic. It felt heavy against her heart. She touched it often that morning while she waited for the steam chariot to arrive.

Sepharia wore a burgundy ionic chiton with a bright saffron belt cinching the waist. Heron would have never picked that dress for her, but she'd sent Plutarch in her place without proper instruction.

At the appointed time, Jarngard led Heron to a vehicle that she couldn't classify as a chariot. It was three times as large as a chariot with two steam mechanics powering it and a large store of chipped wood on the back.

Gilded metal plates had been hammered into various visages of the gods and displayed along the sides, including a couple that Heron recognized as northern ones. A thin cotton awning protected the occupants from the sun. It was an Egyptian Nile barge brought to land.

Heron climbed up the stairs and took a seat on the bench behind the driver. Sepharia sat to her right and Jarngard to her left. At least another twenty people could ride with them. A wooden wall had been placed between the steam mechanic and the benches, providing a quieter space to talk.

Plutarch and Punt had already gone ahead to help with preparations, so the three rode alone.

Heron found it awkward to sit next to Jarngard without speaking so she asked in a smattering of Latin and Germanic, "Do you miss your family?"

Jarngard squinted and then nodded, as he processed her words. "Dead," he said with his characteristic grin and laugh.

Then she remembered Agog's story about the battle with the Romans. She'd forgotten that they'd all lost their families.

Heron grabbed Sepharia's hand. The city passed by them at a comfortable pace. It had a less frantic, compact feel than it had before, like a great load had lifted from its shoulders. The colors burned brighter and the smiles had returned to the people's faces.

"I wish he could be here with us," she whispered,

comfortable that Jarngard wouldn't be able to understand them and the driver couldn't hear them. "You deserve to have your father see you like this."

Sepharia peered up, shaking her flaxen hair from her face. Even with the hint of sadness, she was a beautiful young woman.

"You don't have to say that, Heron," said Sepharia with particular emphasis on her twin's name.

"I understand this has been so hard on you. Since you've been in my care, I've done nothing but keep you locked in the workshop. I've been a horrible aunt," Heron said.

Sepharia squeezed her hand, shaking her head. "Don't say that. You're not my aunt."

Heron recoiled at first, misunderstanding her niece's words.

"When your twin gambled away his profits, you were the one to work on the designs late at night so the workers would have something to do in the day," said Sepharia. "When they killed him for his debts, you took his name and his place, sacrificing your life to make sure we were safe."

"How do you know this? You were too young," said Heron. She'd never intended for Sepharia to learn that her father had been a gambler.

"I figured it out from the accounting ledgers, though I was too mad at you to understand at the time. All I've ever done is make your life miserable as you've tried to protect me," said Sepharia with downcast eyes.

"It's not fair that you lost your father, and I'm sorry I can't be one for you," Heron told her.

Sepharia squeezed her hand again, almost so hard it hurt. "No, Heron," she said again, with heavy emphasis on the name. "You are my father. Not him. You've protected me all these years. You came for me when Ghet took me. You're not

Ada to me any longer, you are Heron. My father."

Heron's heart swelled with those words. Her eyes threatened to tear. She was thankful that Jarngard was too busy ogling the Egyptian women waving to them as they passed.

Heron clutched her twin's token with her free hand. Sepharia leaned on her shoulder for the remainder of the journey.

Despite the cheering crowds that grew as they approached the Royal Palace, Heron remained clutched to her daughter's hand.

With Sepharia's approval, it was easy to think of her as a daughter. In that moment, she knew she'd been longing for that connection with Sepharia. Due to her circumstances, she would never get to have children of her own, so Sepharia was the only child she would ever have.

The steam barge jerked to a halt. A formal Egyptian guard escorted them to the Palace. She'd never been to this section of the city, being of low birth.

The Palace waited on the Lochias promontory. Alexandrians cheered as they walked the hill to the inner wall. The Palace was a site of marble and gilded decadence. Egypt had long been one of the richest countries in the world. A reason for its repeated conquest.

They passed the great theatre and went through the agora, the place of assembly. Free standing colonnades ringed the agora's stadium seating. A high platform denoted the place the King or Satrap might address the land holders.

By the end, Heron barely noticed the opulence as she leaned heavily on her cane and Sepharia's shoulder.

When they finally reached the Inner Palace, Plutarch greeted them with open arms.

"It's good to see a daughter support her father," he said

with a twinkle in his eye.

Heron shared a secret smile with Sepharia. Even Plutarch could see their long troubles ended.

"Dear Sepharia, you look quite delicious in that outfit," grinned Plutarch.

"You did your job too well, my trusted foreman," intoned Heron. "I'm afraid I won't be able to hide her any longer from the eyes of the city."

Plutarch threw a casual swirl of his hand. "A flower needs light to bloom and this one has been in the dark too long."

"Is that a criticism?" asked Heron, narrowing her eyes at him.

Plutarch stiffened with faux-horror, "No, No. Just an unfortunate result of circumstance."

They paused and then broke into laughter. Jarngard had been trying to follow their conversation and just shook his head in confusion.

Heron stepped forward and gave Plutarch a hug. "Thank you, for everything."

After the hug, Plutarch stepped back and bowed with great flourish.

"If only Punt were here," Heron lamented.

Behind her came a gruff clearing of the throat.

"Ah Punt, my master of the foundry," she said.

Punt shuffled in, looking uncomfortable with a shirt, tugging at the hem. "Greetings, Master Heron."

Punt stared at his feet until Heron patted him on the shoulder. "Thank you, Punt." She would have given him a hug too, but he might have passed out from the close contact.

The blacksmith mumbled a response, but she couldn't hear it above the clatter that erupted from the Royal Chamber.

Jarngard started tugging on her tunic. Before she followed him, she turned and said, "You all are my family. Thank you for everything you have done."

With those words, it seemed a hefty weight was lifted from her heart. There was still darkness clouding it, as all had not been resolved, but rays of light now came through.

She didn't get to hear their response as she was shuffled down an empty hallway, guarded by two enormous Northmen.

Jarngard led her to a gilded door. Muffled noises carried to their location. She expected him to go through but he waited with his hand on her arm, head tilted listening for a sign.

After a brief knock on the door, Heron was pushed out onto a high stage. Hundreds of eyes turned toward her. The whole nobility of Alexandria was arrayed before her.

She saw Hortio standing near the front. He gave her a tiny bow.

"It seems our humble miracle worker forgot to consult the gods about the proper attire for a coronation," bellowed Agog to the assembled.

The nobles laughed politely as Heron inclined her head. "Apologies."

A great laugh erupted from Agog. "No, the apologies are all mine. I should have sent you a proper entourage, rather than Jarngard."

Jarngard made a comment in Germanic which, after much time spent with the Northman, Heron translated as: *"you shouldn't send a stallion to fornicate with a sheep."*

Heron stifled a laugh herself while Agog nearly choked. As the nobles watched Agog, Heron glanced out, taking in their awkward embrace of the scene before them. While the Alexandrians were happy to rid themselves of the Roman Empire, they didn't quite know what they had in the Northmen.

Agog turned to her and Heron got to see his royal attire for the first time. He wore an Egyptian tunic that went past his knees and held onto a resurrection staff. His hair kept the top knot and raven feathers had been sewn into his hair, flowing onto his shoulders.

He also wore a smattering of gold jewelry, but none of the darkened eye makeup the Egyptians favored. The Northman King was a strange mixture of Egyptian and Germanic traditions.

Agog pounded his staff on the stage, silencing the murmuring that had taken to the crowd.

Then, he turned and with open arms addressed them.

"Here stands before you the greatest miracle worker of the past, future, and present. Without Heron of Alexandria, your favored son, the oppressive yoke of the Roman Empire would still be around your necks."

There were a great and many murmurs of approval from the crowd. Heron found it hard to believe so many nobles agreed. Usually they were so stand-offish because of her lower birth.

"It is by my decree as the Satrap of Egypt and ruler of Alexandria, that Heron of Alexandria be formally named *Michanikos*, the Chief Engineer of Alexandria. And with that title, comes dominion over all the workshops of Alexandria. To that end, though keeping individual ownership, the workshops of our fair city will be united in the defense against the further tyranny of the Roman Empire!"

The crowd began speaking amongst themselves again. While the workshops were often run by men of lesser birth like herself, they were usually owned by nobles or gifted by the patronage of them.

Agog had come dangerously close to usurping their property and causing a riot within the nobles. But the Northman had shown great nimbleness in his conquest of Alexandria so far, so she was not surprised at his next words.

"Through this uniting of the workshops under our Chief

Engineer, each workshop shall keep the profits gained by it while benefiting from the knowledge of the *Michanikos*."

Heron barely had time to react when Agog continued and his next words above all, gave her pause to think.

"As the Chief Engineer, I bestow the *responsibility and importance* of the Great Lighthouse of Pharos," he said and turning so no one but herself could see, winked.

Then she knew for certain that Agog had been behind the investigation of the fires. She'd come to that conclusion already, but his *gift* to her practically owned up to it.

It was a clever turn as well, because he fulfilled his end of the bargain while dumping more responsibility on her. He'd also avoided the problem with the nobles by letting them keep the profits of her knowledge.

"Lastly," said Agog. "I give a gift of more personal nature, in thanks for the efforts on behalf of my ascendancy."

One of his Northman handed him a long object. Agog motioned for her to move closer.

Quick as a viper, he stole the cane from her hand and threw it into the crowd with a flourish. The nobles laughed and fought for the cane. The Northman had great stage presence.

"For your continued mobility and defense, I offer this new cane," he said and held it out on two upturned palms.

The cane was made of dark luscious wood with an ivory handle and gold inlays. As he handed over the cane, he pulled the hand rest out, revealing to her, the secret shine of a hidden blade.

Heron bowed and then her part of the ceremony was over and she was hustled back through the secret passage. Tired from the walking and the attention of the crowds, she did not try to find her daughter or the others and asked Jarngard to take her back to the workshop.

# 38

Weeks after Agog's coronation (she kept thinking of him as Agog despite his men calling him Wodanaz), Heron decided to survey her final remaining charge and had her horse saddled to make the journey.

She'd spent the weeks afterwards visiting each of the workshops. She knew most already in passing, except for the small shops, but all of them knew her.

At each, she made suggestions for their layouts or tools to help them improve. They took to her words with enthusiasm. Where they had difficulties, she offered abatement in the form of ideas, coinage or manpower. The Satrap had been generous with his funding of her efforts.

In turn, they had to renounce slavery for their works, as she counseled that freemen made for better products. At least half of the workshops had done so, though the remainder were still considering.

She knew it would take time to free them from the easy labor of slavery, for it was the rottenest of sweets.

The ride to the Lighthouse was made refreshing by a southerly wind, washing away the heat of the day and bringing the hint of salt.

Heron glanced behind her more than once to make sure her tails were still there, though she made no intent to lose them. Agog had given her a personal guard, two grim Northmen she'd named Grunt and Stammer by their verbal affections.

They were short on words but quick with a dagger. A Roman soldier disguised as an invalid beggar had rushed her in the Emporium only a few days ago. He hadn't made two steps toward her before he was brought down.

Heron didn't question their presence after that. It would take a long time to root out the Roman spies from the city and until then, Heron counted herself glad of the private guard.

The wind chipped at the waves as she crossed the causeway, leaving them choppy. Galleys and fisher boats tacked across the port in orderly lines, reaching the extensive docks.

Even from a distance, Heron could spot the Library attendants, scrambling onto the boats, scouring them for books and scrolls. Heron had not yet convinced Agog that the Library needed to be copied for safety, but he hadn't turned her down. That was a good sign.

Even in the daylight, the top of the Lighthouse glowed with purpose as she made her way toward it.

Along the island of Pharos, Heron passed the Temple of Isis. The temple commanded the center of the island. Slaves moved swiftly over its gardens and courtyards. Priestesses meandered solemnly through its grounds.

Heron noted the dark crescent moon on the temple designs. As Punt had learned, every temple in the city had a crescent moon. It could be that as the world's nightly guardian, the moon, brought solace to the night, much as religion brought solace to its believers.

Or, as Heron more firmly believed, the Cult of Ur had its tendrils deep within all the temples of Alexandria.

Her workshop made no more miracles for the temples, but she did not forbid the others from doing so. She took the lack of attacks on her as a truce for her decision. With the blame of the fires firmly on Caesar, and the miracles born from the workshops flowing to the temples again, they had no need to be enemies.

Not that she expected them to forget her role in the upheaval of Alexandria. As long as the temples kept to their part of the bargain, she would not trouble them any longer. What people believed was not her responsibility.

Heron pulled up at the gates of the Lighthouse proper. She had to lean back in her saddle to see the top. Her guards seemed equally awed by its presence.

She rode under the wide arch, at least five times as wide as her outstretched hands, that led into the center of the Lighthouse, following a ramp up and around the inside. The horse grunted as it labored up the incline, its hooves not made for such travel.

A few spectators passed her on the way down. She nodded as they murmured and pointed, trying not to draw attention to the fact that they recognized her. Heron had gotten used to being a minor celebrity in Alexandria.

Heron had to leave her horse at the transition to the octagonal portion of the Lighthouse. Numerous sightseers milled about the small market that had been set up to sell food and drink. Small scale replicas of the Lighthouse could be purchased at trinket vendors.

Grunt and Stammer followed her as she took to the stairs, using the railing instead of her cane. She hadn't yet had to pull the blade, but kept it at the ready.

The climb was tiring and longer than she had expected. She stopped twice for a rest. Her guards didn't seem bothered by the effort, but they were much younger and without injury.

When Heron finally breached the walls and entered the observation balcony, her breath was truly swept away by the view.

The winds fired across the stone in dense bursts, blowing her guard's hair about their faces. For once, Heron was glad of her short Roman haircut.

Heron first looked to sea. Distant sails rose and fell upon the waves as they rode toward Alexandria. At that place, Heron felt like the center of the known world. Even more than Rome, which styled itself its capitol.

While Rome had its senators and tales of oration and armies and roads, Alexandria had its Lighthouse and Library. Rome used its power to control its Empire. Alexandria used hers to invite the world to her doorstep.

Heron looked down to the simple buildings that made up the Great Library. In truth, it was hard to even distinguish the Library from the rest of the city. Places of learning and knowledge had spread out across the city, to where even an outdoor café could spark a learned discussion.

Heron smiled. There was no place on the earth she would rather be.

And dotted around the city, often marked by black plumes of smoke, were the workshops that she now commanded. Heron had been hesitant at first, to give direction and advice. But soon, she found it became natural.

She had once promised herself that if given the worth of the Lighthouse, the eight-thousand talents, she would transform the city into a true City of Wonders. Not by the temples, or built on the backs of slaves like the pyramids, but built on the knowledge of its people.

To Heron, machines were logic solidified from thought. With the mechanics and automata she devised, the city would rise up and be a beacon to the new world.

When Agog had dared to throw off their Roman overlords, she thought him a fool. Now with the people united and the workshops humming in tune, she knew Rome could not dare to stop them.

Content, Heron turned away from the city and looked back to the sea, back in the direction of Greece, the place of her father and her twin.

For Heron had not come to the top of the Lighthouse to view the city or ponder upon the Roman Empire. She thought solemnly for a while and then her purpose solidified, pulled her twin's token from her neck.

She hefted it in her hand and let the memory of her twin wash over her for one last time. For if truly she was going to change the world, she could no longer be two people at once. She couldn't be Ada, and Heron. It had to be one or the other.

Heron stretched her arm back and launched the token into the air. The winds grabbed it and threw it far into the sea. Almost immediately, her eyes lost sight of it and it was gone.

And that last bit of darkness, the one that had been lurking over her heart, set itself free.

She knew then that she was no longer Ada. No Greek daughter of a failed merchant or even a twin.

She was Heron of Alexandria.

§§§

Don't miss the exciting second book in the
Alexandrian Saga

# HEIRS
# OF
# ALEXANDRIA

# ABOUT THE AUTHOR

Thomas K. Carpenter resides near St. Louis with his wife
Rachel and their two children. He earned his degree in Metal-
lurgical Engineering from the University of Missouri Rolla.
After finishing up his M.B.A. in the summer of 2006, he
returned to his roots of writing fiction. When he's not busy
writing his next book, he's playing soccer in the yard with his
kids or getting beat by his wife at cards. He keeps a regular
blog at www.thomaskcarpenter.com. If you want to learn
when his next novel will be hitting the shelves, like him on
Facebook at Thomas K. Carpenter.

Made in the USA
Monee, IL
14 July 2021